"The inequities of the justice system, the fortitude of women of color, and the bittersweet struggle to connect are rendered ravishingly in this bighearted novel."

—O, THE OPRAH MAGAZINE

"A fast-paced, intriguing story . . . the novel's real achievement is its uncommon perceptiveness on the origins and variations of addiction."

—THE NEW YORK TIMES BOOK REVIEW

"Timely and important."

—KARIN TANABE, author of *The Gilded Years*

"Disarmingly compelling."

—VOGUE

"An absorbing commentary on love, family, and forgiveness."

—THE WASHINGTON POST

"[An] intimate family saga."

—ENTERTAINMENT WEEKLY

"Engrossing and moving."

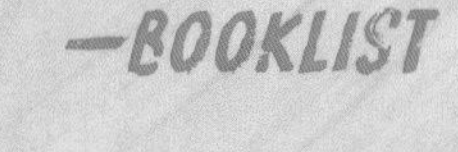

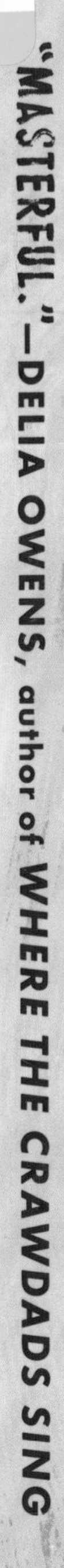

PRAISE FOR

The Care and Feeding of Ravenously Hungry Girls

"The inequities of the justice system, the fortitude of women of color, and the bittersweet struggle to connect are rendered ravishingly in this bighearted novel."
—*O, The Oprah Magazine*

"Gray's nuanced, lyrical debut is a moving examination of the ties that bind and—nearly as often—bless."
—*People*

"A fast-paced, intriguing story . . . the novel's real achievement is its uncommon perceptiveness on the origins and variations of addiction."
—*The New York Times Book Review*

"In her masterful debut, Anissa Gray dissects this disbanded family until the hollow bones lay bare and exposed. From these raw remains, Gray's stark prose reveals a glimpse of the 'why,' which is the only hope for the 'never again.' *The Care and Feeding of Ravenously Hungry Girls* is a poetically written story that guides us through a deep darkness toward a faint whisper of light seeping from beneath a closet door. A light that shows how love and forgiveness can come from unexpected places and triumph over more than we ever imagine."
—Delia Owens, #1 *New York Times* bestselling author of *Where the Crawdads Sing*

"I was immediately taken by the power and honesty of Anissa Gray's voice. She is a writer to watch, and this debut is not to be missed!"
—Terry McMillan, #1 *New York Times* bestselling author of *I Almost Forgot About You* and *Waiting to Exhale*

"Deftly exploring black identity, sibling roles, and emotional trauma, Gray paints a nuanced family portrait you can't turn away from."
—*Entertainment Weekly*

"If you enjoyed *An American Marriage*, by Tayari Jones, read *The Care and Feeding of Ravenously Hungry Girls*. . . . An absorbing commentary on love, family, and forgiveness."
—*The Washington Post*

"As in Tayari Jones's bestselling *An American Marriage*, Gray uses imprisonment as the backdrop for a disarmingly compelling story that skirts easy answers and sentimentality. Conversational in tone and difficult in subject, *Care and Feeding* tells not just an American story but several important ones."
—*Vogue*

"Anissa Gray's debut novel, *The Care and Feeding of Ravenously Hungry Girls*, examines those cracks in the familial glass, giving readers a gripping and sharp story about what it takes to hold a family together when everything is falling apart. . . . Timeless and universal."
—*USA Today*

"Gray's absorbing novel is about family and the things we hunger for."
—*Real Simple*

"Anissa Gray's debut is heralded as '*The Mothers* meets *An American Marriage*.' If that's not enough to sell you on this stunning novel about family and relationships, we don't know what will."
—HelloGiggles

"[A] stark, emotional story you don't want to miss."
—Bustle

"A trio of sisters navigate the tricky waters of forgiveness in Gray's heartfelt, beautifully written debut. This is a wholly absorbing, moving story about incarceration, the mechanics of grace, and the fierce, small wars fought on the landscape of the family and the human heart. The lives of two young girls hang in the balance, stakes so high that I was up late, unable to stop turning pages. Get an extra copy for your best friend or your own sister; this is one you're going to want to talk about."
—Joshilyn Jackson, *New York Times* and *USA Today* bestselling author of *Never Have I Ever*

"*The Care and Feeding of Ravenously Hungry Girls* explores the ache of being torn apart from family and how bad decisions can reverberate for generations. Heartbreaking at times, it is ultimately a story of hope as Gray beautifully captures the way strong women can piece a community back together, taking care of their loved ones while still figuring out how to care for themselves. A graceful debut that feels timely and important."
—Karin Tanabe, author of *The Gilded Years*

"This is perfect for fans of Brit Bennett's *The Mothers*; readers will be deeply affected by this story of a family wrestling to support itself."
—*Publishers Weekly*

"Gray's engrossing and moving debut novel considers secrets and lies and their effect on the families of three sisters."
—*Booklist*

"Gray manages a large cast of characters with ease, sharply differentiating between the voices of hardheaded Althea, shrewd Viola, and hesitating Lillian, who narrate the novel in alternating chapters."
—*Kirkus Reviews*

"A moving portrait of a troubled family that would be an excellent book club pick."
—PureWow

The Care and Feeding of Ravenously Hungry Girls

ANISSA GRAY

BERKLEY
New York

BERKLEY
An imprint of Penguin Random House LLC
penguinrandomhouse.com

ISBN: 9781984802446

The Library of Congress has catalogued the Berkley hardcover edition of this book as follows:

Names: Gray, Anissa, author.
Title: The care and feeding of ravenously hungry girls / Anissa Gray.
Description: First edition. | New York: Berkley, 2019.
Identifiers: LCCN 2018018552 | ISBN 9781984802439 (hardcover) | ISBN 9781984802453 (ebook)
Subjects: LCSH: Mothers and daughters—Fiction. | African Americans—Fiction. | African American families—Fiction.
Classification: LCC PS3607.R3876 C37 2019 | DDC 813/.6—dc23
LC record available at https://lccn.loc.gov/2018018552

Berkley hardcover edition / February 2019
Berkley trade paperback edition / January 2020

Printed in the United States of America
3 5 7 9 10 8 6 4 2

Cover art by Alice Lindstrom
Cover design by Emily Osborne
Book design by Laura K. Corless

For my mother, Mary Ann Wells

We were hungry and lost and scared and young and we needed religion, salvation, something to fill the anxious hollow in our chests.

—Marya Hornbacher, *Wasted*

The Care and Feeding of Ravenously Hungry Girls

Althea

You do a lot of thinking in jail. Especially when you're locked in the box that's your cell. Mine is about as big as the walk-in closet I had back at home, but in place of leather bags and sling-backs and racks of clothes, I've got bunk beds, a stainless-steel sink-and-toilet combo, and a compact, padlocked cabinet. The cabinet's where you keep your valuables, like family pictures, commissary, and letters, including the one from your daughter that's not addressed to you. The letter that, truth be told, you just can't bring yourself to read, so you've got it tucked inside the Bible that belonged to your dead mother.

The Bible's the one thing you read religiously, but not for scripture. You read it for the notes written in the margins. Then, when it's lights out and you can't read anymore, you lock the Bible up in the cabinet and crawl in your bunk. The top bunk, which you're still scared of falling out of. You'd still be in the bottom bunk, if it was up to you, but your new crazy-quiet cellmate asked for that bunk in a way that made you feel like she might kill you as you slept on it, if you said no.

Now you lie here, wide awake, with the compact cabinet across the way and the sink-and-toilet combo near the foot of the bed, thinking and remembering because that's all you've got here in the dark when sleep won't come. And it hardly ever comes. I'm usually up thinking about getting out or what it was like before I came in or why I did what I did and how what I did compares to the next woman's crime.

It's always me versus Inmate X: I did this, but at least I didn't do that.

I used to meet with the chaplain, somebody who's seen everything. We'd sit in a little room that had a view to the outside, with him in his metal chair, black shirted, white collared, but casual in jeans. The type who probably plays guitar to youth groups in parks. He'd sit with his elbows on his knees, leaning forward with his back to the window while I stared past his pink, freckled bald spot to the jail's front lawn and the flagpole.

"Don't go comparing crimes like that," the chaplain would say. "There's no good in it, Althea. What you've done doesn't have to define you."

"Then what does?"

"Only you know that. No one can tell you who you are."

I stopped meeting with him.

Who am I?

I ask myself that question every night I lay my head down in here. Althea Marie Butler-Cochran: round, dimpled face; rounding, dimpled body; smooth, light brown skin. There was a definition of me that went with that name, face, and body, but it's hard to see it now, even though I still look pretty much the same, except for the jailhouse weight gain.

I used to think I was like a river. A mighty force of nature. A real river that I used to watch and dip my feet in, sitting out on the dock behind my house. You can't see the river from the jail, but it's out there past the barred-up windows. Past the recreation yard with the basketball court and beyond the patches of gravel and dry grass you got to cross before getting to the fence. Go over the razor wire, go out past the woods about twenty miles or so, as the crow flies. Touch down on the two-lane road underneath you. That barrenness on either side of you is farmland waiting for its season.

This road, beyond that fence and miles away as the crow flies, looks like it goes on forever because it's flat and straight and all you can see are the miles in front of you. But you're not far now. You'll see the river I'm talking about. The Saint Joseph. I got baptized in that river. I got proposed to there. There's a tree on the riverbank that has, or at least used to have, me and my husband's initials: *P+A Forever.*

That river runs through the place where I was easier to define. The place that made me who I used to be. Althea Marie Butler-Cochran: round, dimpled face; rounding, dimpled body; smooth, light brown skin; wife; mother; daughter; sister; mighty force of nature.

The meeting of the Saint Joseph and the Portage Rivers gives the place I'm from its name: New River Junction.

"One river for each of my girls," is how my mama put it. "Y'all two will run together," she said. That was right after my sister Viola was born.

"Boys and men are earth and stone," my mama used to say. "But you girls, us women, we're water. We can wear away earth and stone, if it comes to it."

I believed her.

And I believed I'd never leave New River Junction. I made promises to her that kept me bound there. But ever since that day the police came, I've been moving farther and farther away from home. It was a Friday afternoon, two Septembers ago. The leaves had just started to turn. I remember the turning leaves not so much because I'm the type to notice things like that but because my husband, Proctor, is. That morning, on the way into our restaurant, he grabbed my hand and stopped me midstride.

"Look at that, Al," he said, stringing his fingers through mine. "It's here."

He pointed over my head to the big, open-armed oak in the yard. Up there, among the rustling green leaves, there was a burst of gold and burnt orange, the first sign of his favorite season. The promise of hayrides and haunted houses and the Halloween candy that he hoarded, always winking and saying, "Don't worry. I'll put it away for the kids."

It was later that day that they came for us.

Me and Proctor were sitting at the long mahogany bar at the back of the restaurant, splitting a turkey sandwich and a beer. The red leather booths and the polished dark wood tables at the front of the restaurant were empty, just like always.

"Do you think this'll be the night?"

Our dare-to-hope question about dinner service, not about getting arrested, was being asked. "Do you think this'll be the night" our dining room fills up again? Even though we knew the answer to that question, it seemed like we'd make our bad luck worse if one of us didn't ask it. We'd been asking "the question" for some three years, going back to when the paper mill started going under. Anchored on the shores of the Saint Joseph for more than a century, the paper mill was a sprawl of red brick and concrete with smokestacks belching into the sky. The rotten-egg stink was the life's breath of the economy. "The smell of money," everybody used to say.

But then came the layoffs and the loss of our regulars. Summer tourists from other lake and river towns disappearing. Other restaurants, stores, and small businesses trimming hours, cutting workers, or closing up.

"What've you heard, Althea? Who else is in trouble?" The few customers we had left would ask me that, as I let them have their pick of the empty red leather booths. "I don't know how y'all are getting by with business being what it is," they'd say, "but I'm glad to see you holding on and still being such a help to people, too. We need that now."

"Do you think this'll be the night?"

I was the one asking our dare-to-hope question in our empty restaurant on that Friday afternoon of the changing leaves two Septembers ago, when we heard the welcome bell jingle out on the door.

"You guys want to grab a table?" I said, looking in the mirror behind the bar at the reflection of the man coming through the front lobby. Officer Hopkins, a big corn-fed white boy who'd played football with Proctor in high school. A regular at the restaurant. Proctor swiveled around on his bar stool and called out, "Hey, Hop!"

Swiveling around, too, I saw a young, creamed-coffee-colored officer coming in behind Hop. A man me and Proctor knew mostly because we knew his family, the Jacksons. They were longtime members at my father's church, where my brother pastors now.

Me and Jay Jackson traded polite nods, like always, as he walked with Hop toward the bar.

"What's the word, man?" Proctor asked his friend.

I got up to grab some menus but stopped midrise when Hop and Jay gave each other a look.

"Um," Jay said, rubbing his thumb along the bill of the police cap in his hand, "I don't know how to say this, but look, we gotta take y'all in."

I heard what he said, no problem, but there was something confusing about it. Like listening to somebody speak a different language but catching enough words to know they're saying something about you, and it's not good.

"You guys have done so much," Hop was saying, sounding like things didn't make sense to him either, looking around like he wasn't really sure where he was. His eyes lingered on the pictures of the mayor, the city council members, and the city's favorite sons and daughters posing with me or Proctor or the both of us. He looked at the two of us again, standing in front of him. "Hell, you're the food pantry people. And everything you did for the people with the flood . . ." Hop said, trailing off. "And this place, do you know how many years me and my family ran through here for the Fun Run and how many times we had your big picnic right out there on the lawn with everybody? The whole community." He pointed outside to the lawn, then his hand moved toward the handcuffs on his belt. "This has to be some kind of a mistake. I know it. But like Jay said, we have to take you guys in."

Jay nodded. But that was the only movement any of us made. We all just looked at each other, me having taken my seat again next to Proctor. It felt like forever, but it couldn't have been more than a few seconds before I finally felt myself getting up again. It didn't feel like I was moving under my own power, though. It was like I was being dragged up by this slow understanding that, Okay, they're here as cops, not customers. Not here to eat. Here for us.

And I felt this loneliness watching Proctor, as he started to realize it, too. He got to his feet slowly, never looking at me, not even one time. It was like something in him was leaning away as we stood there beside one another. When Hop and Jay went to cuff us, the whole time apologizing about having to follow procedure, I put my hands out but Proctor didn't. When Hop said, "Come on now, man," and reached for his wrist, Proctor resisted, not so much fighting as jerking like a child, twisting into a tantrum.

"Proctor, please," I said, as cool metal clicked closed around my own wrists. "It's *Officer Hopkins*."

Maybe saying Hop's title and full last name made Proctor see that this wasn't his friend. This was an arresting officer. Whatever it was, Proctor stopped resisting. But he still wouldn't look at me. He clenched his jaw, and his whole body closed off to me. His eyes filled with tears as he ran his big hand along the smooth, dark wood of the bar, petting it like a dog, before letting his hand rest there. He built that bar himself. Hop stepped back. The cuffs dangled at his side, glimmering in the afternoon light.

"Do what you gotta do, man," Proctor said, finally.

Out in the car, as the cruiser pulled out of the parking lot, Proctor turned to look out the window at the restaurant's taupe, Southwestern-style walls falling away behind us. I could feel the regret radiating off of him. And fear, too.

Bald. Tall and broad. Deep, dark brown. There's a fierceness about Proctor that makes him look like maybe he belongs in the backseat of a police car, and you might assume that a man who looks like that will do just fine locked up. But you'd be wrong. I've known Proctor since we were kids. He's a farm boy who moves to the rhythms of nature. A man nourished by everything that glows in it: bright fall afternoons, burnt orange leaves, and the sun shining through them. But he's prone to a black-hole-in-the-soul kind of darkness that can suck every bit of light from this world.

I tried to imagine just how dark it might get.

But whatever I imagined in that moment, I couldn't have pictured in my mind, not in a million years, what the end of that day would bring. Couldn't have foreseen that I'd find out it all started with one phone call. And I never could've imagined the way I still feel about the caller. That feeling has made me a mother to nobody. And wife? I can't even begin to tell Proctor about that feeling because it would forever change how he feels about me.

The last time I saw Proctor was months ago, when we stood side by side in court as the verdict came down: *We the jury find the defendant, Althea Marie Butler-Cochran, guilty of conspiracy to defraud the United States . . .*

As the reading of the verdict went on and on, guilty on almost every count, I turned and looked at him. But he still wouldn't look at me.

Through the darkness of my cell, I can see Proctor. But through time, to that *first* time. Near the end of summer, 1977. I was standing in a graveyard, listening to a preacher give my mother over to the earth: . . . *till thou return unto the ground; for out of it wast thou taken: for dust thou art, and unto dust shalt thou return.*

I was twelve, hugging my little brother, Joe, to my side. Hanging on to my younger sister Viola's hand, with my baby sister, Lillian, on my hip. All of us Butler kids in pastels, pinstripes, and floral prints. The Easter clothes our mama had made for us just four months earlier. I squinted up into a blinding blue August sky, thinking, *Mama will never be dust.*

I was thinking of women and water.

"She's not dust," I said to my brother and sisters. "She'll never be dust."

Joe was pressing himself into my side, holding on to my leg. He was four years old then. To this day, he still clings a little. Viola, who's always had her own mind with her own notion of things running through it, was six years old but aging fast around the eyes. Lillian wasn't even a year old. She couldn't know what was happening to us. I don't know if our father heard what I told them about our mother never being dust. He was standing off somewhere behind us, basketball-player tall in his black suit with his shoulders stooped. A man already a good ways gone in his retreat to the periphery of our lives.

And there was Proctor, in a boxy, too-big black suit. He was in the crowd of mourners beside his grandmother, peeking around her, looking at me. He found me later at the house with all the other mourners. I was sitting on the stairs by myself when he introduced himself.

"What kind of name is Proctor?" I asked him.

He shrugged. "An old man's, I guess. My granddaddy's." He smiled and looked down at the cuffed sleeves on his suit jacket. "Suit's his, too," he said.

Then he asked if he could get me a plate, and I said yes because I couldn't move. I was disoriented, struggling against this rip current of loss and new responsibility for my brother and sisters. I watched Proctor walk across the hall to the living room that seemed different and dark, even though the curtains were open to that bright August day. As Proctor disappeared into the dining room, headed for the table with the casseroles, side dishes, and fried chicken, he passed my father, who was kissing the wet cheeks of women and patting the padded shoulders of men, telling them, "It's God's will. You can't fight against that."

As I watched the churning, ever-changing circle of mourners move around my father, I thought, truly, if there was a God, He would've healed Mama and none of these people, these locusts, would be here taking over our house. Mama'd be making dinner right about now, like she had been the day I found her collapsed on the vinyl floor. She'd be barefoot, her wheat-colored skin glowing in the heat and harvest gold brightness of our kitchen. She'd be standing over the kitchen sink, wide hips swaying, probably humming "Changed" or something else from *Love Alive*, the album she played over and over. She'd be encouraging Viola to sing along, with Lillian balanced on a swaying hip. She'd be looking around the kitchen to make sure Joe wasn't getting into anything. She'd be pulling me over to the counter beside her with her free hand, her hip bumping against mine as she moved to the music, telling me to put the seasoned chicken in the paper bag with the flour and shake it up. "Now here, take the baby and stand back," she'd say, pivoting from the counter to the stove. Skin-scorching grease popping as she put the floured, salted, peppered, and paprikaed chicken parts in the skillet with steady hands that had done this hundreds of times before. I wanted to see her do it hundreds and hundreds of times more.

How could a God say, No, there'll be no more for you?

My throat clotted up with tears and grief and rage, and I couldn't eat anything Proctor brought back for me. But I stayed there next to him on the narrow stairs, his thigh pressed against mine. He was big for fourteen. As solid and stable as earth and stone.

Here in my bunk, that moment presses in on my chest, a weight so heavy I can hardly breathe. I turn over on my side. I pull the itchy gray blanket up under my chin and stare through the darkness at the cabinet across the way, to where my mother's Bible, with its broken spine and faded gold-gilded pages, sits locked behind the door. To where that unread letter from my daughter, addressed to Proctor, not me, peeks out from the pages of that Bible.

I curl up and close my eyes, trying to feel the pressure of Proctor's thigh against mine. Trying to see him turn his face to me, just like he did when we sat together on those stairs and he said, in a quiet voice still finding its depths, "It's gonna be all right, Althea."

I whisper into the stale air of my cell: "We'll see tomorrow, won't we?"

And we'll see what family of mine shows up, too.

"Besides you, Proctor," I whisper. Unlike everybody else, he's got no choice but to be there. "I bet you wish you'd left me sitting by myself on those stairs, don't you?" I say into the dark.

Lillian

S*tay positive,* I say to myself as I glance back (again!) at the double doors.

"I don't think they're coming, Aunt Lillian," Baby Vi says.

I check the time on my phone. "Sometimes the Universe can surprise us. Let's not give up just yet."

Baby Vi gives me a weak smile and turns away. She folds her hands in her lap and stares straight ahead at the judge's bench, looking weary. Most everything about her these days is a kind of tired, old-ladyish *Why bother?* ennui. And she's only fifteen.

"It's going to be okay," I say to the side of her face.

Baby Vi looks at me again, her eyebrows knitting together, and I see my sister—her mom—in her face. There's Althea's brown-sugar skin, her dark doe eyes. And here they come, Althea's dimples, as Baby Vi twists her mouth in a thoughtful way.

"How can you just keep saying it's gonna be okay?" she asks.

"Because I believe it. The judge, he's looking at a lot of stuff, like the great letter you wrote, asking for a second chance for your mom and dad. And the one from Uncle Joe."

She nods, slowly. Skeptical but hopeful, maybe.

"And I did the best I could with my letter, so, I mean, that could help, too." It would've been even *more* helpful if Althea and Proctor had letters from the rest of the family: Viola, our sister; Kim, Althea's other daughter. If I'm honest, I'd have to admit my letter was pretty hard to write. I said everything I was expected to say but not everything I think. I felt like an accomplice trying to deceive the court by hiding Althea's full identity or something. And worse, I felt complicit in some kind of karma-dodging scam. Because, as much as I hate to say it, when I think about karma, which I do a lot these days, Althea and Proctor are probably in trouble.

"We just have to stay positive," I say, more to myself than to Baby Vi.

I really want to believe what Althea's lawyer, a bookish-looking public defender, told Baby Vi and me when we ran into him outside the courtroom a little while ago. "The prosecution is asking for too much time," he said. "Yes, the community probably wants to see a public hanging, but your sister and brother-in-law are first-time offenders. And for all they've done wrong, well, it didn't start out that way. I think the judge will see that," he said.

Baby Vi turns away again and stares in the direction of the judge's bench. She reaches over and grabs my hand as I look over my shoulder at the double doors again. It's getting way too close to time.

"You wouldn't happen to know where your sister is, would you?" I ask.

Baby Vi pulls her hand out of mine and glances at me, like, *Is that a serious question?*

"I just, you know, Kim said she was coming today, so I thought maybe, I don't know." What? What did you think, Lillian? That this might be different from any other day out of the nearly two years you've had them? Did you think, when you saw Kim this morning, ignoring you in the kitchen, that maybe you finally managed to say or do something right (telepathically?), like those inspirational TV shows and movies where the bumbling relative or coach or teacher suddenly figures things out and becomes a flawed but effective authority figure who turns the troubled kid around? Did you actually think that, Lillian?

I look at Baby Vi, who's still looking away. Guilt hits like a gut kick.

"I'm sorry," I say. "I shouldn't ask you about Kim like that. What she does or doesn't do, that's not on you. That's on her."

And me.

"It's okay," Baby Vi says softly. But she doesn't take my hand again.

Way to go, Lillian.

Baby Vi and her sister, her *twin* sister, couldn't be more different. Definitely fraternal. I mean, Kim is full-on feral now. She's out there who knows where, and I usually try not to make Baby Vi betray confidences. I don't want her feeling like she's selling out her sister. That's something I never would've done. Okay, well, maybe I would sell out Althea, but never Viola, the sister who shares Baby Vi's name. A woman who, like Kim, is a no-show, at least so far, despite promising me she'd be here.

Viola's really going to leave me alone with all of this, isn't she? A wave of nausea hits me. I hug myself, just as I realize I'm rocking a little, like a disturbed person. But isn't all of this disturbing? I stop rocking. I close my eyes and draw in the deepest possible calming breath, but that only reminds me of taking in the deepest possible calming breath this morning as I sat with my cereal (while Kim ignored me), watching the news. The words *The Big Payback* popped up on the screen with dramatic music and video of Proctor and Althea, smiling, leading a reporter through the restaurant in better days. The anchorwoman said: "Disgraced restaurateurs and charity leaders to learn their fate today in court."

They *do* want a public hanging.

People are still coming in, craning their necks, looking around for seats because the church-pew-ish benches are filling up. But there's no reverent silence, like in a sanctuary. There's this sickening, excited buzz as people push past each other to get the last few empty spots. Baby Vi and I have blocked off seats for Kim and Viola with our coats.

"I'm going to go out and try to call them, okay?" I say to Baby Vi.

She starts to say something, then stops and shrugs, like, *Whatever.*

I tell her to give up the seats, if she thinks she needs to. "It's not right for other people to pay for the fact that those two aren't here yet," I say.

I squeeze past the six or so sets of knees between me and the end of the bench, saying "Excuse me" the whole way. As I rush for the door, I spot Joe, sitting near the back of the courtroom. His smile is nervous, but the thumbs-up he gives is steady and sure. I return something close to the same. But I don't stop. I wish he weren't here.

Outside the courtroom, I call Kim and, as the phone rings, I try to think of the right thing to say. I don't want to say anything that might set her off, and that's hard because just about anything can set her off. I mean, just asking her if she wants to talk about what's going on could get you a simple "Not really" or a door-slamming fit. There's also the silent treatment or worse: her wanting to talk, but mostly just to say stuff that she knows will upset you.

I took Kim's phone away after her first upsetting outburst, just after Proctor and Althea were convicted, but then I panicked after she got home really late that night, so I gave it back, thinking, *At least I can reach her if I need to.* Nope, not so. Kim, as is the case now, doesn't answer when I call. I leave what I hope is a neutral message: "Hi, just wondering where you are. We're at the courthouse waiting for you."

Then I text: We're at court. Where are you? Let me know you're okay. XOXO

She will, at least sometimes, text back. But I bet she'll do what she usually does: show up at the house tonight, give me a look that dares me to punish her (and I wouldn't dare because I haven't figured out how without feeling like an oppressive overlord), then disappear into her room for the night and blast her stereo (the stereo that used to belong to her dad and is now considered government property, therefore, illegal).

I call Viola. No answer there either, which worries me. If she says she's coming, she's coming, even though she doesn't come home from Chicago anywhere near as much as I'd like her to. And she always answers her phone, even if it's just to say: "I can't talk now, I'll call you later." I've been getting a lot of "I can't talk now" lately. But this is the first complete no-show.

I stuff my phone in my back pocket and rush back into the courtroom. Our bench is full now, except for the space Baby Vi has saved for me. I squeeze past all the knees again, settle in next to her, and hold our coats in my lap like a security blanket. Baby Vi pulls her long legs up to her chest, like she's trying to make herself small.

Lawyers are getting themselves seated at their respective tables.

And now, here's Proctor being led out, shoulders squared and ready. He looks around the courtroom. His steady, bright eyes find Baby Vi and me. He smiles. Like always, it's a smile that makes you feel like he's got this. Like everything will go our way.

Baby Vi's hand shoots up, and she waves excitedly at her dad.

Proctor smiles wider and nods in her direction.

As the marshal points to Proctor's seat next to his lawyer, Proctor keeps searching the crowded benches, looking for Kim. Not finding her, his eyes come back to Baby Vi and me again. He's struggling to keep that smile now, I can tell.

Here's Althea. That jail jumper gets me. Not that it's easy to see Proctor in one, but it's especially hard to see Althea that way. During the trial, she wore "very traditional" dresses that I got for her: "Maybe something an older woman might wear," she'd said, telling me how to choose. As somebody who happens to have a lot of experience with the elderly (thanks to recent, unrelated events), I was definitely qualified to pick out something appropriate. Althea wore those flower-covered monstrosities, literally the most old-ladyish dresses I could find at Dress Depot (really, you just may as well call them muumuus), like a drape over a nice piece of furniture you want to keep under wraps. Because the truth is, Althea's all about looking good. She's all blue jeans and blazers and swing skirts and heels. But more than that, she has this kind of straight-backed, proud way about her. That, she could never hide. I can see it now, even with her in that jumper, as she scans the crowd, with her chin raised and her head tilted. She sees us and smiles. Baby Vi waves again, but it's a little hesitant this time. Althea keeps looking, searching the benches. She smiles again, I guess at Joe, but then her face falters as she keeps searching. I wish I could say she's looking for Kim, but I doubt it. I think she's missing Viola. That's who she's been asking about lately. She takes her seat next to her lawyer.

We get the order to rise, and the judge walks in. He's a big Santa Claus–looking guy (but more white stubbly than beardy), which I'm hoping is a sign that we're about to get a sentencing gift.

We sit.

The judge says a few words about a case that, "after the longest time, is finally giving a wounded community closure." The rest of what he's saying is just courtroom garble to me, but now he's nodding toward Althea and Proctor, asking if they'd like to say anything.

Proctor and Althea walk up to the lectern, with their lawyers close behind. The two of them look at each other, then Proctor speaks. "Thank you, Your Honor," he says, his voice radio announcer rich. "I want to say to the people of New River Junction how sorry we are. It's a community we've worked in and loved our whole lives." He nods in

Althea's direction. "Me and Althea were born and raised in the Junction. We stayed to raise our family there." His voice breaks. He lowers his head, clears his throat. He looks up again. "In the midst of some hard times, hard times for everybody, I know that." He glances back at the rest of the courtroom, his steady brown eyes promising: *I do care about people, despite what you've heard in this courtroom.* He clears his throat again. "I hope we get a chance to make up for the bad choices we made." He looks at Althea, signaling her to speak.

She shakes her head.

"Please know that I speak for the both of us, Your Honor," Proctor goes on, "when I say, we take full responsibility. We never meant to hurt anybody."

The judge nods. He looks from Proctor to Althea and says, "Throughout this trial, we've heard a lot of testimony about hard times and the choices people made. You had a whole community suffering in the aftermath of the Great Flood, and that community chose to come together to help each other. But the two of you, you chose to prey on the suffering and generosity of those people. And what's more, you used your position as leaders in the community. You abused the trust people had in you."

My stomach knots up.

"Before I go further, I would just like to read something here," the judge says, as he puts on half-moon glasses and picks up a creased piece of paper from his desk. "It's a letter from one of the people who suffered because of the choices you two made. I'd like to read something here that I think really speaks to the heart of things:

"'The Great Flood did its worst. It washed away my family's property and things we can never get back. That was an act of God, and we must accept that. But it was Althea and Proctor Cochran, people we trusted, who laid waste to the faith and loyalty of this whole town, holding their fund-raisers, taking our money, promising to help, but never delivering. We want to see justice done.'"

I whisper a mantra to brace myself: *Everything works out for the highest good.* I repeat it over and over in my head because, as the judge slowly folds up the letter, it's like I can see the karmic wheel turning, roulette-style, over Proctor's and Althea's heads, spinning toward something terrible.

My mind goes into a kind of spin of its own, but I come out of it when I hear the judge say, "Having considered all of the factors, the court sentences you, Althea Marie Butler-Cochran, to a term of one year in the custody of the Federal Bureau of Prisons for one count of conspiracy to defraud the U.S. government, to be served consecutive to a sentence of one year and three months for obstruction of justice. For wire fraud, the court sentences you to a term of one—"

But I can't hear the rest of what the judge is saying because of what I'm seeing: Althea, swaying in a wind that only she can feel. There's a loud *crack! bam!* and gasps all around as Althea slams into the table and collapses.

Somebody's screaming, "No!" I glance over my shoulder to the back of the courtroom. It's Joe. He's pushing past people to get to the end of the bench, to help Althea.

The judge bangs his gavel, calling, "Order!"

Baby Vi grabs on and folds herself around me. I wiggle an arm free to hang on to her, covering her ear like I can somehow keep everything out. I whisper, "Everything's going to be okay," hoping my voice gets through.

Hugging her is like holding a scared, whimpering puppy just as the storm rolls in. And I think of her feral sister out there, grateful to God, the Universe, whoever's listening, that Kim isn't here. Because how much worse would she feel? After all, she was the one who called the police in the first place. The one who tipped the first domino that touched off the investigation, toppled her mom and dad, and caused a cascade of devastating losses that we've only just begun to see. Kim will find out the sentences soon enough, but I can't imagine what she'd do or what she'd be feeling, watching this: her mom, dazed, being helped up from the floor by lawyers and a marshal; her dad, helpless and defeated, standing there watching.

I get my other arm free and hang on to Baby Vi as tightly as I can and whisper, "Safe," willing that thought out to the Universe to Kim, wherever she is, as the judge picks up where he left off with Althea: "For making false statements . . ."

Viola

I sit on the floor and rest my back against the bed. Glance down at my watch. Six thirty. Eva will be home from work any minute. No, this very minute. There's the door.

"Hello? Viola?"

And there's her voice.

"I'm back here," I yell in the direction of the front room. I catch myself squeezing and rubbing my fingers, nervously. A bad habit. I stop and slide my hands under my thighs.

There's the quick *click-click* of Eva's heels on the hardwoods. She appears in the doorway. I note the ponytail, a desperate, rushed, stop-gap styling measure. And there are the puffy eyes. She's not sleeping. Neither am I. She looks down at me, leans against the door frame, and crosses her arms. "What are you doing here?"

"I thought maybe I left a pair of shoes behind."

"I'm pretty sure you took everything." Her voice nicks, with its knife's edge. She glances around the room as if to be certain all traces of me were removed when I moved out. Her gaze rests on what used to be my dresser, which was uncluttered by ornamentation even before I left. Her eyes return to me on the floor. "Do you want to tell me why you're really here?"

I feel caught in a lie, but still I go on: "I guess those shoes could be in a box I haven't gotten to yet." In point of fact, I haven't gotten to any of the boxes yet.

"What are you doing here, Viola?" This time her voice is quieter. The knife, sheathed. "What is it?" She looks at me closely, her eyes roaming over the topography of my face, and I worry that she'll arrive at the truth. Isn't it right there in the sharp, high ridges of my cheekbones? In the gaunt gorges of my cheeks? In the squared-off formation of a jawline that's unusually pronounced? She hasn't seen me in days. She'll notice.

I get to my feet quickly and turn my face away. "I just came for my shoes, like I said. I'll just . . . never mind. I'll go."

"Wait," she says. "You're supposed to be in Michigan. You didn't go to the sentencing?"

"I got held up. Work. I couldn't make it in time."

"You promised Lillian you'd be there."

"I know," I say, about to sit on the bed but catching myself. That bed doesn't belong to me anymore. Nothing in this room does. I lower myself to the floor again. "Like I said, I wasn't able to leave town in time." I look over at our two khaki-colored reading chairs sitting expectantly by the window. At the books on Eva's nightstand: *Written on the Body, Dream Work*. At the empty nightstand by what used to be my side of the bed. "But I'm going to head up to Michigan when I leave here," I say.

"Right." Eva sounds unconvinced.

She sits on the floor beside me. Takes her pumps off and massages one of her high arches. She's short, even in heels, but she has this particular kind of stature—self-assurance, genuine earnestness—born of boarding school and Ivy League breeding. She stretches, and I smell home: the faded flowers and vanilla of her perfume; sweat from teaching and student meetings and all the things a good academic does in a day. A good academic. A good, honest woman.

I taste the lies at the back of my throat.

A confession comes up from out of nowhere: "I saw coverage on television. I watched it—stop looking at me like that—I watched it on my laptop." Sitting there paralyzed on one of my moving boxes. With my car keys in my hand.

She gives me a look that says, *It doesn't have to be this way.*

"Would you like me to go with you? Back home?" she asks. "You know I will. Even with things, you know, the way they are."

"No. I'm good. It's fine."

She closes her eyes and pinches the bridge of her nose. Typical exasperation. "Viola, if you'd only—" She stops and shakes her head. "Never mind."

"What? If I'd only what?"

If only you'd be more open; if only you'd go to couple's therapy, like I've asked; if only you'd get any *therapy at this point; if only you were a little less you; if only; if only; if only.*

But Eva doesn't say any of that. She shakes her head and says simply, "Your face. You look thin. I'm worried about you."

She's seen. I get up and head for the door. "I should probably get going."

"Wait," Eva says, raising her hands and wiggling her fingers for me to pull her up from the floor. When I have her back on her feet, she says, "I have mail. I was going to drop it off at work for you." She stops and examines my face closely again. "Hasn't anyone at work noticed? How thin you are?"

"No," I say. "Because there's nothing to notice. I'm under a lot of stress, clearly, and like any normal person, my diet is, well, it could be better."

She shakes her head. "I'll get your mail."

I sit on the bed, suddenly too exhausted to care about the division of formerly joint-owned property.

"You have something," Eva says, coming back into the bedroom, flipping through the mail pile, and pulling out an envelope, "from Althea. It got here yesterday."

"Thank you," I say, accepting the pile. I look down at the envelope written out in Althea's lovely, calligraphic handwriting. I trace the letters of my name and touch upon a memory. "She taught me cursive," I say. "Or, rather, she made sure I was good at it. Did you know that?"

"No," Eva says quietly, sitting down on the bed next to me and resting her hand on my thigh, like older, easier times. "But I'm not surprised."

I nod, picturing Althea back then, when we were younger, with her Angela Davis afro, her bell-bottoms and butterfly clogs. "She made me practice, relentlessly. And she would teach me new words, too. Simpatico. She taught me that word. Where would she have learned that? She wasn't a word person." I pause, thinking. I was the word person. I think sometimes she learned things she had no interest in, just for me. We'd sit together at the kitchen table, just the two of us. Practicing or talking or whatever. Even when we didn't have any electricity, which was a regular occurrence, she'd grab a flashlight or light candles.

"I imagine Althea was a pretty dedicated teacher," Eva says.

I'm thinking of what Althea used to say to me sometimes, as we sat together at that kitchen table: "You and me, we run together, Viola. Mama used to say that, and it's true."

"Althea was more than a teacher," I say.

"I know."

Althea was sister, mother, friend, all the world to me.

"I bet she wants to make things right, Viola," Eva says, looking down at the letter in my hand.

"I don't know." Althea isn't the contrite, introspective type. The last time I saw her, no, I mean the last time I *argued* with her, I told her as much.

You have too many blind spots, Althea, I said, deeply upset. *And I worry that, even when you're shown, you still refuse to see.*

Actually, the last time I *saw* Althea was today, while I was sitting paralyzed on one of my moving boxes, watching that Michigan news report on my laptop, feeling something in me give way. I look at Eva. "The reporter said Althea collapsed while the judge was reading her sentence," I say. I glance down at the letter, my throat tightening. "The reporter, he counted up all the years they got. Althea got five. Proctor got seven. They weren't supposed to get that much time!"

She grabs my hand and holds tight.

"The twins. They're effectively orphans now." Just like we were.

"Viola," Eva says, "you need to get home. Immediately. Lillian must be beside herself."

I look down at my hand in hers and murmur, "She is."

"I'm so sorry," Eva says, raising my hand to her lips to kiss my fingers.

I squeeze her hand and hold on for a moment. Then, I let go. I tuck my pile of mail under my arm and get up, looking again at our reading chairs by the window. Wanting nothing more than to sit in my chair while she sits in hers, both of us with a good book, like we used to. Me, blocking out crimes and punishments and the misfortunes of orphans.

"And really," Eva says, "I can—"

"No, I'm good. Everything's going to be fine."

"Do you see what you just did, there? Don't cut me off like that, Viola. I'm worried about you, okay? I'm worried about your family.

People, *some* of them at least"—she takes a beat to illuminate a truth about Althea—"some of them," she repeats, "who've been my family for a long time. Why don't you, for once, let someone help?"

"I told you, I'm fine."

We stand, facing each other, on the edge of yet another precipice.

"I don't want to fight with you," I say.

Eva presses her fingers to her eyes, spent before we even begin. "Neither do I," she breathes.

"Look, this thing with Althea and Proctor, it's unexpected and terrible," I say. "But it's done. So there's nothing to do now except get up to Michigan and make some decisions about the best thing to do going forward."

Eva lets out a resigned breath. "Fine. Go do that. By yourself."

I start for the door.

"Wait," Eva says. "I know I'm not in a position to make demands on you anymore, but we spent fifteen years together. I know you better than just about anybody, yourself included right now. So I have to insist: Call me while you're there, okay? Check in."

There are the chairs, together. The bed: my side, her side. My empty dresser. Our room in our dream home that we shared for three years. A condo downtown, after years of living in an actual house in the suburbs for most of those fifteen years.

My eyes find her again. "I will. I'll check in."

"I mean it, Viola."

"I *know*."

"Promise?"

"Promise."

I head out the bedroom door and stop in the kitchen. I take my keys out of my pocket and look at them for a moment. I slip my house key off the ring and leave it on the cool, concrete countertop. I hug my week's worth of mail to my chest and leave. But not bound for Lillian's.

Oldham County Correctional Facility
Proctor Cochran
720 Smith Avenue, NE
Park Point, Michigan

Saturday, November 16, 2013

Althea,

You okay? I'd be lying if I told you I'm not still trying to get my mind wrapped around this. So much for the hopes of first-time offenders. Yesterday, I heard this brother say, "The community wouldn't have stood for nothing less." I acted like I didn't hear him and went on about my business, but I wanted to pop him one because all I could think about was you in that courtroom, falling out like you did, down there on the floor, gone, and seeing Baby Vi back there crying in Lillian's arms and Lillian looking at me like DO SOMETHING! And the whole time, I'm worried to death about where Kim is. I swear to God, I've never felt so useless. It brought me to my own knees inside. In a lot of ways, I'm still there, this close to popping the next person who tells me what we deserve. I know we did wrong and we'll pay for that, but you can't tell me that that judge couldn't have found something between a smack on the wrist and a beatdown. My man went for the beatdown with us, straight up.

I tried to write you the other day, right when I got back from sentencing. I started a couple of letters, but I couldn't finish them. I was in my Darth Vader Space, all darkness and doom, writing crazy stuff. You know how I get. I tell you, being able to play the "community guitar" is truly therapy for a brother's soul. The guitar's not a Gibson, but it'll do. Your boy would play all day every day if they'd let me. But man can't live on guitar alone, so there's the Prozac, which, I got to say, doesn't look like it's doing a damn thing. But I need to know, are you doing any better? I saw our friend up here today. He said he saw you and you were talking to him about his son and family like you usually do. He said you seemed okay. Is he right?

Anyway, I'm glad I waited a couple days to write. Guess what I saw this morning? We were finally able to get out after all that rain, and you know me, I was chomping at the bit while some people were complaining about the damp and the cold and this and that. I made it outside first and there it was, a deer standing out there past the fence on the edge of the woods. It was over on that end with the basketball courts. The deer was picking around in the brush, and there was sun coming down through the breaks in the clouds. It was the kind of thing you see on a postcard or something. Can you picture it? And before the rest of the guys came out and scared her off, that deer raised her head and looked at me across all that distance between the woods and where I was in the yard. And I swear, this calm came over me that I get sometimes when I'm out hunting and I've been still for a long time before seeing something. It's like me and whatever I have in my sights are both part of this natural order and there's a rightness to everything. Feeling some-

thing like that when I was still so torn up from the sentencing, it was like nature was saying, There's still beauty and light, man. That's nature. That's your <u>true</u> nature. What do they say? The better angels of your nature?

But enough of my philosophizing. It's time for the most important thing, which is getting things set up for the girls now that we know what's what. I just can't get my head around the fact that we won't be raising our own kids. No driver's training, no prom, no dropping them off at college.

I hope this finally makes you see that you need to let the girls come up and see you. It was one thing to say "I don't want them seeing me this way" when we were going through all of this waiting and the trial. But I'm not stupid. I know why you won't see them. Well, I know why you won't see Kim. But they need to see you. You got that now, right? <u>Especially</u> Kim. Did you read her letter I sent you?

And I may as well go ahead and say this. It's time to stop going over and over which one of us did what and this and that. I made my choices, and I can live with them.

Before I close out, though, I wanted to tell you that that picture you sent was nice, so thank you for that. I'll give it to her, your girl Mercedes is some kind of artist, but, still, please be careful. You know crazy can't help but do crazy, so watch yourself with her, <u>please</u>. I wish you'd stay away from her like I asked you to, but when have you ever listened to me? Anyway, the picture of you is beautiful, and I'm happy to have it. I couldn't imagine a better anniversary gift. It looks a lot like you, and I see you're standing in your special place, "River Girl." There's even our tree in the background. I'm looking at the picture now while I sit here writing to you. I have it taped up over my bunk. When I look at it, it reminds me of all the things that have survived through all this. That tree *was here before either one of us, and it stood right through the Great Flood. Remember that because that has to be us, right? P+ A. Can you believe we've been married 30 years? And we made us two kids. That's something we did right, isn't it?*

I've had this song running over and over in my head like a reminder that things can't change us so much. Not for the bad, if we're careful. Time for the hint. And yes, I still like doing this, which means, yes, we're keeping it going, so stop trying to quit. Here we go. Hint: First time, end of time, flack.

I know I hit you with some B-sides the last couple times, but I'm taking it easy on you with this one. You know this song, young girl.

We'll see each other when we do.

All my love,
Proctor

Althea

The walk to the kitchen is a slog past sealed windows and closed doors. As I pass through the high-ceilinged dayroom, ringed by two stories of cells, the reverb of voices ricocheting off cinder-block walls and stainless-steel tables surrounds me. Stepping heavy, in no hurry, I move into the hall. There's always some rotting, mildew funk under the surface of the antiseptic air out here. I imagine the cleaning crew spreading that stink around like a virus with their dripping, gray mops.

I hear my name. It's C.O. Jordan, walking right beside me. I forgot he was even here, which is hard. He's a big bulldog of a man with broad shoulders and bowlegs and squeaky shoes.

I work up a smile.

"You still hanging in there?" he asks.

"You know me."

He nods. "Yeah, I do."

No, you don't. But like the woman he thinks he knows, I ask, "The family okay? Your son liking first grade any better?"

"Everybody's good," he says. "And Little Stanley wanted to go to school this morning, so I'm guessing first grade's finally starting to agree with him."

"See, I told you he'd be fine. It takes some kids longer, that's all." My lip trembles from the strain of making myself smile. "Make sure you tell everybody at home I said hi."

"Most definitely."

I don't know what else to say. He clears his throat, no doubt feeling the same way. It was easy talking to Stan on the outside when him and his family would be in town and come to the restaurant, but he's C.O. Jordan to me in here, not Stan. He'll sometimes have a word from Proctor, but he doesn't really ask anything about my family like he used to back in the restaurant days, when I'd come out of the kitchen in my chef's coat and red clogs and everybody'd be waiting to see me. He never makes me think about how it used to be or what's happening out there in the free world, more than I already do.

"Look," he says, "I know you said you were okay after that fall in court and everything, but, you sure? You hanging in?"

"I'm fine."

He slows down, looking at me like he actually expects me to say more. But how do you tell somebody what it's like to have reality rolling in on you in waves, knocking you to your knees as a judge ticks off the charges against you, taking years of your life like it's nothing? There aren't words, so I don't say anything else. I keep walking, at my speed.

He falls in step with me again and glances up at the brown-stained drop ceiling. "I saw your boy the other day." Proctor is two floors up in the men's block. I look up, too, like I might catch him looking down at us. "I saw him last week, after the sentencing. I hope it helps to know that he seemed all right. I think he's handling it."

"It does help. Thank you."

I look up again, imagining Proctor in his element. While I was back in the kitchen, he'd be out front, like he loves, working the room, turning up his quiet charm a little when him and his band would play for the late-night crowd, taking all requests. If somebody hollered out, "Etta James!" Proctor would play "I'd Rather Go Blind." Clapton? He might lay down a slow, acoustic "Layla." But mostly, he just played whatever was in his heart, which, these days, has to be "Serves Me Right to Suffer."

I hear myself ask, "If I said, 'First time, end of time, and flack,' to you, what song would come to mind?"

He blinks at me, confused. I'm confused. Why'd I say that? His forehead scrunches up, and he shakes his head. "I don't know. Should I know that?"

"Sorry. No. I don't guess you should. It's for me. I'm cheating. I guess I'm just being, I don't know."

"It's all right." But his uncomfortable laugh says it's not. It says he thinks there's something wrong with me, which he might be right about. "Hell, we're all 'just being,' aren't we?" he says, putting his hands in his pockets and looking down at the floor, then back at me. "Look, I just wanted to say that if I can do anything, you know I'm here. You still got a friend in me. And Proctor, too. You got any sense, you know, of your timetable? How much longer you got before your transfer?"

"They'll probably be shipping me out in the next few weeks. At least, that's what my lawyer thinks. Maybe around Christmas. But you know how it is."

"Yeah," he says. "I was hoping that maybe you'd at least be here, you know, close to your family for Christmas."

"We'll see," I say. "Anyway, I'd probably better get on in the kitchen for work. Lunch won't serve itself." As much as I hate passing out trays, at least it's something to do. At least it keeps my mind from wandering off too far.

"Right, right." He waves me off. "Get on in there. I'll see you later."

I walk fast, my hand going up to my breast pocket like a reflex. I've taken to keeping Kim's letter there, instead of in the back of my mother's Bible.

And there goes my mind . . .

What kind of family does this man think I have? There are the daughters that I can't, *won't*, see. And the sister, Viola, who I raised like a daughter, who wouldn't even come to my sentencing. Who hasn't so much as responded to my letter. Who won't see me.

Viola

I close my eyes. Rest my head on the porcelain. It feels exceptionally cool against my face. It's like an ice pack soothing a relentless ache. Peaceful white noise fills my head. I feel light enough to float on air. I could fall asleep.

But the sharp, sweet-sour stench wafting up from the toilet bowl hits my nose like smelling salts, and I'm awake to the carnage around me: food flecks dotting the wall of the tub and the tile behind the toilet; the chunks of doughnuts, Ding Dongs, and hot dogs clinging to the lip of the commode; and the orange trickle of disgust streaking down the side, close to where my face rests. I scramble to my feet and flush the toilet. Wipe the back of my hand over my mouth as I wait for the toilet bowl to fill up. Flush again to get the remains. It's going to need a third flush.

While I wait for the toilet to collect itself for another flush, I go to the sink, still feeling light as air. Still enjoying the fuzzy, white-noise sense of calm. Xanax couldn't make me feel any mellower, I don't think.

I splash cool water on my face, but I don't look up in the mirror. I stand here, enjoying the moment, because I know what comes next.

I flush the toilet again and shuffle out to the room, my T-shirt damp down the front with what I hope is just water. I don't inspect myself. I survey the hotel room instead.

"Clean up, Viola," I say, my throat scratchy and raw. "And get back on the road, please."

I push potato chip bags, a pizza box, and candy bar wrappers out of my way and flop down on the bed. *"Please,"* I beg myself again, as I lay on my back, staring up at the bright popcorn ceiling. My body has a mind of its own and remains supine. But my eyes travel over to the desk and stop on the letter. Its pages are flared up as if to fold itself away from the seesawing fits of guilt and blame I feel every time I read it. Althea's letter. It's the thing that, eventually, got me out of my new apartment and into my nearly as new car. Next to the letter sits my phone, with text messages and voice mails from Lillian. They're what kept me driving northbound, toward New River Junction, when I wanted to turn around. That is, until I felt like I was getting low on gas at about the halfway point. Which made me exit the highway to fill up. Which triggered a craving for a gas station hot dog. Which should have been the proverbial canary in the soul-killing k-hole I'd been inching down for days. Now I find myself trapped at the very bottom of that hole, here at the Days Inn.

I haul myself up from the bed and go to the desk.

"Fine," I mumble, grabbing my phone.

Maybe this will give me enough lift to get out of the hole this time.

I read Lillian's text from this morning. It's the most recent, though thematically the same as the ones that preceded it: Where are you?????

There are, what, four voice mails now?

"I'm coming," I say to the phone. "I'm on my way."

But my eyes drift and my stomach flutters. I'm losing that little lift. Slipping back to the bottom of the hole. That calm I felt, the fuzzy white noise? It's leaving, too. And here arrives what always comes next: this need, nothing short of crotch-grabbing desire, spreading up and seizing my brain until I can think of nothing else.

The zombie stirs.

There's only the table where I've carefully organized, by height, what's left of my hoard: an unopened package of Oreos; half a large pizza, still boxed; half a dozen glazed doughnuts; the last three jumbo honey buns from the vending machine, stacked one atop the other; a two-liter bottle of Orange Crush, minus a few chugs.

The zombie walks.

There's no taking this dead-eyed monster down with a good head-shot, a good blast of rational thought. I'm alive with it. Pulsing with adrenaline, desire, and dread.

I reach for the Oreos.

Stop, stop, you can still stop! says the dread.

But it's no match for desire and adrenaline, especially after the first bite. I'm reaching, grabbing, pulling everything down to the floor, crouching over my quarry protectively. A gorging, hunchbacked creature.

But it's not enough. As I reach for the pizza, my mind is already out hunting for more, roving up and down the street outside. It's late. After midnight. Everything around the hotel is closed. It will have to be the vending machine again. How much cash do I have? Shit. I spent it all! Just credit cards. The machine's old. It doesn't take credit cards!

But I don't slow down. I don't ration. I can't. I devour the jumbo honey buns. A gob full of sweetness and mush. I eat until I'm tight. I eat until everything is gone, then I chug down some Orange Crush. I'm packed tight, ready to pop. I grab a cup for water. It helps me flush myself out, particularly the doughy doughnuts, which I find exceedingly difficult to expel.

As I head for the bathroom again, I touch my drum-tight belly like it holds life. But in my mind, what I see is a wasted little girl with the empty, distended gut of the malnourished. I'll feel better soon, though. Light as air again and there will be that soothing white noise. There will be at least a moment's peace and calm before the crash into self-loathing, which is another hole entirely.

Showered.

Freshly washed face.

Dry, clean shirt.

I look at my phone on the desk.

Come on, Viola. This is bad again. Please make the call.

I make myself pick up the phone and thumb through the list of names. I find the one I need, but my thumb hovers there.

Come on!

My thumb still hesitates.

You are not okay! You are not going to be *okay! Do it!*

My thumb drops on *Therapist*. I hear the ring.

Don't hang up, don't hang up, don't hang up.

There's the voice mail, as expected at this hour.

Speak! Say it!

"Hi." I clear my throat. "This is Vi—Dr. Butler. I'm calling to make an appointment. For as soon as possible, if I can. I know it's been a while, but I can't actually come into the office. So, a phone appointment, please. I need to go home to Michigan, and, well, it's an emergency. I need, see, I could use a tune-up. As soon as you can. If you can call me back when you get this, I'd appreciate it. Thank you."

I let out a heavy breath and drop, with my hands on my knees like I've just finished a run.

Good girl.

I stand up straight again and look at Althea's letter, still trying to fold itself away from me: *I've been thinking about things, and I'm sorry for everything I said to you,* she wrote. *With everything that's happening, I need you to come home, little sister. Will you? We need to talk.*

I fold up the letter and put it in my purse, which hangs from the chair.

I pick up my phone again. I need to call my best friend to meet me when I get to town, but that conversation is going to take some time. He'll want an explanation. I'll have to talk him into helping me do something that I haven't even convinced myself to do.

I text Lillian first: Coming tomorrow. Will call before I leave. Still held up with work. Again! Sorry!! A nightmare. Love.

TASTE OF HOME

Lillian

A chill runs through me as I look out the window. It's one of those days that feels like night. All gray skies and ominous clouds, with house lights and streetlights and headlights glowing in the gloom.

I take a sip of my tea and look over my shoulder (finally) to see that it's still pretty gloomy here in the kitchen, too.

"Any suggestions on how to handle her?" I ask, looking down.

My cat, an orange tabby, blinks up at me and tilts his head to the side. He's got nothing.

"Same here," I say.

He yawns, stretches, flicks his tail against my leg, then trots over to his water dish.

I look over at the *her* who needs to be handled. My little gray cloud of an ex-grandmother-in-law, who actually looks more like a little Michelin Man, sitting over there across the room in the breakfast nook in a white puffer jacket and a white hat with earflaps.

"Are you going to let me help you off with your coat now?" I glance at my watch. "I mean, we've been in the house for, like, twenty minutes. I know you're hot, and you know I'm not changing my mind."

Watery black eyes peek out from the heavy folds in her face. A usually sweet, flat face if not for the fact that she's seriously pissed off.

"Look," I say, "this isn't my fault. It's for your own good. No more McDonald's. You heard what the doctor said."

She looks away from me, crossing her Michelin Man–padded arms.

"Please, Nai Nai," I say. "The doctor told you. He's worried about your cholesterol."

"Last favorite in life," she said to the doctor after his fast-food fatwa. Then she complained to me (silently, but belligerently) on the drive home and now here in the kitchen over the tea she won't drink in the coat and hat she won't take off.

But I'm putting my foot down this time. I mean, she's my ward (my word). My roommate (her word). My responsibility, no question.

Nai Nai turns and stares at me. "I eighty-eight," she says finally, in broken English, meaning, *What do I care about cholesterol at this point?*

She knows the age card is usually the trump card with me. I've always said, "She's an old lady, let her live a little." Having outlived two husbands, a son, a daughter-in-law, and a grandson, she should have whatever she wants. And let's face it, she's hard to kill (not that I've tried, yet). She's survived cancer, two broken hips (a few years apart), and growing up in rural China in a way that she described only as "very hard," but maybe "not as hard" as her first years in this country. By my count, it's Nai Nai, four; Death, zero. But then, Death only needs one win, and with the doctor saying, in really guilt-inducing terms, that the takedown could come any day now at McDonald's, I'm rethinking what it means to "live a little."

"Why don't we try something different for breakfast tomorrow?" I ask, going for an old-school favorite. "Some porridge. I'll make it. I still know how." She taught me how back when my ex-husband was still alive and still my husband, but only after she resigned herself, somewhat, to him having married "a black." Rice porridge, she said while teaching me, is what *we* (read: Chinese people, not you black people) eat.

"I like sausage egg biscuit now," she says, looking away and mumbling something in Mandarin. I don't speak it, but that doesn't stop me from doing berating translations: You're doing everything wrong, Lillian; I'm going to die miserable because of you, Lillian; shouldn't be a surprise since you're screwing up with your sister's kids, too, Lillian.

I try to breathe through it.

Finally, I get ready to do some more pleading, but there's the key in the front door and the click of it closing. I hear shuffling feet and the *thud-thud* of shoes tossed in the front closet. There's the soft padding of socked feet. My other roommates/wards. Althea's girls. The nieces I'm screwing up, home from school.

When I moved back home from Brooklyn almost four years ago—after the affair(s) and resulting divorce—I never imagined that this would be my life. I came home to regroup. Spend time with my dad. Reconnect with my better self. Renovate the house I grew up in. A life rebuild in every way. But then the Universe had other plans. Taking in Nai Nai two and a half years ago when my ex-husband died. Then Althea and Proctor's arrest and custody of the girls after Althea and Proctor's bail was revoked for talking to a witness ("tampering with a witness," prosecutors said). Now here I am at thirty-six, no kids of my own, both parents dead, yet somehow I'm a member of the sandwich generation.

Baby Vi comes through the wide, arched entry to the kitchen, hugging her book bag to her chest. She's like a tall, knobby-kneed foal, folding in on herself. Her head's tucked down, and her narrow shoulders are hunched up, still locked in a defensive block against the cold. Michigan, rushing into winter, is not for the faint of heart or the underdressed. Baby Vi's both, standing there in a jean jacket and black leggings.

"You didn't wear your heavier coat, did you?" I ask her.

She lowers her book bag to the floor and reaches down to pet the cat, Thelonious, waiting at her feet. "No," she answers, in a voice so quiet I can barely hear.

Why do I even ask?

Baby Vi looks at Nai Nai in her white Michelin Man coat and raises an eyebrow. "Aren't you hot?"

Nai Nai nods like this is the first time the issue of overheating has come up. Baby Vi goes over to her, but not before looking at me, appalled, like I should be arrested for elder abuse.

"She wouldn't let me take it off." My voice sounds suddenly babyish and whiny. "Never mind."

I lean against the counter and sip my tea while Baby Vi unzips Nai Nai's coat and gently pulls out one stiff, spindly arm, then another. As she removes the coat, there emerges a woman who's like a tiny comma, back hunched, head just about at chest level. She's wearing a white T-shirt with sparkly stitching that says: KEEP CALM AND HIRE AN INTERIOR DESIGNER. A shirt she saw and liked when I took her with me to an interior design show in Chicago last month. (I wanted the same T, given that I'm the actual interior designer, but I let her have it.)

She has pretty good taste in clothes, for her age. When she and I were at Dress Depot with Baby Vi picking out Althea's old-ladyish muumuus, Nai Nai squinted at one of the tight floral patterns and leaned on her walker, like just looking at the thing took it out of her. Then she eyed me, like, *Seriously?*

Nai Nai smiles up at Baby Vi. Baby Vi looks down, her dark eyes soft, as she tugs off the cap with the earflaps. "There," she says, arranging Nai Nai's thin, white, sweaty hair so that it looks like spiky bedhead.

"How was school?" I ask.

Baby Vi shrugs. "It's school."

Nai Nai wraps thick-knuckled fingers around Baby Vi's thin wrist and demands to know, "They still all the time making fun?" She says this like there's something she can actually do about it.

Baby Vi gives a weak smile and pats Nai Nai's hand. "It's fine," she says gently, pulling her wrist from Nai Nai's grip.

I look at the empty archway.

"And Kim?" I ask, trying to sound casual. "I thought maybe she might walk home with you. They said I didn't have to come pick her up this time." I feel instantly guilty and irresponsible. I try to explain. "I'll go back to school with her tomorrow. I have to. I mean, I had Nai Nai's doctor's appointment, see, so the principal said it was fine. I thought she might've walked home with you."

Baby Vi shakes her head. "I went to find her, but the detention monitor said she was gone already."

"It's okay."

She chews on her bottom lip.

Both of us know things aren't okay.

I set my now-lukewarm cup of tea on the counter and pull my phone from the back pocket of my jeans, thinking maybe I missed a text from Kim. I check the screen. Why do I even look?

I shove my phone back in my pocket.

Baby Vi has moved to the pantry to stare inside. On one shelf, there's her and her sister's food (potato chips, cookies, cereal, etc.); on the one under that, Nai Nai's staples (dried rice noodles, dried black mushrooms, dried prunes, and other dried stuff); under that, mine (goji berries, granola, quinoa pasta, quinoa itself, and so on). On the other shelves, the things we have in common, which isn't that much (peanut butter, crackers, raisins, cans of corn).

"I got groceries this morning, so you have plenty to choose from." I hear way too much upbeat torque in my voice.

Nai Nai gives me a look. Translation: Do you always have to try so hard, Lillian?

"Yeah, I can see that," Baby Vi mumbles, but not like a sarcastic kid. More like an exhausted old lady.

She pulls out a box of Cap'n Crunch Crunch Berries and reads the nutrition label. She puts it back.

"There's plenty of other stuff in there, too," I say. "Healthier stuff." It's like I can't buy the right thing for her anymore. If it was right before, she all of a sudden has some reason for why she doesn't want to eat it now: "I'm thinking about becoming a vegetarian," or "I think I should start watching my carbs," and so on. But she loves those Crunch Berries. I can tell by the way she keeps going back to the box, then rejecting it.

"Go ahead," I say. "They're your favorites, aren't they?"

She looks at me, chewing her lip. "I'm good. I'm gonna go up. I have homework." She makes another stop by the table and gives Nai Nai a peck on the cheek.

Nai Nai pats her arm. "You good girl," she says.

"Thanks," Baby Vi murmurs as she heads for the archway, grabbing up her backpack with her free hand and disappearing.

Nai Nai shakes her head and clucks her tongue, watching her go. "How much she can take?"

The taunting, teasing, and the silent treatment at school. More than two years of it. "I don't know," I say quietly.

"She tough girl. She tougher than she look. She be okay." She quickly adds, "The other one, too."

We look at each other.

Nai Nai looks down at the table and shrugs.

I take a seat at the table with her. Thelonious jumps up in my lap, and I stroke his back as I close my eyes and send positive energy, thoughts of resilience, up the stairs to Baby Vi. I send those same thoughts out to the Universe to Kim, wherever she is, and whisper, really low so Nai Nai can't hear, "Safe."

I open my eyes and look at Nai Nai, her head haloed in white, partly matted, partly poking-out hair. "I still can't believe this is happening," I say. "I mean, it's not fair."

Nai Nai shrugs again. "Life not fair." She reaches for her cup of tea.

"It's cold," I say, grabbing up the cup before she can get to it. "I'll make you a new one."

As I get up to refill the kettle, she says, "You *mèi mei*. Little sister." She raises a trembling hand, holding up a crooked index finger. Third sister. Fourth child. *Mèi mei.* Little sister. "You do duty for first sister," she says, pointing the finger at me to emphasize my place at the end of the pecking order. "No fair when you flesh blood."

Flesh and blood. I'm at least that to Althea. But Althea's heart? That's the brother, Joe. And her soul? The other sister, Viola. Being just flesh and blood, fourth child, never seemed like enough with her when it came to me. The only reason we're in regular touch now is because I have her kids.

Just as I put the kettle on to boil, I hear the front door. Nai Nai and I look at each other. I tense. There's the heavy clomping of boots. Kim never takes off her shoes or boots. I'm going to have to say something. Again.

Kim clomps through the entryway, a large, cinnamon-skinned girl in a long, black puffer coat. Behind her is her boyfriend. A tall, dread-locked, round-glasses-wearing cross between Urkel and a Rastafarian. To his credit, he *always* remembers to take off his shoes, thanks mostly to good home training from his mother, who happens to be my very best friend.

"Hey," I say, smiling, like Kim hasn't walked on my hardwoods with those boots on. Like I didn't get that call from the principal today: "We're going to put her in in-school suspension"—(again)—"but we'll need you to come in with her in the morning, to talk about behavior"—(again)—"before we can put her back in her classes."

Kim's boyfriend, Junior (who's actually a senior), says hi and asks how I've been. As I tell him that everything's good, he nods and says, "Cool, cool," in his usual, absentminded way. I could tell this kid that I'm dying, and I think he'd just stand there, all dreamy, nodding and saying, "Cool."

"It's chilly out there," I say, looking at Kim. "I'm glad you wore your heavy coat." P.S.: I wish you'd listen when it comes to other things.

"Trying to stay warm," she says. Her voice is heavy and hoarse. Her eyes are red and glossy. She's blinking slowly.

Something's up. "You guys doing okay?"

Junior smiles, flashing braces-straightened teeth.

"Yeah, we're good," Kim says. She drops her notebook on the counter. It's a blue, spiral-bound, bulging monster stuffed with God knows what all and held together with rubber bands. It's been her constant companion since the arrest. With it safely where she wants it for the moment, she bends and gives Thelonious a quick pat, then moves in Nai Nai's direction.

I look down at Kim's feet. "Remember the, um, remember about wearing shoes in the house?" I try to avoid the word *rule*. It feels too overlordish. "Remember how we want to keep the hardwoods in good condition? Remember how I just laid those floors?"

"Right. Sorry." Kim stops and leans against the counter to pull off her combat-style black boots, glancing up. "Hey, Nai Nai."

Nai Nai nods at her, then looks at me.

"So." I look into Kim's red, glossy eyes. *Is she high?* I glance at the still-smiling Junior. Yep. Same red eyes behind the silver wireframes. "Kim, we need to talk." I turn to Junior. "Junior, would you mind?"

"He can stay," Kim says.

"Okay. All right. No problem." I try to think of the best way to approach this. "You know the principal called today, right?"

"Yeah," Kim says, grabbing up her boots and putting them by the garage door.

"He told me you were giving your history teacher a lot of pushback?"

She rubs the chubby rings around her neck. "I'm not really feeling that into people right now."

"What does that mean?"

"It means I'm not taking a lot of shit from people." She walks from the garage door back over to Junior by the archway and grabs up her notebook.

"Look, I know it's hard. I—"

"Teachers need to show respect, too." She hugs the notebook to her chest and narrows what I'm almost one hundred percent sure are weed-reddened eyes. "It's two ways. It's not only for me to do all the respecting."

"No, you're right," I say. "So, look, we have an appointment with your principal tomorrow, okay? We'll get to the bottom of everything. But, Kim, this can't keep happening, you know?"

I look at Junior. For backup, if I'm honest.

He rubs his fledgling, feathery mustache as he looks down at his big toe, which is peeking out of a hole in his sock.

The teakettle goes off, sounding less like a whistle than a scream. I go over and turn down the flame as Kim tells Junior, "Come on."

When I look up to stop them, there's Baby Vi, as quiet as a cat, back from upstairs.

"I heard you down here," she says to Kim. "I looked for you after school."

"Yeah, I got out quick."

"I wanna ask," Baby Vi says, glancing from Kim to me, then back to Kim. A silent question is being asked between them.

Kim scrunches up her heart-shaped face. "If you must."

Baby Vi looks back to where I'm standing, over by the stove. "We were thinking—"

"*You* were thinking," Kim cuts in.

"It wasn't just me, but fine. *I* was thinking, when are we gonna get to go back and see Mama? Because, it's like we all thought they'd be coming home soon, but, obviously, they're not, and nobody's even saying anything."

"I'll have to talk to your mom and dad about it," I say. "Soon."

Kim looks at Baby Vi and shakes her head.

Baby Vi lets out an angry breath. "It's not right to not talk to us about things. Or pretend like nothing's going on. Or that it's 'adult' things. We're not blind babies or something. We can see things. Like we could see what was going on at the minimarket when we worked our shifts. Obviously. They tried to hide it, but—"

"They have stupid customers," Kim finishes. "She thought she was so smart."

She being Althea, I'm guessing.

"Kim, *stop it*," Baby Vi says.

Kim looks down at her socked feet and shrugs. "I don't care. It's true."

"Look," I say. "We'll call Althea. It's just—"

"See!" Kim interrupts, her head snapping up to look at her sister. "*It's just*," she mimics me. "Didn't I tell you? She doesn't wanna see us. She never calls us, does she? She hardly writes us, and you write her all the time! She doesn't care! Not even about you!"

"Kim, please," I say.

Kim whips her head around and looks at me again. "'Kim, *please*'? This isn't my fault. It's *her*. Not me!"

"Kim!" I say.

She pushes past Baby Vi and stomps off.

Junior stands there wide-eyed for a second. He blinks, like a flash has gone off in his face. He turns around and follows her.

Thelonious looks startled, too, as we all listen to Kim thundering up the stairs. I flinch at the sound of a slamming door and the blast of bass suddenly thumping through the floor and vibrating through the walls.

Baby Vi has a faraway look as she goes over and picks up Thelonious, burying her face in his softness.

"Your mother," I say, "you know she absolutely loves you. She's just having a hard time."

Baby Vi looks up at me, tears dropping, dampening Thelonious's orange fur. She glances up at the ceiling, toward the sound of music. "So are we," she says.

And she goes the way of her sister, but quietly, cradling Thelonious.

I turn to Nai Nai and point in the direction of where the two of them last stood, with Junior. "See?" My voice is trembling, my whole body shaking. "That's not fair."

Nai Nai nods.

Still shaking, I try to take in deep, calming breaths. Try to figure out what to do. I'm blowing it, blowing it. I look out the window over the sink. Thank God Viola's finally on her way. She'll know what to do. I grab the teakettle and pour the hot water over the tea infuser to steep, as the ceiling above our heads vibrates even more with rhythmic *thump-thump-thumps*.

Nai Nai makes a throat-clearing noise: the sound of disapproval.

"I know," I say. "But what do you want me to do? That stereo is everything to her."

Nai Nai's eyes soften into a look I've never seen before. "Girl have to have something," she says, looking down at her gnarled hands on the table.

I feel a stab of sadness as I think about what little the girls have left. Kim has the same love of music (obsession, Althea would say) as her dad, along with that stereo that used to be his. A stereo that I helped Kim and Junior smuggle out of her parents' house before it, along with the house, could be seized and tagged for auction by the U.S. government, like most everything else "bought with ill-gotten gains."

I imagine the speakers vibrating above our heads and think of Baby Vi in her room, probably putting her earplugs in. She has her books and her need for quiet. In that way, Baby Vi's like the other sister, Viola. Both of them named for my dead mother. The two surviving Violas are both readers. Solitary types with souls that seem as old as Nai Nai.

"It's really coming down now," I say, rubbing my arms, feeling chilled as I look out the window over the sink again, out to the front yard and the road. It's been threatening sleet all day. But now, it's here. "I hope Viola's okay driving home in this."

"She okay. No worry."

I turn and Nai Nai's looking over her shoulder out the windows behind her, watching the change in weather that's blowing in at her back. The patter against the panes is off beat. Way out of time with the *thump-thump-thump* coming from above.

Althea

"Had a visit with my mom, and she told me she drove through some real weather to get here," says Mercedes, motioning up to a tiny, rectangular window. "For once, it might be better to be in here than out there, wouldn't you say, ladies?"

"No," I answer.

A few of the women laugh.

"Hey, I'm trying," Mercedes says, looking around at the ten or so of us circled up together, sitting B.O. and bad-breath-breathing close; all of us look-alikes, after a fashion, in our black-and-white-striped, jail-issue jumpsuits. Most of our minds likely on the same thing: how long it'll take to get back out there, no matter the weather.

"Well, anyways, ladies, anybody got anything to say about today's scripture? We got some new faces, like our sister Althea here." She nods toward me, sitting next to her on her right. "It'll be good to get some new perspective and whatnots."

"I liked this scripture," says the beaky-nosed, birdie-looking girl who read the verses for us. She closes the Bible and puts it on her lap. "It speaks to me."

Mercedes, who's filling in for the chaplain today, leans forward, her anemic blue eyes examining the girl. Adira, I think she said her name was. Mercedes says, "You wanna say more about what you liked about what you read?"

"I meant to say it speaks *for* me," Adira says, scratching nervously at a space between her neat, oiled cornrows, looking at the floor.

Mercedes stares at her with a bushy eyebrow raised. "Right," she says, giving up and looking around. "Anybody else?"

Not me. God knows, I shouldn't even be here. I let Mercedes talk me into it: "Just this one time," she said. "If nothing else, it'll keep you from sitting in your bunk stewing with old Crazy-quiet, while she sleeps."

Sleeping your time away, like my bunkmate, Crazy-quiet, sounds better and better every day, especially since every waking hour, wherever I am, I'm stewing. I look up at the little window. What I wouldn't give to be able to see through the frosted, chicken-wired glass or, better yet, open that window to get some fresh air. It's stuffy and suffocating in here. When I walked in, this room didn't strike me as small at all, but now it feels as cramped as a closet. Or a cell.

"All right, all right, ladies, I get it," Mercedes is saying. "Like I said, some of you are new, like our sister Adira here. Feeling a little shy. I get it."

Gale, the woman sitting to my right, elbows me in the ribs. "I think I'mma have to get this party started," she says, her voice rattling with phlegm. She's a tiny-eyed pygmy of a woman who's spent most of her fifty-nine years in some kind of bondage or other. Her face, like mauled mahogany leather, literally shows the scars. And so does her mind, sometimes.

"Please don't," I whisper.

Mercedes raises a long, E.T.-looking index finger, pointing to the sign taped to the wall. Bold block letters spell out: SPIRITUAL SAFE HAVEN. "I wanna remind you ladies: This is a safe space. You can be free in here."

A snorty laugh cuts in from across the sharing circle. A short, squared-off Mexican chick repeats, "Safe space," and "Free." She's new, too.

"You think this shit's funny?" Mercedes asks, blood rushing up her neck, filling her pink, pockmarked face. She pushes back overgrown, dirty-blond bangs so there's nothing between her glare and the woman, who's shrinking back in her chair. The woman looks to be about forty, maybe. It can be hard to tell. Some of these women in here are aged in ways that defy the normal passing of time. As I sit here, at forty-eight, I wonder what five years of prison time will do to me.

The Mexican mumbles something about being sorry.

"Yeah, you should be," Mercedes says.

"All right, ladies," the guard warns, distractedly, from his chair in the corner, where he's working a crossword puzzle. "I don't mind shutting it down."

Mercedes sits back, crossing her arms, her short sleeves showing off the sleeves of tattooed crosses and roses and vines snaking down from her elbows to her hands. "Hell, I'll go ahead and get us going. Our scripture was about Jacob wrestling with the angel, right? So I'm thinking, but ain't we all wrestling with something? And for some of us, it sure as shit ain't angels. Am I right?"

"You ain't never lied," Gale says, clapping. "Speak it!"

Other women throw in some amens.

"I guess I'm like Jacob," Mercedes says. "I'm somebody that never minded wrestling. Mixing it up. Hell, I could always take a beating, if it came to it, but you better believe I gave as good as I got."

"Me, too!" a brittle, witchy-looking old white woman shouts out.

Mercedes flashes her a meth-mangled smile.

Most of the women are laughing now. Nudging each other, reminiscing about the times they gave as good as they got. Mercedes raises her hands to quiet everybody down. "The way I handled things," she says, through the dying chatter, "was I knew how to separate my mind from my body, right? So, if somebody came at me, I could take it. They call that mind over matter." She points to her temple. "But what always got me, what always fucked with me like crazy, wasn't really the fighting and everything like that. It was people talking shit to me, right?"

Murmured agreements and nods all around.

Mercedes's face is tight, and I can see she's mad just *thinking* about "people talking shit." On the outside, I'd probably be just as nervous about her as anybody else with any sense, which includes Proctor upstairs. She was the top story on the news before I got arrested and took her place. She likes to remind me that she's back on TV now that her trial has started up.

"Words can either feed you or eat you alive," I offer. "My mama used to tell me that. Well, she wrote it. In her Bible. I've got it here with me."

Some of the women are nodding. The Mexican says, *"Que Dios bendiga a tu mamá."*

Mamá is the only word I understand in all of that.

"You don't wanna hear what my mom would say," Mercedes puts in. "She ain't the poetic type." She looks around. "Anyways, I got us started. It's somebody else's turn now. Like they say, confession's good for the soul."

"I don't know about that," Adira says, barely above a whisper.

Everybody looks at her, surprised. Like seeing an animal learn to speak.

"What's that?" Mercedes says, cupping her hand around her ear.

"I said, I don't know about that," she repeats, a little louder. "See, I wrestled with an angel one time, like Jacob. A real live angel, with wings and everything."

Everybody exchanges looks.

"I don't care what people say," Adira says. "It was real. What you call a *visitation*." She opens her mouth to say more, then closes it. Tries again, then stops, like she's wrestling with herself, now. "And that's the problem. I try and talk about it, I try and tell why. I try and *confess*, but people never get it." One of her hands flutters up to her mouth, and she chews on an already bitten-down nail.

"Give us a try," Mercedes says.

Adira looks so young. Not much older than my daughters. Living in line with the normal passing of time, I bet. Impulsive and too quick to do something stupid, maybe, like Kim. And I wonder what this girl's done and how it compares to what I did to get in here.

When the girl doesn't speak, I say, "Sometimes it's best to keep things to yourself."

Mercedes laughs, and some of the other women do, too.

"I'm serious," I say. "Nobody can say what's good for somebody else's soul or anything else."

Mercedes's smile goes into a slow fade. Her pale hand goes up to rub her neck and chest like she's checking for the disposition of *her* soul. She shrugs and says, "Hell, Althea, I don't know. But that's what they say. Confession's good for the soul, and I don't argue about it." She looks up and checks the clock in its cage, agitated. "Let's just get in a few more and wrap it up."

They keep at it, the women a lot less shy now: "I have problems trusting." "Nobody trusts me." "Trust God."

And I think again: I shouldn't be here. Their God and their angels and their Bible stories may as well be dolls and unicorns and fairy tales to me. I always promised myself I'd never be one of those crisis Christians, running to God or Jesus or whoever in times of trouble. But here I am. In trouble. In crisis. Sitting up here in jail Bible study. I haven't been in a church, or anything like it, since I left home, when I was about the same age that Adira looks. Eighteen. Running away to marry Proctor, thinking I'd never have to do anything I didn't want to do again. That's how young I was.

That's a long ways from here, but it's like I can see it, beyond these dingy walls with their gray streaks and black scuffs and yellow spots. Like I've got a view out past the razor-wire fence, miles away as the crow flies. And there's that house. Not the big, beautiful ranch me and Proctor had on the river, but the one I ran away from. The white brick two-story with wide, weathered steps leading up to the porch and the paint-chipped front door. I can hear my father yelling at me, out on that porch, on the day I left to be with Proctor: "You think you got everything all figured out, with your little plans! Don't come running back home or to the Lord when you find yourself starving, out there on them streets!"

And as he raised his hand to me to make his point, I thought, *But I'm starving now. Living off meals made from charity and church food or whatever me and the kids can lift from the grocery store. I'm cold, too, in clothes passed and shared, worn almost to threads. And I'm tired of living in a house that goes dark whenever you forget or can't leave money to keep the lights on or the heat running.*

But I never had a real plan—little or big. I've had to make things up as I've gone along since I was twelve years old, younger than my own daughters. Since the days after my mama stood me up in front of the stove and said: "I want to get you ready, Althea. There's a few things I need you to know."

It was springtime, and I could hear everybody outside next door playing Red Light, Green Light, which was my game. Quick reflexes and speed, that was me. Mama wouldn't let me go, though. "Let's start with learning how to cook a good meal, Althea."

But things didn't go like she planned. That would be her last spring, and she wouldn't make it through summer. So, I never learned to sew, like she could. She never taught me how to separate and wash clothes, like she meant to. She wasn't able to show me how she stretched a dollar or how she made do when there was even less than that. I never learned how to raise the kids she left behind. Or how to live with the husband, my father, who wasn't any more ready to lose her than I was. I figured all of that out on my own.

At most, there was only time enough to teach me how to make that one good meal.

"You're the responsible one, okay?" she whispered to me, as I sat beside her bed, in the days before she died. When she drifted off to sleep, I stayed there next to her, flipping through her Bible, reading something she'd written in the margins, in her cramped but careful hand: *Dry bones. Read Revelation? (Then the angel showed me the river of the water of life.)*

Quiet *amens* pull me back into the sharing circle. Mercedes taps my arm and I jump. She looks at me, like, *Don't lose it on me,* and stands up, Olive Oyl tall, skinny and knobby jointed. She glances up at the clock. "Let's close out with a hymn. And something with a beat. I think we could all use a little toe tapping right about now."

Gale starts singing "Do Lord" in her smoke-wrecked rattle of a voice. We stand, hold hands in our circle, and sing along. As the last bit of discord fades, Mercedes barks out a prayer, calling out for mercy, demanding that God hear her, commanding God to bless us and surround us in His abundant love. Ordering Him to watch over every single one of us, but most especially me: "God, that devil in a black robe worked his tricks on our sister Althea. Now, show that judge that You're the ultimate judge for Your children. Let her confessions be forgivable and understood. Make her way from here easy."

Viola

"This looks like a derelict hacienda," I say aloud.

The "adobe" bricks, left over from the restaurant's former life as Don Juan's Cantina, are pitted and broken. Some of the plywood covering the boarded-up windows is pried away in places. There's graffiti scrawled all over the walls. My eye catches on the phrase: *Prison: Food for thought*. Between the restaurant and its attached mini-market, the big sign that used to say ALTHEA'S KITCHEN AND GROCERY is gone. There's nothing left but an empty, rusted pole.

"Good luck getting this place sold," I say to the restaurant in front of me and the street behind me. My words condense into a cloud and disappear into the night air. There's no one around to hear me, not even a car on the street, except for mine. The silver Lexus sedan parked down the road. The one functioning streetlight shines above it, a glowing dot of honey.

This is, in point of fact, a terrible location for a restaurant. The street's too quiet. That's one reason Don Juan's Cantina failed. That and the hepatitis A outbreak. But Althea and Proctor managed to make this place into a destination even though neither of them had any experience food-service-wise beyond hosting big dinners for friends and family. You have to give them that much. Althea, quitting her bookkeeping job, and Proctor, leaving the paper mill to start their own business. That was almost twenty years ago. This restaurant was their dream.

I walk up to the entry and look out to the icy parking lot and the street. I check my watch. A quarter after ten. David is running late.

"Do you really think this is a good idea?" he said, when I called from my hotel room and asked him to meet me here.

"Probably not," I told him.

I hug myself against the cold as I think of the drive into town on chewed-up, potholed roads. Driving past the shell of the shuttered bowling ball factory, where half the town worked when I was growing up. Rolling past Althea and Proctor's empty ranch house on the river.

It wasn't so long ago that Lillian and I watched the prosecutor on television, standing out in the restaurant parking lot in front of the media, making his case against Althea and Proctor. Althea's Kitchen and Grocery had not killed anyone, not like Don Juan's with the hepatitis A outbreak, but the restaurant and its proprietors were, in his view, even more of a public menace.

The prosecutor, a big mafioso type, stood there under a steely sky, pointing to the restaurant behind him, saying, "This very building is a crime scene. The site of so many of those fund-raisers for the Cochrans' sham charities. It's an absolute travesty to use the plight suffered by this community to prey on good, honest people who just wanted to help their neighbors. A community already living with the budget cuts, layoffs, and economic ruin of the Great Recession is now a victim of the Great Fleecing."

He paused. "For years, the Cochrans bought food stamps from people at their minimarket here." He pointed to the little darkened store attached to the restaurant. "They used those benefits to go out shopping to resupply this restaurant. That's where our investigation started. With a tip that put us onto food stamp fraud. But as we dug in, we saw the Cochrans were up to a whole lot more. Hundreds of thousands of dollars—money that was supposed to go to the operation of their food pantry charity and their charity for victims of the Great Flood—went to line their pockets. In the final analysis, hardly any of the money the generous people and businesses across this great state and beyond donated ever made it to the people who needed it. People who lost their homes, people living in shelters. We can never forget. If it was about keeping their business afloat, like the Cochrans claim, they could have stopped at the food stamp fraud. So, ask yourself, where did the rest of that money go?"

I see movement in the parking lot. David, emerging from the shadows of a press conference past and an ever-present question, more than four years now after the flood and this town's slow recovery.

David approaches, tall and gangly. With his black knit cap pulled down to his eyebrows, he looks more like a killer than the periodontist that he is, as he crunches across ice patches in heavy boots with a chain saw gripped in his gloved hand.

And I think, *No. This is in no way a good idea.*

"You know this is illegal, right, Viola?" David grunts, prying off the last loose board covering one of the windows on either side of the double-doored entry. "And even if you're hell-bent on doing this, does it really have to be tonight? You literally just got to town. Lillian and the girls have been waiting." He props the board against one of the chained, padlocked doors to the restaurant and looks at me pointedly. At my left eye, specifically.

"I know," I mumble.

They've been waiting since the missed sentencing last week. Waiting through days of manufactured delays and excuses. Waiting through the day and a night that I sat lost in a hole in my hotel room. My left eye, the bloody glob in it that I discovered this morning and that David is looking at now, is a visual reminder of where that day and that night went. I know this, but this isn't the issue at hand, so I ignore David's pointed look at the eye and the point he's trying to make about my delays and the detour on the road home.

I use one of the freed boards to knock more glass out of an already broken window as carefully as I can, jumping back when shards fly. David and I work until only a few pieces of glass, as jagged as shark's teeth, remain along the window frame. The whole time, I can feel David's disapproving thoughts, radiating out like the stink waves and dust clouds around Pig-Pen.

Finally, I say, "Yes, this needs to be done tonight. If I give myself any time to think this through, my better judgment will kick in, okay?"

He mutters something about me being impossible as we peer through the mostly glass-free window. The dim light from the street barely penetrates the darkness of a room that's been all but sealed like a tomb. David and I look at each other as if to say, *You first.*

"Fine," I grumble and step through the tall window. I've known David since we were little, and I've always gone first. And usually not because he's being a gentleman. He hands the chain saw to me through the window and gets ready to come in.

"Do you even know how to use this thing?" I ask, looking at the saw he borrowed from his father. I'm holding it away from me, as if it's capable of somehow turning itself on and attacking.

"More or less," he grunts as he comes through, stooping down to make sure the glass teeth don't bite into the top of his head. "And shouldn't *you* know how to use it? You're the lesbian."

"You know I'm not gifted in power-toolery."

He laughs, and we move slowly through the front lobby, using our phones for flashlights. Our breath appears in white puffs, leading like ghostly guides. Glass cracks under our boots as we pass the shattered remains of a gumball machine and busted display cases that once held mugs, T-shirts, and key chains printed with ALTHEA'S KITCHEN AND GROCERY. We step into the even darker dining room, a jumble of toppled tables and chairs and odd shapes. I stumble over something. A stray board. With a closer look, I see that stumbling and stopping was an exceedingly good thing. There's a hole in the tiled floor.

"Careful," I say, grabbing David's arm and shining my phone flashlight on the place in the floor.

He nods and we step around the hole to stand in the center of the room. "So, we're really doing this?" he asks.

My eyes settle on the bar a few steps away at the back of the restaurant. "Appears so."

David stares at the bar, too. In defeat.

The bar, built by Proctor, a good handyman and amateur carpenter, is the focal point along the back wall. Its gentle curves were inspired, Proctor once said, "by my girl," which made me gag a little. Stained a deep mahogany with brass footrests, the bar is imposing, sure, but nothing fancy. Inspired, in my view, by Proctor himself: a kindhearted, straightforward, nothing-fancy kind of guy. Despite my recent issues with Althea, Proctor and I have, until lately, pretty much always stayed in touch.

I look away from the bar and up at David. "See, we can easily just saw off a chunk from somewhere. And then I can take it someplace to have it whittled down to something the prison will let him keep. See?"

I wait for an endorsement, as if hearing this idea standing in front of the bar makes it sound somehow less ill-conceived than it did over the phone.

"Does Eva know you're doing this?" he asks, a skeptical eyebrow raised.

I haven't told him about the "separation," and I'm not about to now. "What do you think?"

He lets out a heavy breath and hands me his phone. "I'm going to need as much light as I can get while I check it out, so double beam me." He reaches in his coat pocket for his goggles and hangs them around his neck. He walks up to the bar, pounds on the already distressed wood like he knows what he's doing. Which he doesn't. Frankly, I'm surprised he even remembered to bring goggles, and I say as much.

"I'm more butch than I look," he says.

David looks nothing if not average, though he's well over six feet tall. He has a long, narrow face, and under that killer's cap there are tight, dark curls clinging to his head. Horn-rimmed glasses sit low on a large, hooked nose. He pushes those glasses up on that nose as he walks around to the back of the bar, stepping over and around the jagged remains of the mirror that once hung behind the bar. A few shiny shards still cling to the wall. David squats down behind the bar, his disembodied voice rising up. "I just need a good, clear place to cut with nothing in the way."

This is the right thing, I say to myself, feeling my better judgment trying to do an override.

I think of the letter from Althea folded up in my purse. She wanted me here. Well, not *here* in the restaurant, necessarily. But the last time I spoke to Althea, really spoke honestly to her, was right here, two years ago. In the restaurant. We argued. We treated each other in the way that people do before a calamity reorients them. Before a multiyear prison sentence forces a rethink.

I'm sorry for everything I said to you . . . she wrote. She also wanted a favor: *If you won't do anything for me, can you at least think of something to do for Proctor?*

She knows there isn't much I wouldn't do for Proctor. He's the closest thing to a father I've known. And of course, I called David to help because there's not much he wouldn't do for me. David is more brother to me than my actual brother is.

"ThankyouDavid," I blurt out in an overloud, run-together rush, suddenly beyond grateful for him being here with me.

He stands up again and looks across the bar at me. "Why are you getting weird?"

Weird? I've gone way past weird. I've been out of my mind these past few weeks.

As I stand silent, David's face softens, like he feels sorry for me. "You're under a lot of stress, Viola." He looks at my left eye again. "You haven't been yourself."

"I know."

He pushes his glasses up his nose. "What do you say we just get this done, then erase the whole night from memory?"

I nod. "Yes, I think this qualifies as a clean-slate night."

He smiles and tries to fit his goggles over his glasses. I go over, deposit our phones on the bar, and help him. "There," I say, straightening the strap on the back of his head. Then I look at the chain saw. "Do you really know how to use this thing?"

He holds it off to the side, away from me, then fiddles around with something on it, inexpertly, and pulls the cord. I jump back as the saw buzzes to life in his hand. He jumps a little, too, which is all the answer I need. But he says, with a sinister grin, "YouTube can be quite instructive."

"Right. I'll just be over there." I motion toward the center of the room, then grab up our phones and put a good five strides of distance between us. I shine light on him as best I can but otherwise leave him to it. David moves to push up his glasses, apparently having already forgotten that he has on goggles and that the saw is running in his other hand. He goes back to gripping the saw with both hands and gives it a look like it's a disloyal pet. But he goes to work on the bar, sending wood chips flying.

Looking at David, there's a flash of him as a boy and the memories of me always going first. The first ever to even befriend him at school. It was a forced friendship that turned out to be the last, best gift my mother ever gave me. She was a teacher's aide who would sometimes bring home mildly disabled and/or special ed and/or otherwise outcast children. David was an outcast.

"He's Jewish," my mother said to me, by way of introduction. "I want you to play with him."

Who knew my mother had a soft spot for Jews? Who knew of our similar histories of enslavement and discrimination? Who knew that, as a people, our histories, theoretically, should have made us natural allies in commiseration, thus fast friends?

I didn't. I was six. David was five and three-quarters.

Like my classmates, I didn't want anything to do with David, but not because he was Jewish. He had pop-bottle-thick glasses and wore floods, the hems of his pants riding up an inch or more above his ankles, safe from high water. What's more, he seemed at a loss on the playground. As it was, I was a black girl among too few of my kind. Shy, bookish, "oversensitive with an overactive imagination," too, according to my teacher. All of which made for tenuous peer relationships: I was in a forced friendship with the redheaded, severely freckled Ketchum twins, the daughters of, I suspect now, white-guilt-ridden liberals who likely told them, "She's black. I want you to play with her."

My first adventure with David came just months after my mother brought him home. When she died, David told me she'd gone someplace other than heaven. He gave me hope that I might find her here on earth.

"They said dead people go to Olam Habah," he said.

When I asked him where that was and if we might go there to bring my mother home, he looked at me through his perpetually smudged glasses, pushed them up, just like he does now when he's nervous or thinking, then shrugged and said, "They wouldn't tell me where to find it." There were tears in his eyes when he spoke.

With a tender child's hope, we looked for Olam Habah together. I led him on that very first adventure, trekking through my overgrown backyard to his well-tended one to search the toolshed and behind the aboveground swimming pool. From there, it was on to points beyond until we concluded that Olam Habah had to be somewhere near Battle Creek, which was the last place he saw his baby brother, who had disappeared in the same way my mother had.

David finishes up at the bar and smiles wide, raising a jagged-edged square of wood about the size of a small pizza box over his head in triumph. The bar, once such a thing of beauty and built with such care, is now a hacked-up wreck. On either side of the missing piece, there are deep gouges from David's repeated do-overs. He walks over to me, sees the tears in my eyes, and lowers his prize.

I've gotten weird again.

"Hey, Viola," David says, looking down at me. "It's okay. I know I've been giving you shit, but this is a really special thing to do. It'll mean the world to Proctor once we, you know, make it into something, that, I don't know . . . that's not prison contraband." He holds the square out and looks at it in a hopeful way. "I think we can have it whittled down to something that'll have real meaning to him."

I look at the square, unsure. But I say, "Thank you."

He gives me a hug, rubbing my back with his wood-free hand. With my cheek pressed to the rough, damp wool of his coat, I allow myself to really look at this place. To really see the booth where Althea and I sat together in the days before her arrest. She was watching with her usual pleasure as I sat across from her, enjoying a bowl of chicken noodle soup. Althea always had her homemade chicken noodle soup—with double noodles—waiting for me whenever I visited because it was my favorite. Its rich stock, made from roasted bones, is the taste of care and tenderness and home. Althea says it is the one dish she learned from our mother, and she immortalized it on her menu.

Across the restaurant is the booth where Kim sat with Proctor that day. It was just the four of us in the restaurant. Baby Vi was at the movies with a friend. Kim, who's never really had many friends, was hunched over a salad, glancing across the room at Althea between fork stabs at her lettuce.

"You know, you don't have to be so hard on her," I said, looking from Kim to Althea. "What's she on punishment for this time?"

"She needs to learn how to watch her mouth."

I looked at Kim again. She looked at me, then down at her salad, and said something to Proctor. Our tables were too far apart to hear each other. As diplomatically as I could, I asked Althea: "Do you think maybe you put too much pressure on her? That maybe it makes her act out more?" I wanted to add: And don't you think it's as obvious to Kim as it is to everyone else that you treat Baby Vi better? But what I said was, "Like, just today, you didn't have to call her out on her outfit in front of the staff. You must know how humiliating that is, Althea. And besides, that's what the girls are wearing."

"Not girls like her." Althea's eyes darted over in Kim's direction with unmasked disdain. "She's too big for *skinny* jeans."

"Maybe you can talk to her in a gentler way? In a way that doesn't devalue her."

"Viola, being a therapist to girls with issues doesn't qualify you to be anybody's mother, so don't talk that stuff to me."

"Why do you always have to be this way?"

"Why do you always think you can tell people their business?"

"Althea, I—"

"You always think you know better," she interrupted. "That you *are* better. If that's what all your degrees add up to, I'm telling you right now, you've got the wrong number. And don't forget who helped make all that possible, by the way."

"I've always been grateful for your help, Althea, and I've always *told* you how grateful I am. How many times do you need to hear thank you?" I refused to go any further down that road. As it was, the one we were on was fraught enough. "Look," I said, "all I'm saying is that Kim is upset—that much we can agree on, okay? It would be nice if you could affirm her sometimes. That's all."

Althea rolled her eyes. "Viola, life doesn't *affirm* anybody. I want my kids to be prepared for life. They get the truth from me, not lies. That's the same way I was with you, Lillian, and Joe, and you were all fine."

"Were we all fine? Really?"

Althea glared at me. "If you have issues, take them up with the man who should've been around to raise you. Or when he was around, who should've learned how to act. I did my part."

I looked back across the restaurant to the table where Kim sat with Proctor. Her father. He'd managed to coax a smile out of her. I swallowed hard against a swelling throat and looked at Althea again. "All I'm saying is, Kim isn't fine. Look at her."

Althea wouldn't, which made me even angrier. Tears stung my eyes. Were they for Kim? Were they for how *not* fine we all were? Finally, I said, "You have too many blind spots, Althea. And I worry that, even when you're shown, you still refuse to see."

Althea looked at me as if to say, *How dare you?* She hissed through her teeth, "The day you and your little *girl*friend can make some babies, you come back to me and talk about how to be a mother. But until then, you can feel free to get the hell on, like you always do."

I scrambled out of the booth, jostling the table, sloshing chicken noodle soup over the side of the bowl into puddles. I stood, seething, looking down at her.

Proctor called out from across the room, "Hey, you two, everything all right?"

I walked out, like I'd done many times before, and headed home to Chicago. After past arguments, I was never able to stay gone. Althea, the restaurant, chicken soup—they were home to me. This time, though, apart from almost formal, form-letter-like Christmas and Thanksgiving texts, then cards after she and Proctor had their bail revoked, there's been very little communication between Althea and me. There was a brief visual exchange in court on the day Kim testified, the one and only day I attended Althea's trial. Althea looked back at me, smiling like nothing had happened. I wanted to pretend with her, given the circumstances. Given that that is how we've always been with each other after arguments and spells of silence. But for some reason, I couldn't. Then, finally, there was her letter the other week, which was something new for her. For us.

"This is the last place I talked to Althea," I whisper, still locked in David's embrace.

"I know," he says into my hat.

"It's going to be strange seeing her again. After so long and with all of this. What will I say?"

"Whatever it is you need to say." David pulls away and holds me at arm's length, examining my face, his gaze lingering on my left eye. "It'll be fine, okay?"

"I'm not really at optimal performance levels, you know?" I feel a tremor in my lower lip as I try to laugh at what is not a joke.

He hugs me again.

"Right now, Lillian and the girls are waiting. And above all, they need you to be okay. I need you to be okay, too."

"I'm working on it."

He hugs me tighter. "Okay, then." He pulls away and looks me square in the eye. "So, once more unto the breach, dear friend?"

It's one of our lines from dweeby days gone by.

"Once more," I say.

I pull up in the driveway and cut the engine. Turn off my headlights. Slide the jagged-edged square of the bar under the passenger's seat. No need to get into all of this with Lillian tonight. I sit staring straight ahead, not quite ready to go in, even though the house, all aglow, looks warm and welcoming. It's all Lillian.

She's done a lot with this place, both inside and out. The house is like the unimaginable "after" version in one of those makeover shows: a white-bricked, black-shuttered, two-story stunner. Nothing like the rodent- and roach-infested heap of wallboard it used to be. When Lillian started her renovations—what, about three years ago?—not long after our father died—she told me the house was a nightmare in all respects.

"You know I tried to get Daddy to do something for years. Now the house is barely even structurally sound. I mean, I'm going to have to prop the thing up and put in new supports, which could've totally been avoided if he'd only listened."

Lillian's salvage mission. But she could never do enough to reclaim this house for me and probably not for Althea either. Althea left when she married Proctor, and the rest of us Butler kids would end up being sent to live with the newlyweds. I never came back here. Not to live. Of course, Lillian came back after her divorce. But that was the second time. The first time was when our father came for her and Joe. She was twelve, and I, at seventeen, was about to make my escape to college.

Our father, a traveling evangelist, was suddenly off the road, for the most part. He'd been like a phantom of a father to me. A moody, window-shaking poltergeist of a parent when he came home on weekends and found things not to his liking. But when he came home for good, just as I was about to move on, he manifested as something different. To Lillian, he became corporeal. A flesh-and-blood father who was still moody, but mellowed in some ways. He became a near-constant presence for her. And this house, where Lillian and, for a short time, Joe lived with him, is a home. Passed on to our father from his father, our father left the house and a big life insurance payout to Lillian, and Lillian alone, when he died.

"It's the last I have of him," she said, "and the closest thing I'll ever have to Mama."

As I get out of the car and slam the door shut, the porch light comes on and there's Lillian, coming out the front door. In some ways, she, herself, is the closest thing to Mama. Out of all of us, she looks the most like her. Her features are delicate, neither exceptional nor objectionable. They're set against skin that's neither light nor dark. Average looks, like our mother's, make Lillian uncommonly beautiful.

Standing on the porch, with her cat trotting out behind her, Lillian waves. I wave back. She smiles, showing the small gap between her front teeth. Our mother's gap. Then she goes back to hugging herself, rubbing her arms to stay warm. Her foot, worrying the welcome mat into place, even though it appears perfectly placed from here. She's wearing the blue-and-green-plaid flannel housecoat I got her for Christmas seventeen or eighteen years ago and fuzzy slippers. Her cat has settled down at her feet, looking at me with what I imagine is contempt. The cat and I aren't on the best of terms. Our relationship has never been good, but it got worse after Lillian moved back home and told me the cat had developed "separation anxiety, brought on by the divorce."

She tells me "natural therapies" and "environmental enhancements," some New Agey nut-jobbery, I'm sure, are helping. My diagnosis is simply this: The cat's insane. And I say this as a licensed therapist, even if I'm in no condition to practice right now.

I give the cat, Thelonious, what, in my mind, is an alpha-cat warning look as I walk to the porch with my bag. I notice that Lillian, the baby girl, is going gray. Just a few sprigs among the ropy, neat dreadlocks that hang just past her shoulders. The gray wasn't there when I saw her last. She's worrying too much. And now I'm worried. More than usual. Sad, even. And looking beyond her through the glass panes on the front door into the house, I'm sadder still. Thinking about everything that happened here, both real and imagined. Every time I go through those doors, it's as if the walls whisper reminders.

I walk up the wide porch steps. Drop my duffle bag and purse and reach out to hug my little sister.

She reaches back, then recoils. "Your eye!"

"Oh," I say, having forgotten. "Right. That." I move my hand to my face. But of course, I can't touch it. It's in my actual eyeball. The bloody glob that David made note of earlier tonight. The visual reminder of my day and a night in the Days Inn. It wasn't the issue at hand with David, he'd already been well informed, but it's the issue now. And looking at Lillian, I can see she knows what I did, so there's nothing to do but just say it and have it over with.

"A capillary," I say. "It, you know . . ." I do the universal hand sign for "explosion," then wave the word away, like it's a nuisance. Like it's some annoying little thing that could happen to anyone.

But Lillian puts her hand to her mouth and shakes her head, No. *This* doesn't just happen to anyone.

"I know, I know." I can barely say it. I mumble, "Ihadarelapse."

Her eyes slowly widen as her mind, apparently, separates the jumble into distinct words: I. Had. A. Relapse.

"A small one, Lillian," I quickly add. "I'm fine."

She grips my chin between thumb and forefinger and turns my

head from left to right, examining the eye, interrogating, "What happened?"

"You know what happened, Lillian. I purged, and with the pressure, I got a rupture."

I leave out the hotel room and how long I spent holed up in my apartment before that, instead of being here. Just the physiological facts, nothing more, because my mind has been building up a neat little wall around the most vivid mental specifics, trying to block them from my own view. Even though I know better. Even though I can see exactly what my mind is doing with that wall. "But I'm okay now, Lillian," I say. "Really."

She looks unconvinced as she stares at the bloody glob between my pupil and the corner of my eye, so red and fresh she probably expects a bloody tear to drop with the next blink. I saw the rupture this morning. The first time I'd looked at myself in the mirror. But at least I stopped, I told myself. At least I picked up the phone and called my therapist and David. True, I haven't called Eva, but it could be worse.

I peek over that wall in my mind. Maybe it is worse.

"I'm okay," I say again, removing Lillian's fingers from my chin. "But I'd like to go in now. You have to be freezing. I know I am."

She crosses her arms and doesn't move. "So, you're getting treatment?"

"Yes. I'll make more concrete arrangements as soon as I get back home to Chicago. In the meantime, I really *am* okay. I have my therapist in my Favorites now. We had a phone session before I got on the road today. And we'll be doing FaceTime sessions while I'm here. It's under control."

"What about work? Your clients?"

"I'll have to take a leave of absence," I say. "Obviously."

I just haven't taken one yet. I wonder if I will. I wonder if I'll say anything at all to my colleagues, because what would I do without my work? My refuge. Work with girls like I used to be. Gaunt girls. Skin-clinging-to-the-bone-like-plastic-wrap girls. Gorged-out girls. Flesh-bloated-and-bulging girls. And "perfect" girls. Healthy, as far as the eye can see.

"You've done so well," Lillian says. She pauses and I feel all my years of recovery and all my years of work with those girls are now in doubt. "What happened?"

I manage something like a smile at the sweet, worried face of my little sister. "I think there was a thing or two too many, Lilly, and not enough, on my part, to manage." I reach down to pick up my bag and purse. "But we can talk about that another time."

She regards me, her face a mix of skepticism and sadness that I can barely stomach. She reaches out to pull me into a hug. "I'm so glad to see you. You have no idea."

I hug her back with my free arm. "It's good to see you, too," I say, tears springing to my eyes. Good eye, bad eye. "I'm messing up, Lilly."

"You're getting it back together."

I give her another squeeze and start to move past her, toward the door. But she puts her hand on my arm to stop me. "Wait." She glances over her shoulder to the front door, her smile faltering. "Joe's here."

"For what?"

"He wants to talk about 'next steps.'" She does air quotes. "With Althea and Proctor's situation."

I hear the hesitation in Lillian's voice. It's almost always there when she mentions Joe. My gaze goes over her shoulder, through the glass panes on the door into the foyer. Muted browns, white marble, crystal chandelier. Everything so warm and well-appointed. So beautiful. I take a deep breath, cold singeing my lungs. Coughing a little, I say, "This is your house, Lillian. You know you don't have to let him—"

"Yeah," Lillian cuts in. "I know."

She opens the door and leads me in.

Lillian

I feel kind of stalkerish, tiptoeing around in the dark, listening at doors. But I can't sleep. I stop at Baby Vi's door (Althea's old room). Muffled murmurs and flickering light from the TV are leaking out through the cracks. I rest my palm on the cool wood of the door and whisper, "Safe."

I creep across the hall to Kim's door (Joe's old room), with the hallway window throwing squares of soft, silvery light under my feet. At her door, I hear the soft words of a song I don't know: . . . *Do you want the truth or something beautiful?* . . . I touch the door and whisper, "Safe."

I go down the hall to my room. Viola's in there. There's no light under that door, and I don't hear anything. Half an hour or so ago, I came to the room to get ready for bed and walked in on a heated conversation. Viola was pacing and whisper-yelling into her cell: "Come on, Eva! You don't have to tell me—" She froze when she saw me in the doorway.

"Sorry," I mouthed, pulling the door closed again. But as it shut, I heard Viola say (not that I was eavesdropping), "Look, I've been here for days, and I've been taking good care of myself. I just haven't had a chance."

And I was, like, *Here for days?* But she just got here. From Chicago.

Standing there with my hand on the doorknob, I thought, If she wasn't in Chicago and she wasn't here, then she was somewhere doing something worth lying about.

A thing or two too many, she'd said.

Standing there, stock-still, holding that doorknob, I resisted the urge to go back in the room and say something to her. Instead, I went on with my nightly routine, more on edge than before. Doing my checks of windows and listening at *other* doors. My rounds.

Now, having rounded my way back to our bedroom door again, I stand here, wondering what to do. I'm too wound up to go in and go to sleep. Obviously. When we shared this room as kids, before we were taken to live with Althea, Viola was always the restless one. "Go on to sleep now, Lilly," she'd say. Then she'd put her head under the covers, turn on her flashlight, and read. *The Hobbit*; *A Wrinkle in Time*; *The Lion, the Witch and the Wardrobe*; whatever. And I felt safe knowing she was there. To this day, I need a little light like that to sleep.

With my ear pressed to the door behind which Viola now sleeps or sits awake in the dark, I whisper, "Safe," and leave again, heading down the stairs. The rosewood floors, a replacement for nasty green carpet, are cool and creaky under my bare feet. That carpet was made to look like moss. (Maybe to be some kind of calming, natural element in the harsh environment of our home?) It was one of the first things I got rid of when I renovated, but sometimes I still feel it, like figments of the past under my feet, sending pinpricks of fear right up through me.

I touch my left ear, my fingers tracing the ripped-up, jagged skin along the top ridge. There's something calming about the feel of that ragged cartilage and delicate skin. Althea used to say my ear rubbing was like thumb sucking. She said it was a miracle my ear ever healed with all my fiddling with it. It healed, but it's hideous, and I wear my dreadlocks long to hide it. No short, Halle Berry haircut like Viola's.

No ponytails or tucking either. Not behind that ear. The rat got to me (to that left ear) on that carpet. Althea got cats to get the rat. I was too little to remember the rat mauling my ear, but I have the scar. And probably because of hearing the story of it, I was always scared of those stairs and that green carpet, as a kid.

I pad toward the family room, where Joe's sleeping.

"We need to talk about next steps," he said to me earlier, as he set up for the night in here. He glanced toward the window. Viola was somewhere out there. He'd decided to stay over, rather than make the forty-five-minute drive home to the city, since it was late. "It's probably best to wait until the morning when we're all fresh," he said.

He's sprawled out on the sectional now, wrapped in the smell of leather, wood, and faded paint fumes. And the cashmere throw that I really wish he wouldn't use that way. I mean, I gave him a blanket, but now it's just balled up there by his feet.

I look around, annoyed. I redid this room only a few months ago. Saved it for last because it was Daddy's favorite place and hard for me to change. It used to be a mash-up of the worst design hits from the seventies and eighties (gold shag carpet, dark wood paneling, pastel lamps), but it's a balance of earth tones now with a faux bamboo finish on the walls. And a nice big fish tank that the vet recommended as a natural therapy for Thelonious's anxiety (but I'm worried about traumatized fish now).

In the corner, where the light comes in best, I've kept Daddy's big leather chair (even though it doesn't go with anything in the room) and, beside it, a table with pictures I know he'd like: the two of us out trout fishing when I was around fifteen; him going for a layup when he was a high school basketball star; and him with Mama on their wedding day, sitting side by side on a love seat right here in this room, smiling. I smile. Until I look at Joe again on the sectional. He's on his back, snoring lightly, with *SportsCenter* playing low in the background, flickering light and shadow over his body.

He jerks and flips over on his side.

In his slack, relaxed face, I see shades of the skinny, bucktoothed boy with the lopsided afro, standing in the middle of this room with a bedsheet tied around his neck, dragging behind him like a wedding dress train. "Get ready for me to Blow. Your. Mind!" he'd say, waving his arms around dramatically before making a quarter disappear or having you pull a card from his card deck and put it back, then finding the exact card you picked.

"I still don't know how you did that," I whisper.

He's all grown up now, here at forty, with a barrel chest and a bald face with teeth that now fit it. I think: *You did kind of blow our minds when we were kids, didn't you?* I remember Althea sitting on the floor, smiling and clapping, as she watched him. She was always entertained by Joe (whether it was magic tricks or one of his dance routines or whatever), and I think he lived to entertain and make her laugh. Even Viola, who usually treated Joe like an annoyance (because he was annoying as a kid), would give him her attention when he put on that bedsheet to show us some new trick he'd taught himself.

By the light of the TV, I notice a small pile of coins grouped with Joe's stuff on the coffee table. I pick up a nickel and make it "disappear." It's the one thing he was finally willing to teach me, after my endless begging.

"But you've made it impossible to feel happy in memories like that, Joe," I whisper, so angry at him, no matter how hard I try not to be.

He moves and mumbles something in his sleep.

I put the nickel back on the coffee table, grab the remote, and turn off the TV.

I look back out to the foyer at the zigzagging outline of the stairs. Under them, I see the contours of the closet door, and feel little pinpricks of fear all over me.

"The past is past," I whisper.

* * *

I had to make myself use that closet in the way you're supposed to. And I had to force myself to reclaim the color green, starting with plants. Living things.

When I renovated, I went after the dusty, fake moss carpet and the memories bound up in its fibers with a super-sharp carpet cutter. And it was like everything that disturbed me when I climbed those stairs and opened that closet door rose up in the dust of decomposing carpet padding and disappeared out the open window in the hallway upstairs.

It was sparkly and beautiful. But then the sun went down and the glow was gone.

I go down the hall to Nai Nai's room. There's light under her door, so she's probably up. I listen. Knock, while turning the knob. "You sleeping?"

"If I was, I not now," she answers. "Come."

I open the door just wide enough to slip inside. She's sitting in the chair across from her bed, knitting. In her pink nightie, she looks little-girlish, so small in her rocking chair that her feet don't touch the floor. The sound on the TV is down, but the CD player's going. Wu Man's "One More Day." The girls got that CD for Nai Nai for her birthday this past summer. She plays it a lot. Enough for me to know every song, which isn't really a good thing. A little of that pi-pa goes a long way. But this song is nice.

"Sorry to interrupt," I say. "Can't sleep."

"Me neither, but I old lady."

I plop down on the bed.

She gives me a look: *What's wrong?*

I shrug. "Joe's here. Viola's here." I gesture toward the family room and up in the direction of my bedroom. "It's a full house. And, well, not the most comfortable."

"But nice to have family," she says, her knitting needles *click-click-clicking* as she goes back to her work. Knitting is something she does by feel instead of sight because her vision's pretty bad now. "Need family," she adds, nodding in agreement with herself.

"Yeah, but not like this."

She puts her needles on her lap and looks at me again, her eyes watery like always. It's always like she's about to cry.

"I just mean, it's crowded. Like I said."

Nai Nai's creased forehead scrunches into outraged wrinkles. "What? He your brother. She your sister. They come here! You should be glad!"

I wince a little, sensing the nerve I've struck. Reminded that what little I know (what little she's ever said) about her life revolves around family. The loss of it. I know she's the third born of four (three girls, one boy, just like us) and the only one left. I know that she's the only one who came to this country, brought here by her first husband. And I know how much she must miss everybody. Especially Sam. Her grandson. My ex-husband. The last of her family, here.

I remember her calling on the night he died: "Sam in accident. You come back."

And I went from here, back to the home we'd shared in Brooklyn. Everything made me cry: the photo album/scrapbook Sam had put together after our "trip of a lifetime" to Bodh Gaya, saying, "Watch, Lillian, you're going to thank me for this when we're in the old folks' home trying to remember how great life was"; the top tier of our Neapolitan ice cream wedding cake, still sitting in the back corner of the freezer; his one navy blue suit, his pressed, dark blue jeans, one pair for each day of the week, and his pressed white oxfords, hanging above the small cubbies that held plain white T-shirts. The whole time I sat in our old apartment with our old friends, making fun of Sam's decision-free wardrobe (and his lectures on the dangers of decision fatigue), I cried. Up until Nai Nai grabbed my shoulders and shook me violently, yelling, "Stop it! Stop it! Crying don't help nothing!"

Her eyes were wild and angry but clear of any tears because Nai Nai never cried. Not in front of me, anyway. But I know she grieved. Still grieves.

Reminded of all of this (and the fact that she couldn't even begin to understand our family situation), I say, "I'm sorry. You're right. It's fine for Joe to come here, and I'm glad everybody's here. It's just . . ." But, again, there's nothing I can say that she'll understand.

"What? Had nice time. Tea. Cakes."

"Sure, that was nice." I guess. If this is your idea of nice: Kim showing up without saying where she's been; Viola, just arriving, saying a too-quick and clipped "No, thanks" to an offer of cupcakes from Joe; all of us, including the girls, sitting around the glass table in the breakfast nook, talking about everything but Althea and Proctor; Viola excusing herself after sitting through about fifteen minutes of it, saying, "I'm just tired after the drive and a long day at work," then promising Kim and Baby Vi that they'd hang out tomorrow; Viola, still awake and on the phone when I went up more than an hour later, only to go right back out to do my rounds, worried about what I'd overheard her saying to Eva about being here for days. If you call that a nice time, then, okay. Sure.

"You worry too much," Nai Nai says to me. "Mind everyplace."

I smile. "And where should my mind be?"

"Here. With family."

It is. That's the problem. "You're right," I say.

She nods like she does when she's said all she has to say about something. In a shaky, thin voice, she starts humming to the music.

Sitting on the bed, I sway to the beat, looking around the room. It's yellow, her favorite color, but it's a muted, creamy yellow, not the sunburst-bright one she wanted (sorry, Nai Nai). The woods in here are deep, rich browns. Her bedspread is a field of bright red poppies, where I now rest. I went American modern in here, but this is totally an old-lady space. Sometimes, like these times, it's the only place in this house where I feel at home.

Up near the head of the bed, there's a "grip and grabber" thing Nai Nai uses to close the curtains and pick up just about anything she can't reach. There's this half-cylinder thing for putting on socks. It's beside the longest shoehorn known to man so she can get into her shoes without throwing out her back. Perfume, powder, and prescription bottles crowd the dresser. Collections of porcelain figurines encroach on the collections of framed family pictures on the bookshelf and on the bedside table.

And on the wall, there's a framed picture of the Atlantic Ocean as seen from Miami Beach. It's something I'd *never* pick for this room, but it's special to Nai Nai for reasons known only to her. Sometimes when I come in here, I find her looking at that picture with a smile that makes me think at least part of her is there on the beach. I've asked her about that picture, and about Miami, a few times. She only says, "That was best time for me."

I look away from the picture of the ocean and sniff the air. Something's off. That's talcum powder, definitely, but I think I'm getting some pee in there, too. I reach out and feel the bedspread. Get up and check the sheets, trying not to make a production out of it.

All clear.

I sit down again, wondering where the smell's coming from or if maybe I'm smelling something else. I checked her when I walked in (a quick, stealthy sniff). That's how we deal with these kinds of things. Action, without a lot of words.

That was how I dealt with my dad, but he wasn't as old as Nai Nai and didn't have as many physical things going on (that he let me see, anyway). He was seventy when he died, and I'd only been back home for six months. He just went to bed and didn't wake up. Like my mom, he died right here in this room. Viola came for the funeral, but I think she was mostly there for me. Althea wouldn't come for anybody. Most especially not for our father.

I watch Nai Nai, knitting and humming. I've never told her about the deaths in her room. She's superstitious. Always on the lookout for the supernatural. She'd worry: Are these restless souls? Lonely spirits? Hungry ghosts? Condemned to wander the earth, never satisfied.

"Hungry ghosts got to be fed," she told me once, describing the plates of food she left out when she was younger, for lost, wandering ancestors. "Bring them peace," she said.

I bet my mom and Sam are at peace. But I worry about my dad. He was unsettled (*unsettling*, Joe, Viola, and Althea would say) and restless, even when he was alive. This makes *me* restless. I get up and give Nai Nai a light kiss on the top of her head, do another quick sniff. Nothing but powder from her shower. Just another unidentified pee smell, I guess. That happens.

"All right, Nai Nai. Don't stay up too late, okay?"

"I stay up late as I want." She pauses. "You lucky I want to go to bed soon." She winks.

I squeeze her arm. It's so skinny I can almost close my thumb and middle finger around it. She hasn't gained back the weight she lost after the hip break over the summer. It worries me.

"What you waiting for? Go. Go to bed." She shoos me away.

I move toward the door but pause, finally paying attention to her knitting. She's working from a ball of red yarn. Her gnarled fingers and the oversized knitting needles that make things easier for her are moving slowly, repeating over and over the motions she learned as a girl.

"What're you making?"

"Afghan for Thea," she says. "So she don't have bad time."

I think for a second. Right. Red for luck. The color of the poppies on her bedspread. Tears rise as I wonder, *Do prisoners get to have homemade afghans?* The tears surprise me because I'm not really one to cry for Althea. God knows, she's never been one to cry for me.

I remember Althea sitting me down on the bed that Viola and I shared at her and Proctor's apartment, right after our father came in off the road. She told me, "He says he wants you home." She had tears in her eyes, but, even at twelve years old, something told me they weren't for me. Especially when she said, "You're going with him now. I've done all I'm going to do for him."

But what about me? I wanted to say.

Nai Nai looks up at me. The doctor says she can still see faces, for the most part, if she turns her head just so. With her head turned just so and the yarn ball held up and trembling in her shaky hand, she says, "I make you scarf later, okay?" There's quiet tenderness in her voice.

"That'd be great. I can use a new scarf." I squeeze her bony arm again. "See you in the morning."

"Breakfast?"

And there it is. An English word, not Mandarin, but still, translation: McDonald's. The exact meaning, based on context and the *I shouldn't be asking, but . . .* inflection: sausage and egg biscuit.

Be firm, be firm, be firm.

"We'll see," I say.

Not firm.

I leave, her quavery humming following me out through the door.

I go back through the foyer to the entryway and check the porch light (yes, still off). I check the front door (yes, still locked). Viola's car, the Midlife-Crisis-Mobile, as Eva calls it, is in the driveway (right where it was when I checked the last time). This is the fourth time I've done my checks. Reassuring myself, Yep, everybody's in. We're all here.

I pull the fraying belt of my robe tight around my waist as I stare out the glass-paned front door, thinking about standing there in the family room with Joe before Viola got here. His voice, always gravelly and hoarse from years of preaching, was light, but his eyes held me in place as he mentioned "next steps." I wanted to know right then what he thought they were, but I felt like I sometimes do when I'm alone with him: a mix of trust and panic; a compulsion to cooperate, the reflex to run. And I replied, "Yeah, sure. We'll wait." No further questions. Then he unpacked a few toiletries from his bag: Right Guard deodorant, toothpaste, toothbrush, mouthwash, Gucci cologne. He set it all on the coffee table, then turned on the TV and settled in, in Daddy's chair, to wait for Viola.

The man of the house.

My brother. My tormentor.

I'm in charge now. You do what I say.

"The past is past," I whisper, my breath fogging up the glass windowpane.

When my father came home, he wanted me with him. I was the baby of the family; there was more raising to do with me. He left Joe and Viola to make their own choice. They were almost finished with high school, practically grown in his eyes. Joe chose to live with Daddy and me: "It shouldn't just be you, Lillian," he said, his jaw set. "I have a right to know him, too."

The day Daddy came home, Viola and I stood hidden, just outside the family room, watching him sink into his big chair and stare off at nothing, with tired, red eyes. He was sweaty, his suit wrinkled, and his tie undone after God knows how long behind the wheel. Viola whispered, "Look at him. I don't think he will do like he should. He won't stay."

She'd just been accepted to college. You could see the first signs of her eating disorder: sunken cheeks, dark circles under her eyes, always claiming she wasn't hungry. But nobody knew anything about that at the time. As far as anybody could see, she was just an overachieving high school senior. So focused on going away to college that she collected university catalogues like vacation brochures. But unlike Althea, she was always focused on me, too. Viola's plan was to sneak me off to college with her. What did we know? I packed some clothes, pajamas, and underwear in garbage bags along with a toothbrush, my *Birds of America* book, a couple of Little Debbie Oatmeal Creme Pies I'd been saving, and a map of Ann Arbor.

Those bags never left the house. Neither did I.

But Viola, she went.

And Daddy, he stayed, for the most part.

Even though I've never blamed Viola for going (or imagined she could've done anything if she'd stayed), she's never forgiven herself for leaving. Or what happened after she went away. It's hard for her to come back home, because of how she is.

When we were kids, Althea told us a story about water and women and Mama giving her and Viola a river (there was nothing for me). Althea got the Saint Joseph and Viola got its tributary, the Portage River. Viola offered to share her river with me, but it's all hers. The name, Portage, comes from the French word *porter.* To carry.

That's how she is.

Viola is the self-appointed bearer of things. My worst memories, mostly (even though she's only just guessed at them). Everything I'd forget, she'd remember. Everything I'd forgive, she'd avenge.

"The past is past," I say, as I stop in front of the closed door of the closet under the steps in the foyer, remembering some of the words carved into the other side of that door. My voice is almost too quiet to hear as I touch the doorknob and say, "Safe."

Viola

I should go along the River Walk. It's a nice run.

In the spring and summer. Early fall, maybe. But now? It's a little before five in the morning and freezing. Do I really want to go out there?

No. But I don't want to wait for the gym to open either. Outside is fine.

I'll warm up once I get going, I guess.

And how about a couple of turnarounds? That would make it, what, two hours?

I shouldn't go that long, it's not healthy.

But it's okay. A nice run, remember?

But two hours. Tops. And just this once.

Of course. Just this once.

I'm standing in the foyer in the silent hours before first light. The only voices to be heard are the ones in my head finishing up an argument over a morning run that I've now both won and lost. If this were a therapy session, I'd describe the arguing parties this way: the strong-willed Child-self once again winning out over the Wise Woman–self, who, let's face it, seems to get less sensible by the day.

But it's agreed. Permission granted. So, I'm out the door before my selves have time to say anything more. Running head-on into the biting cold.

I beat the sun home, but just barely. A blush was spreading across the sky when I got to the front door. A three-hour run, clearly more than the two hours agreed, but I've been agreeing to all kinds of things that would have been out of the question a few weeks ago. Win/losing arguments with myself over how much exercise I should do, over how much I should and shouldn't eat, and over whether I should keep what I do eat down. Little by little, giving in to the deceptive, yet decisive: just this once, one last time, what's one more? My stay in that hotel room and the days leading up to it were the worst losses, so far. The predawn run, my way of balancing the scales. But I should know that it's yet another weight, another loss.

I peek over that wall I've constructed in my head: I do know that.

You won't work out that long tomorrow, Viola. And you'll eat right. You'll eat, says my Wise Woman, giving it all she has.

I go over to the counter to pour myself a second cup of coffee and, out of the corner of my eye, I notice movement. I look up from my cup, smiling, expecting to see a sleepy-headed niece. But it's Joe. My smile becomes fixed.

Joe pauses at the threshold to the kitchen.

"Morning," I say, cordial enough.

"Morning." He yawns, scratching his stomach under his gray sweatshirt, looking half-asleep. As he staggers toward the refrigerator, mumbling, "Lemme see what we're working with," I take my coffee over to the breakfast nook table and pull out a chair. At the sound of the chair moving, Joe, who's staring into the refrigerator, glances over his shoulder at me. "You want some breakfast? I'm about to hook something up real quick."

"I'll stick with coffee for now. But thank you."

He goes back to the refrigerator.

I sip my coffee. A tongue-singeing gulp. Too fast. Be mindful, I remind myself. Pay attention to what you're drinking. I'm supposed to be savoring things. So says my therapist. So I say to my clients. So says everything I know. The coffee would be better with milk and sugar, but that's out of the question. A calorie savings, certainly, but this is also the bitter palate punishment I deserve.

"How are Tanya and the kids?" I ask.

"The kids're getting big, getting into devilment, like you'd expect." He flashes a proud-father smile, as he puts a stick of butter on the counter. "But nothing too bad. And Tanya, you know, she's taking on more and more with the ministry."

I nod, but, in point of fact, I don't know. I don't know much of anything about Joe's life.

"Yep, she's about the best helpmate I could have. I think it's our season." He pauses. "You ran off awfully fast last night." An unnatural casualness has seeped into his voice. "I didn't hardly get a chance to say anything to you. But how've you been? It's been a minute, hasn't it?"

About three years. Our father's funeral. That's the last time I saw Joe. "Yes, it's been a while."

"Well, you look good, and it's good to see you."

He turns to consider his breakfast again. I look out the windows behind me. There's the sun, its rays buttery and warm. This is a sensory feast, isn't it? A thing worth savoring in Michigan here in late November.

Be present in this moment.

The past is past.

I can hear Lillian saying that to me right now. Her mantras, mottoes, and truisms. Words she wears like talismans, as wards against negative forces. But the sun that I should be savoring is, at present, eclipsed by an uncomfortable silence in the room. And Joe, a large mass, opening the refrigerator again. Taking out bacon: four. Eggs: three. Two slices of bread. Zeroing in on the toaster. He rummages through cabinets until he finds a skillet. He's moving like a maestro now with his arm out, leaning back from the stove as bacon sizzles. Swaying forward as eggs are whisked and scrambled and finished with a flourish of cheese and parsley.

My stomach grumbles. Looking at Joe's plate, I feel that feeling. As piercing as any hunger pang, as all-consuming as the desire to feed. It's the fear: *What if this wakes the zombie?*

I take another sip of coffee.

Joe takes his plate to the other side of the room and leans against the counter, crossing one white-sweat-socked foot over the other. When he digs in, it's more like an angry clenching and unclenching of the jaw than actual chewing. He looks up from his plate and asks, "Where's everybody? Guess the girls are at school?"

"Baby Vi is. Lillian has to take Kim later today. They're meeting with the principal. There was an incident, apparently."

"That girl," Joe says, shaking his head.

"A handful, that's for sure. Anyway, Lillian and the grandmother are at breakfast."

He points to the refrigerator with his fork. "They have a full fridge. Why do they need to go out?"

I shrug. "They have their routine." Their own booth, even, at their McDonald's.

There's the sound of clinking charms and chains. We both look up. Thelonious enters the kitchen. He has on his bright blue "cat bib," which makes him look ridiculous.

"It's not for food spills," Lillian told me the first time I saw him wearing that thing, which hangs around his neck like an actual baby bib. "It stops him from pouncing on birds. I like to think of it as the must-have accessory for the outdoor feline."

Thelonious pauses in a pool of sunshine, gives a long, languid stretch, bird-killing paws forward, bottom and tail thrust in the air: downward-facing cat. He comes out of it and yawns, looking from me to Joe. I wonder what he sees. Lillian once told me cats have a wider field of vision than humans, but in bright light, like the morning light flooding this kitchen, they don't see details as well as we humans do. But even the best human eyes would have a problem seeing through to the details of who Joe is.

As a boy, he was something of a showman. He had a need to be seen, which sometimes made me sad for him. I remember when Joe was in middle school, he invited our father—like he always did—to come see him break-dance in a school assembly. As anyone could have told Joe, as Joe himself had to know from all of the letdowns in the past, our father would not come in off the road to watch him perform. I caught up with Joe walking home from the assembly alone, every bit the B-boy, in a black Adidas tracksuit and white sneakers he'd saved up for. But everything else about him—his sloped shoulders, the barren expression on his face, the way he seemed to drag himself along the sidewalk—cried utter heartbreak. I told him how sorry I was for him and that he should stop having such high expectations of our father. He shook me off, almost violently, telling me to mind my own business and, "Don't touch me! I don't need nobody feeling sorry for me, especially you. Don't you got homework to do or something?" Later, in high school, Joe would disappear into himself, showing off a lot less. He was a mediocre student who never stood out in sports, and he blended in in the hallways at school, apart from the occasional fight. Then, the next thing I knew, Joe was gone to the army. Now he's a man with whole stretches of his life unseen by all of us, except for maybe Althea.

Thelonious blinks and moves on from his pool of sunshine, stopping to sniff at his water dish and the complicated "interactive feeder." One of the "natural therapies" that's supposed to help with his anxiety, I'm guessing. The cat looks up at Joe and me from the feeder. He turns and leaves out the cat door.

"I really don't like that cat," Joe says, frowning as he watches him go.

On this we agree. "Lillian says he's dealing with"—I do air quotes—"'divorce-induced separation anxiety.'"

"It's been years! Get over it, cat!" Joe yells in the direction of the cat door. "That's why I've always been a dog person." He laughs, shovels some eggs into his mouth, but speaks anyway. "A high-sadity city kitty." He shakes his head. "Too good for us."

We're both laughing.

Lillian comes through the garage door to the kitchen, the grandmother ahead of her, pushing her little red walker. They're laughing together until they notice us: me sitting, Joe leaning against the counter on the opposite side of the room.

"Good morning," Lillian says, but her usually open, plain face scrunches up with a question: *What's going on?*

"Breakfast," I answer.

She looks at Joe, holding his plate. She looks back at me. "Where's yours?"

I raise my mug of coffee as if to say, *This is it.*

She looks at me hard. "I think you need more than that."

"I'm fine," I say, squirming out from under her gaze and going over to the coffeemaker for a warm-up that I don't actually need.

"So, what were you guys laughing about?" Lillian asks.

"We could ask y'all the same thing," Joe replies. "Miss Nai Nai, you working on your comedy act again?"

The grandmother smiles but doesn't answer. I wonder how well she can even hear, and I think, *What a burden.* I tried to talk Lillian out of tying herself down after Sam died. Told her that the grandmother would probably be more comfortable in a good assisted-living facility. And Lillian almost listened, but guilt speaks louder than common sense. The grandmother had lived with her and Sam when they were together. Nai Nai had watched the implosion of their marriage. Did she see that Lillian was the one who detonated the charges? Lillian said she could never be sure, but she felt plenty guilty about it anyway.

Lillian asks again, "Seriously, what's so funny?"

"We were just laughing about Thelonious," I say, warming up my coffee and pouring a cup for her. "You know. His inflated sense of self."

Lillian smiles. "I think his sense of self is just the right size."

Joe laughs.

I laugh, too.

The sound fades into an expectant sort of silence.

Joe looks at his watch, then at Lillian and me. "We need to talk."

"Why don't I get you set up in the family room?" Lillian says to the grandmother, her hand resting on the walker. "I can grab your knitting stuff."

The grandmother disengages the hand brakes on her walker and propels herself forward. The little woman shuffles along but looks sharp in her khakis and a rhinestone-collared, red cardigan that matches the red of her walker. Even stooped over, there's a kind of steeliness-in-the-spine quality to that woman. I wish Lillian had more of that, sometimes.

I take my warmed-up cup of coffee and the cup I've poured for Lillian to the table.

Joe goes back to finishing his breakfast, leaning against the counter. It's otherwise quiet. The silence, somehow more excruciating than it was before we laughed about the cat and chatted with Lillian. And I wonder what it would be like if the talking and the laughing were authentic. If that were our regular way of being together, assuming we ever tried to be together at all. I wonder what it might be like to spend time with your brother without it being a betrayal of this guarded part of yourself and your selfless sister.

Lillian returns and takes a seat at the table next to me. I slide her cup of coffee over just as Joe says, "Lillian, you've done a really good job holding things down with the girls, I hope you know that. But me and Tanya have been talking, and we're thinking it might be good for them to come and live with us."

Lillian grips her coffee cup tight, with both hands. "Althea and Proctor haven't said anything to me about that. Isn't that up to them?"

"The girls are here," I add, "because Althea and Proctor wanted to keep them in a familiar environment. Their same town and school. Surrounded by all the things they know."

"But a new town, a new everything is what those kids need. Althea and Proctor just can't see it yet. They got a lot coming at them right now. I'm gonna talk to Althea about moving them when I go up for my visit, but I wanted to game it out with y'all first," he says, his eyes moving between the two of us. "I think those kids need to be in a family environment, and I know y'all gotta see it, too." He nods toward me. "Viola said Kim was in trouble at school again. I think it'd be best to get them started making new friends, someplace new. And getting active in church, too. A real church." He keeps his eyes on Lillian, who sometimes visits the Unitarian Universalist church in the city where Joe lives and commutes in from to pastor the church our father left to him, here in New River Junction.

Lillian mumbles something about everything being fine, but I doubt it's loud enough for Joe to hear. I, on the other hand, hear more than what she has said. I hear intimidation. I put my cup of coffee on the table. "I don't think so, Joe," I say.

He looks at me, uncomprehendingly. "What do you mean, you don't *think* so?"

"Just what I said. The girls are comfortable here. They shouldn't be uprooted."

"Well," he laughs, "let's let Althea be the judge of that."

There's something in his smug laugh. That dismissive tone. I wait for Lillian to speak up. Nothing, of course. Frustrated, I just say it: "I don't trust you, Joe."

Lillian looks at me. Alarmed.

Joe laughs again, but not smugly. It's something between a laugh and a surprised gasp. In his eyes, there's a flicker. Memory? He blinks, shaking his head. "I don't even know what you're talking about, Viola."

"I bet you do."

His eyes dart over to Lillian.

Her hand is raised. She's rubbing her ear.

He shakes his head. "Don't go there, Viola."

I stand. "I'm already here. You—"

"Kim'll hear this!" Lillian says in an urgent whisper, as she gets to her feet.

Joe ignores her. "What do you know about me or anything, Viola? Huh? You show up here, trying to bring up old stuff. You don't *trust* me? You think I care?" He looks to Lillian. "You know me. We talk. It's . . . everything's all right, right? Everything's normal."

Lillian gives a vague shrug and looks at the table.

Anger snaps through me like a whip. "Nothing's *normal*," I say to Joe. "Walking around each other *pretending* at normalcy doesn't make it 'normal.' What the hell happened here?"

"That's enough," Lillian says in a small but firm voice, glancing at the arched entryway to the kitchen. "I mean it. Kim could come in here any minute. Stop it!"

And we three stand silent, so much spoken in glances. In a touch. I feel Lillian's hand at my sleeve. I recall her fingers, the nails bitten back and ragged, reaching for me. She was fourteen. I was nineteen. The nails are well-manicured now, but the *tug-tug-tug* on my sweater sleeve pulls me back in time.

"He's so mean," Lillian whispered.

"What happened?"

She wouldn't answer me.

I looked down to where she had hold of me, and I could see bruising, there on her wrist. It was faded by then, but there were still livid smears of black and purple and yellow.

"Did he do that?"

Still no answer.

"What did he do, Lillian?"

She shook her head. "He's just mean, Viola. Like nobody else. But he's gone now. That's all I can say." It's the most she's ever said—and it's the most I've ever asked.

Joe was eighteen at the time, and I did not know then, but it would be years before I would see him again. As someone used to walling off the worst in my mind, part of me has been happy to leave it at "Joe's gone." But now, with my distrust of him, my disgust with my own weak, willful ignorance . . . Suddenly I want to smash my cup of coffee into his face. But it comes to me: No, Viola. Control. After a few seconds, I test my voice: "Look, you know what I think, Joe." I hear the reserved, clinical tone I use with clients.

"You don't—"

"What's going on?" A young, sleep-sanded voice cuts Joe off. Kim stands in the entryway in a pink do-rag and Hello Kitty pajamas.

"We were just talking," Lillian says. She turns to Joe. "Maybe you should go. We have to get Kim to school."

Joe looks from Lillian to me, his face unreadable. He goes over and pats Kim's shoulder. "Good luck at school today."

She crosses her arms, shooting a sharp look at Lillian and me. "Glad everybody knows."

"You make sure you stay out of trouble, young lady," Joe says. "You hear?"

"I hear," she mumbles.

"Why don't you go up and take your shower," Lillian tells her. "We need to get going soon."

Kim grabs a couple of granola bars from the pantry and leaves without a word. Joe follows her. I hear their voices out in the hallway. He says something about the importance of school and doing as you're told.

Lillian is rubbing her ear again.

"Stop it with the ear, please!" I say. "Is that all you're going to do? You just sat there!"

"*Don't*, Viola," she says. She grabs our coffee cups and fast-walks them over to the sink.

My anger quickens into guilt. "Lilly," I say. "I'm sorry."

She doesn't respond.

I look out the windows behind me, where the sun is still bright, falling on dormant grass. I'm remembering when that grass was green and overgrown and weedy. Pulling at my ankles as I ran through it, with Lillian at my heels. In our own world. Our *olam habah*. A place David and I could never have found because, I learned later, in Hebrew, it means "the world to come." An undefined place. I'm thinking of it now as the world you make. And whenever it was for Lillian and me to make, it was a world built around forts, fairies, and a mother resurrected as Glinda the Good Witch.

"What kind of world are we making, Lilly?" I say.

She looks across the room at me, irritated. "What?"

I start to explain. I start to ask all the questions I should have asked when she said, "That's all I can say," about Joe. "Nothing," I say, finally.

Now's not the time.

A voice in my head says, *See, even after all these years, after all your talking like a therapist, you still don't have the words to talk to your sister about what happened to her in this house.* It's the thing implicit in the silence around a shared memory of a fading bruise. But always, always, "What's past is past." Lillian's words, not mine.

There are sounds coming from the family room and the hallway. Shuffling and slamming and Joe saying a polite goodbye to the grandmother. The front door slams, and I imagine the lovely glass panes shaking in their frames. Cracking. Then, quiet. The kind of quiet that reverberates with every troubling sound, every intimated word that came before it.

I should have stayed home. I'm of no use here. I look at the clock over the principal's desk. It's just past noon, and already it's been a day. Kim is sitting next to Lillian, with that battered, busting-at-the-seams notebook of hers on her lap, staring at the wall in silent complaint. I stand here by the window, waiting for the principal to come back with a chair for me.

The school has been updated and renovated, but the principal's office sits exactly where it was when I attended school here. I wasn't the kind of student who generally found herself in the principal's office, but there was that one time. Eleventh grade. I'd been deemed "unfocused" and "uncooperative" and possibly "depressed." They'd called my father's house instead of Althea's, where I actually lived, and he happened to be home for once. I was terrified when he walked in the office, so imposing he seemed to fill the entire room. He sat in the chair beside me, warning, "I'll give you something to cry about if you don't cut it out." Because

I was crying. He promised the principal this would never happen again. "I'll get her under control. Nobody's got time for this nonsense."

Shaking in my chair, swallowing the tears, all I could think about was what kind of whipping I'd get. Joe, who dabbled in minor vandalism and petty theft, was punished with the extension cord, down on all fours, his head held between the vise grip of our father's knees, defenseless against every *thwack* of the cord on his back. For Althea and me, it was mostly the belt or a switch that cut into you like a whip. But beatings were rare for me. I generally stayed out of trouble. I didn't have that shield of defiance and rage Althea and Joe threw up to at least blunt the blows.

With those worries running around in my head, I was marched out of the school, almost running to keep up with my father's long, pigeon-toed strides. I kicked snow off of my beloved orange and silver moon boots as best I could before getting into his beloved white Chrysler New Yorker. A car that you didn't dare spill, drop, or leave anything in, including excessive amounts of snow and slush. During the drive, he occasionally looked over at me and lectured me on how to "act like you have some sense." The next thing I knew, we pulled up at Burger King. He got out and motioned for me to follow him.

He ordered Whoppers and fries. Orange pop for me and a strawberry shake for him to settle his stomach, which was upset almost all the time. My stomach was upset almost to the point that I couldn't eat because I was still worried about my punishment. But I was even *more* worried about getting in trouble for wasting the food he bought, so I ate what was in front of me.

Even apart from the fear and the forced feeding, I don't imagine it was anything like a normal father-daughter lunch. Our conversation was mostly monosyllabic and stilted:

"Your grades still good?"

"Yes, sir."

"You know to mind your teachers, right?"

"I do."

"Good."

Awkward silence while we chewed and sipped. For a long time.

Then he looked up at me, his mustache speckled with pink milk shake. He looked around the Burger King and out the window to the parking lot, where his car was nested in black and gray slush. "There's nothing for you here, Viola. Don't be acting no fool up there with your teachers. Ain't no such thing as 'depressed.' You just make it your business to get something in your head, you hear me?" He leaned in and tapped his finger to my forehead three times. "Feed your mind. Keep them grades up, then get out there and make something outta yourself, you hear?"

I told him I heard.

There was no whipping. But I had this sudden longing to know him and an understanding that I never would.

That talk in Burger King stands as the longest conversation I ever had with my father and the finger taps, the longest touch, apart from an awkward hug and head rub when I graduated. It's a moment I pick up and turn over in my mind from time to time, like an artifact from another age. Both comforted and grieved by its existence.

I hear the principal coming and carefully put that moment back in its place: a snowy day in November; junior year of high school; a few months before I'd start a "diet" that would come to consume me.

Principal Davis is tall and rangy like a runner, with a head full of coarse, graying Einstein hair. He's carrying in one of the waiting room chairs. "I apologize again, ladies, for the seating situation. Sometimes it's musical chairs around here," he says, putting the chair in place on the other side of Kim and motioning for me to sit in it. "Thanks for joining us, Viola. Again, it's nice to meet you." He perches on the edge of his desk in front of us. "Sorry for the holdup. Had to chat with a student out there." He smiles, looking at Kim. "But now it's time for this student. It's good to see you, Ms. Cochran."

She cuts her eyes in his direction briefly and murmurs, "Hi, Mr. Davis."

He looks somewhere between amused and not. "That's our Ms. Cochran, isn't it?"

"Yeah," Lillian says, shifting uncomfortably in her chair.

"Why don't we get right to it?" Principal Davis says. "We want to get Kim out of in-school suspension and back in class. But"—he addresses Kim—"we need to talk about what you can do on your part, young lady, to make sure we don't keep repeating the same behaviors that got you pulled out of class in the first place. We've talked about de-escalation tools before. We just need to try to use them more, right?"

Kim crosses her arms across her wide, protruding chest and rolls her eyes.

"This is serious, Kim," I say, not entirely sure I should be interjecting, but Lillian begged me to come. To help.

"Your aunt is right," Principal Davis says. "I'm afraid we're seeing an escalation in how . . . well, in some of your responses to challenges that come your way. For instance, this latest incident."

Kim glares at him. "What was I supposed to do? She wouldn't stop talking to me like that! Then she spit on me!"

"Right. I know. I get that. But we've talked about coping mechanisms and, again, de-escalation. Reaching out to your teachers. Coming to talk to me. Or walking away."

"How is somebody supposed to have 'coping mechanisms' when they have somebody all up in their face like that? All the time! Talking crazy! I'm supposed to just walk away?"

"Yes," the principal says. "And look, I know it's hard."

"No, you don't, otherwise *you* wouldn't be talking crazy." She crosses her arms tighter.

"Kim," Lillian admonishes.

"You either," Kim says, cutting her eyes at Lillian.

"All right, Kim," I say. "Enough."

The principal raises his hand to me and Lillian, as if to say, *I have this.* "Kim, you had a teacher trying to intervene when your classmate got out of line. But you turned on her, too."

"She wasn't helping me." Kim waves an arm, pointing out toward the hallway. "She doesn't even want me in her class. You don't even want me in your sorry-ass school."

"Kim," the principal says, "first of all, if I didn't want you here, you'd be gone. The fact of the matter is you used some very strong language with your teacher and then got physical with your classmate. You know we have zero tolerance for that kind of behavior."

"Then kick me out!" Kim grips the armrests, leaning in toward the principal. Her face, pure fury. "Go ahead!"

"*I* want you here," he says. "*We* want you here. I know the challenges you have at home."

"No, you don't," she snaps, sitting back, crossing her arms and looking away. Tears rise, but they don't fall.

He opens his arms. "Okay, Kim, if I don't, tell me. Please. I'm listening."

But it's Kim who doesn't appear to be listening. She's looking just past the principal, over his desk where a stack of manila folders sits. She's looking toward the bookshelf behind the desk, where a gray and blue Detroit Lions paperweight and foam finger are scattered among the books and family pictures. She has that same empty stare some of the girls I treat get. Those breakable, self-protective girls go to places I can't reach. I think Kim's there now. There's a defensiveness in the way she's sitting, holding herself tight, her jaw locked. Maybe less defensive than deeply distressed. Like some kind of torture sufferer. One thrown into isolation and affection deprivation as punishment for informing on her parents. Now, practically waterboarded by the steady *drip, drip, drip* of daily frustrations. I would reach out and hold her hand, if I thought she'd let me.

We wait for her to speak, but she says nothing.

"It's all right," I say to her.

Lillian reaches out and rubs her shoulder. Kim neither shrinks away nor welcomes Lillian's touch.

The principal says, "We're all on your side, Kim."

But even as he leans in, trying to get her to look at him, her eyes stay fixed on that distant spot, just past his head.

He looks from me to Lillian.

"Kim," I say, trying to call her back.

No answer.

"Kim," the principal says quietly, "would you mind giving me a second with your aunties?"

Here, she nods and stands.

"Thank you," he says, but I can tell he's disturbed by Kim's unbreakable, impenetrable silence. Still, he smiles. "How about grabbing a seat out there with Mrs. Babcock for a minute, if you don't mind?"

She goes.

As soon as the door closes behind her, I ask Lillian, "Is this normal? Is this how she behaves now?"

Lillian eyes me over Kim's empty chair, clearly upset. "They're in a bad place, Viola. I've told you that. But obviously, you don't listen."

"Well, how does Baby Vi manage?"

"She keeps her head down," Principal Davis says. "She doesn't, let's say, *engage* in the way Kim does. And you know, she does have some friends who've stuck by her. Kim's always been kind of, well, an insular kid." He glances at the door Kim just went out of. "Aside from the obvious, the sentencing and what have you, is there anything else going on that I should be aware of?"

Lillian lets out a breath. "Their mom, I guess. They want to see her."

The principal raises an eyebrow, like, *Well?*

"She won't see them. I take them to see their dad, then we come home. That's it."

"Althea loves her daughters," I say, feeling defensive on Althea's behalf.

"I didn't say she doesn't love them, Viola, I said she doesn't want to see them. Kim. She doesn't want to see Kim." She explains to the principal: "After the one time I took them to the jail, she told me not to bring them back. With the girls sitting right there, mind you." She turns and looks at me: "If you had been there, you would've seen. You'd understand."

Principal Davis's eyes move between us.

"We're going to see Althea first thing next week," I tell the principal. "And I do think, with Althea and Proctor knowing what they're facing, in terms of their sentences, it changes everything." I think about Althea's letter to me, her attempt at reconciliation and my response. "What we're experiencing now has a way of focusing the mind on what's important. I think this will be resolved."

Lillian shakes her head. "Please listen to me for once, Viola. Don't go getting your hopes up or the girls' hopes up about reunions. Trust me." She turns to the principal, her eyes pleading. "What should we do?"

He grimaces. "I have to be honest with you: There's no magic bullet." He pauses, his expression sliding into something like thoughtfulness. "She's a good kid. She really is, once you get in there. I've seen it. But I'm also seeing that goodness less and less, and I have to tell you the truth. I'm worried because I'm not entirely sure how to proceed." He looks out the glass door of his office, out to the waiting area where Kim sits, writing furiously in her notebook.

Oldham County Correctional Facility
Proctor Cochran
720 Smith Avenue, NE
Park Point, Michigan

Tuesday, November 19, 2013

Althea,

I've been thinking about where we might end up. I was talking to our friend the other day, and he was naming off a couple of possibilities. He mentioned a prison out there in Virginia. In a place called Hopewell. That's a name for you, isn't it? He was going on about how he heard it was easy time out there in the federal system and I said, man, I don't know what "easy time" is. He got me, and tried to make up for it by telling me about a ladies' prison out in West Virginia, and he said, wouldn't it be nice if Althea ended up there? He said, you two would be close. And you know what? For a minute, your boy was happy, just imagining it. I even went to the library and looked it up. And there it was, West Virginia with what looked like a little arm, snuggled up there with Virginia. Then, it hit me: This is what it's come down to. I sat here on my bunk thinking, I can't believe that this is the best we can hope for at this stage in the game. Ending up in states that are side by side. It breaks my heart, Al.

Do you remember when we were talking about getting that RV? Well, I guess I was the one talking about it. I haven't thought about that in years. But remember standing out on the steps of the courthouse after we got married? Me, you, my granny, and your little shadow, Viola? It was cold as hell, but there we were, posing for pictures and taking a minute to stand there and dream. Talking about how once we got on our feet, we were going to see every state in the union. What happened to that? I bet we thought we had all the time in the world to be together.

I know I shouldn't think about what was and what could have been, but that's where I am these days. So deep in Darth Vader Space that I can't hardly see out. And it doesn't help that I haven't been sleeping the greatest. I keep having this dream where I'm doing laundry and you and the girls are there with me folding stuff. You're fussing at the kids about how they're folding everything wrong. But then you stop fussing and the girls start singing. But they've turned into really little girls, and they're doing their "Battling Beyoncés" routine. Remember that? They have those yellow towels on their heads for "hair," swinging it all around. They have on their matching Barbie pajamas, and they're using brushes for mics like they used to do, singing "Say My Name." But all I can recognize is the tune. I can't make out any lyrics.

Then they break out with something from this girl Kim turned me onto. She sent me the song a couple months ago. It has some nice strings, all moody and angelic, and I can hear the girls' little voices high and clear, singing two-part harmony, and those lyrics are easy to make out about wanting the truth or something beautiful and how easy it is to deceive people. Then they start laughing and jumping on me, knocking the laundry all over the place, climbing me like a tree, like they used to do when they were little. But then, we're all of a sudden outside with bright, white snow all around us, but you're gone. We can't find you. Then I wake up with this really bad feeling, like a black fog in my head, like I haven't slept one bit. I've been walking around with that feeling for days with those violins and the voices of the girls going over and over in my head like a mourning song.

It doesn't help that you didn't say a word about Kim's letter when you wrote back. Did you read it? What's going on? I've always had to be the referee with you two, and here I am again. I wish things could have been different, God knows. Not just so that she wouldn't have called the police. That is what it is. But what I wish is that there hadn't been the kind of feelings for her to even think about calling in the first place.

I'd better go. As for a song for this week, I'll wait for your best guess on the last one I sent. I promise, it's one you know, if you sit with it and think on it for a minute. If you think about us.

To tell the truth, I don't have a song in me right now. I can't explain it, but it's like there's a receiver in my head picking up on every bad vibe out there. This picture of you over my bed is like a window to see out to you. It usually feels like a good thing, but I got to be honest. Right now, it doesn't. I think it would do me good, <u>IT WOULD DO ALL OF US GOOD</u>*, for you to do your part with the kids.*

We'll see each other when we do.

Love,
Proctor

Althea

I'm coloring in the *b* in *Goodbye*. I've done every letter in a different color: green, orange, yellow, purple. I'm doing the *b* in blue.

"It's tacky," Mercedes grumbles for the umpteenth time, looking at my sign like she might do something to it. "Seriously tacky."

"This isn't an art show," I say.

Mercedes just sits there, giving me and my sign dagger-eyes from across the table. They've moved into the "battered-woman defense" in her trial, and it's made her touchier than usual. She never liked that defense, and she flat-out hates it now that they're looking at the evidence, especially the pictures of her bruised-up arms and back and the black eye she got from her victim.

Gale, who's sitting next to Mercedes, raises an eyebrow to me, like, *See?*

The other day, Gale said, "I think it's getting too real for Mercedes. Real's good for personal inventory types like me and you, but it damn sure ain't the best for somebody with, let's say, impulse control issues."

Then she made her fingers into scissors and pretended to cut off her tongue, miming what they say Mercedes did to her victim.

Gale looks Mercedes up and down, giving her one of her "checking-for-crazy visuals." Mercedes's current levels must be more or less in range, because Gale goes back to coloring her sign, which says: *Good Luck, Big Chit!*

"Chit's going to Sober Home?" I ask.

"It's a *sober house*," Mercedes corrects, sounding irritated. "A sober living community."

I look at her, hard. "Thank you for clearing that up."

"Sober home, sober house, call it what you want to," Gale says, her voice phlegmy and thin. She coughs and pats her chest, trying to clear her throat. "It's all the same. Just another prison with curfews and the twelve-step cult." She stops and studies the little colored pencils in the middle of the table. She takes a red one out of the bag to fill in the big bow she's drawn.

"That's a long way from home for her, isn't it?" I say, thinking about Chit's husband and two boys, the pet rabbit she talks about, and the three-bedroom house with the changed locks where the husband, boys, and the rabbit still live, but without Chit. "Nobody's waiting for her out there," I say.

"At least she got someplace to go, 'cause, Lord knows, Chit can't handle them streets," Gale says, coughing again and pounding her chest.

I want to say, *Stopping that smoking would help more than the chest pounding*, but I'd be wasting my breath. When she gets out, all somebody has to do is dangle a cigarette in front of Gale and she'll follow them anywhere, coughing and trying to clear her throat the whole time.

She shrugs out of the coughing and throat clearing and in a rattling voice says, "DUIs, blackouts, and bad checks? I seen way sadder cases than Chit's, trust."

As Gale colors in her bow, I think, *I see sadder right now*. My eyes move to the raw half-smile carved up from the right corner of Gale's mouth to her earlobe by "a client."

"Crazy nigga thought I wasn't a happy enough hooker," Gale explained one time, sounding confused about it but not surprised. "The smile," as she calls it, has healed, but her leathery, mahogany skin is so pulled and raw in that place, it makes her hard to look at. My eyes go from that serrated smile to the deep gouge in the center of her forehead and the tracks on her arms.

"Chit'll be all right," Mercedes says. "The Lord'll watch over her, but we'll make sure we give her a good send-off at Bible study. She's good people."

"Even though she only come to Bible study when she feel like it," Gale mumbles.

Mercedes stops midcoloring. "Why do you got to hate all the time?"

"I ain't hating. I'm just saying it damn sure must be nice getting a goodbye party. Who's gone be around to give my ass a send-off when I roll up outta this bitch? Y'all two gone be—"

Gale cuts herself off at the familiar sound of wheezing and the *swish-swish* of fabric on rubbing thighs. But we all know what she was about to say: Me and Mercedes will be off in our prisons somewhere by the time what's left of Gale's one-year sentence, served right here in jail, is done.

We all look in the direction of the sounds that made Gale shut up. Here comes a mountain of a woman, heaving herself at our table. She stops and looks at our signs with the sweet smile of a baby on her chubby, apple-cheeked face. But you can see the calcifying around the eyes and the creases in her forehead. The first signs of cracking, and the girl's barely thirty.

"You guys planning Big Chit's goodbye party?" she asks, talking about herself.

"Look like we are," Gale rattles. "Go on 'head and grab a seat for a minute while I bust this sign out right quick. We got plenty of time to go for meds."

As Gale speeds up her sign coloring, Chit lowers herself into the seat next to me with a grunt, still catching her breath from the walk across the room. Her skin is pink and moist, which reminds me of the name somebody gave her here in jail: Big Chitterling. She looks up at the clock, grabs some paper and a couple of colored pencils, and starts making her own goodbye sign. "It's going to be a new life," she says, the tone of her voice matching her happy sketching. "I'm going to get my job back and everything."

"Hold up. You mean to tell me they gone let you go back to working in a courtroom and whatnots with your case?" Gale motions around the oval dayroom, taking in the two stories of cells behind us, the guard station, and the other inmates. "Seem to me you outta second chances."

Chit's smile wobbles. She starts sketching again, a dog. No. I think that's a rabbit. "It's true," she says, glancing up. "I had a low bottom, but I hit it. This is me on my way back up. I'm going back to school. I'll get a new job, if I have to. Everything's going to come together." She stops coloring. "Did I tell you my youngest is turning four next month? They're going to let me come to his birthday party, I think." She smiles. "And I'll get to spend Christmas with my boys, too, if things go my way." She raises a plump hand to wipe her eyes and smiles again. It's the kind of hopeful smile you can't help but smile back at.

"That's right, Chit," Mercedes says. "Speak that shit into existence."

"Always," Chit says. Her face goes soft. "And thanks, you guys, for the send-away. I know it's not a usual thing. It kind of feels like I have somebody pulling for me, you know?"

"Well," Mercedes says, "the chaplain is the one allowing it. He said he thinks it'll be good for *everybody* to just have something fun." She shoots a glance at Gale. "Anyways, you know, it's still officially Bible study and all, so make sure you thank him." Mercedes looks down at the table. "Give me this tacky-ass thing," she says, snatching my sign away. "Let me do it."

She flips the paper over to start from scratch, tracing out *Go with God, Chit!* in rainbow colors, and already the letters look better than mine ever could. The outlines are like little puffballs doing a bouncy, happy dance on the page.

"You don't got to show off," I say.

Mercedes shrugs, but she's smiling. She used to be a sketch artist, working carnivals and fairs, doing caricatures, mostly. If you catch her in the right mood, she'll sketch you. Your true self. Or how you'd like yourself to be. She drew a picture of me before my trial, earlier this year. I was sitting right here in the big, oval dayroom with cells all around. But Mercedes drew me sitting out on my dock, looking out at my river with my feet in the water, just like I'd described it to her. It was all in black and white, but it had this feeling of living color and real life to me.

"You'll be back out there before you know it, sis," she said, when she gave the picture to me.

I look up at the ceiling, thinking of that picture and Proctor. I sent it to him for our anniversary earlier this month. He said it was his window to see out to me, and I wonder, *Is he in his bunk right now looking out to me, thinking his dark thoughts? Is he writing another letter telling me how I ought to be?*

I touch my breast pocket and feel the stiff square of the letter that he sent, folded inside of his letter, two weeks ago. The square of lined notebook paper has the word *Private* written on it in Kim's rounded, pillowy handwriting with a little circle floating above the *i* in *Private*. I took it out the other day and turned it over and over in my hands before finally making myself read it.

"Where your head at, girl?" Gale asks. "You ain't paying attention to a word we saying."

"Daydreaming," I say.

"You're thinking about your transfer again, ain't you?" Mercedes sounds like she's accusing me of a crime. "The two of you are gonna land okay, watch."

It's the last thing I talked to her about and the last thing I want to be thinking about right now.

"We'll end up where we end up," I say, trying to sound like I can take whatever. But it's starting to get to me. Through the trial, through the conviction, even at the sentencing when I realized I was going to spend years in prison, for some reason, I wasn't thinking in terms of *we*: me and Proctor. That *we* won't even be in the same building anymore. That *we* are going our separate ways, even if we end up in states side by side. How do you live for so long without somebody who's always been there, even when you didn't want him to be? Even when he didn't want to be? Proctor's all I've known since I was twelve years old.

Stop wallowing, Althea, I tell myself. *Just stop it. It is what it is, and it could be worse.*

You could be Mercedes. You could be Gale. You could be any of these women. That's worse, isn't it? Remember, you built yourself something from nothing, out there in the real world. And talk about parties? You put together parties and fund-raisers like none of these people have ever seen. Even when it wasn't anything fancy, everybody came. People showed up for you at your barbecues, at the balls you put on, sponsored you in that *Dancing with Our Stars* fund-raiser because they knew who you were and what you could do. Everywhere you went, people had something nice to say to you.

"All right," Gale's saying. "I think it's about time for me and Chit to roll out."

They get up and gather their signs while Mercedes keeps coloring. The letters are bright and fun in pinks and greens and yellows. She's working on flowers now. Daisies.

I hear a high-pitched laugh. It's Adira, one table over. Instantly, I feel the need to know her crime and how mine compares. She's playing cards with another girl, Tina the Talker, her new best friend. Everybody knows Tina's crime, thanks to her constantly running mouth: "They say I stole a car and busted through somebody's garage in the getaway," is how she tells it. "But I don't remember none of it. I was on Ambien. They could accuse me of doing anything in the night and, believe me, they have."

I can't tell what the Talker's saying now, but Adira thinks it's funny. It's been a couple of days since that Bible study when she spoke. I turn to Big Chit, who knows just about everybody's crime, because just about everybody who knows her treats her like some kind of jailhouse lawyer because of her past life as a court reporter. "Do you know what Adira's in for?" I ask.

She glances over at the table. "Some killings. But she's not a real killer."

There's a quick hit of awkwardness. All of us, suddenly aware of the "real killer" in our midst.

"We all know the score," Mercedes says, not looking up from her coloring. "But 'some killings' sure as shit sounds like real killing to me."

"Adira gave some people in a home a bunch of sleeping pills," Chit says. "A mercy-killing thing."

"Naw, she put the sleep on just her neighbor or somebody," Gale says.

Chit looks at Gale with a raised eyebrow. "I'm pretty sure I'm right."

"Did she tell you this herself?" I ask.

"Big Chit never reveals a source."

"Well, I'm revealing that whoever your source is, she wrong. Trust.

My intelligence always tight," Gale says, looking up at the clock. She slides her and Chit's signs toward Mercedes. "Come on, Chit. Let's mount up."

As Gale limps and Chit lumbers and wheezes away, I'm reminded there are a lot of bad sources in jail, usually the very person who's telling you about their crime or what they're accused of. You can never be sure of people, especially in here.

What I do know is Adira, a girl who claimed she wrestled angels, doesn't look like she'd hurt anybody. She's holding her hands up miming something, and I see green, fancy swirls on her wrist, but I can't make out what they are. She lowers her arms, nodding at Tina the Talker like she never understood anything so clearly. Now she's looking at me. She smiles and waves a timid wave.

I smile back.

"All I know," says Mercedes, "is, whatever the hell that girl did, if they send her ass up for it, she's gonna get eaten alive. Just look at her. That's what you call a lamb to the slaughter right there."

"Maybe we all are," I say.

She rolls her eyes. "You'll be fine. You're going to Club Fed. That's a vacation compared to where that one'll end up."

"For somebody who's never been to prison, federal or state, you sure do seem to have it all down."

Mercedes smiles, showing her gray, jagged teeth. "Well, I guess we'll get a chance to compare notes when they send *my* ass up, won't we?" Her smile fades. "You know this battered-woman bullshit's not gonna get me off, right? For one, I ain't no battered-ass bitch. I ain't *nobody's* victim, and they need to know that. I give as good as I get."

She rakes a hand through her hair, pushing it back from her face. I notice the shadows under her eyes as she looks off at the guard station. There's a silence now. A very long stretch of nothing but angry breathing.

"You got a ways to go before the jury has its say, Mercedes."

"You sound like my mother," she says, still looking at the guard station.

I saw a picture of Mercedes's mother one time. She's a ground-down, razor-boned woman who doesn't look like the encouraging type, but that woman and Mercedes's brother never miss a visit, even if sometimes one or both of them are drunk and denied entry and sleeping it off out in the parking lot.

"You know," I say, "for somebody always talking about speaking stuff into existence, you're pretty good about speaking yourself into a prison cell instead of freedom."

She shrugs and pulls another stubby colored pencil from the bag. Green, to color in a flower stem. Her hand moves fast, making tiny strokes, bringing the daisy to full bloom. "You know, I was gonna be a cartoonist," Mercedes says. "That's what I wanted to be." She only ever talks about what she was, a caricature artist, never what she wanted to be. And I think, *What did I want to be?* Definitely not a bookkeeper. That's something I just ended up becoming after years and years of night school. And a restaurant owner? That was Proctor's dream, at first. A mother? I think I just *became* everything I am. Was. But at least I was somebody out there.

I look down at Mercedes's picture with the bouncy letters, the beautiful daisy, and the outlines of daisies still waiting to be brought to life. "You're talented enough to be a cartoonist," I say.

She smiles, but her lips are tight. "Not bad for some battered-ass, weak-ass bitch, is it?"

"Stop that."

"I had this teacher," she says. "Fifth grade. The year my mother started going down the tubes." She mimes lifting a glass to her lips over and over again. "Ms. Peterson was her name. A real sweet lady. Real fat, though. You know, the kind that'd be pretty if they lost some weight?"

She nods toward Chit's empty chair. "Like Chit. Anyways, she'd stop by the house when I didn't make it to school. And she started taking me to the library and everything like that. She took me to the movies sometimes, too. She took me to see my first Disney movie, right? *The Fox and the Hound*. You remember that one?"

I shake my head.

"It's about this dog and this fox that make friends. It was my favorite movie in the world. Ms. Peterson took me to it, like, three times, believe it or not. I drew pictures of the characters. I still remember them: Tod, Copper, and Boomer." She smiles. "Anyways, Ms. Peterson saw my drawings and said, 'You're a real artist, kiddo.' She called me that all the time. 'Kiddo.' Like a pet name. She told me I could go work for Disney when I got big, so I decided right there and then, yep, that's what I'm gonna do. I talked about it all the time, right? Hell, up until I was in high school." Mercedes pauses, and there's that tight smile again. "But certain shit ain't got no hope of coming into existence no matter what you're told or how many different ways you speak it. Some of us just got Kick Me signs tacked to our backs straight outta the womb, and, sure enough, life just rears back and puts its foot clean up your ass. I'm talking ankle deep. And ain't no getting it out."

I think of Mercedes's Kick Me–sign life, as reported on the news: Twenty-eight out of her forty-one years were spent huffing, snorting, smoking, shooting, and drinking anything that could alter her consciousness, if not her reality; she finished high school by the skin of her teeth; stole, traded drawings, or sold herself for whatever she could get.

"But I think there's hope for Chit," Mercedes says, "and you, too, even with prison. At least you got something real and good out there if you want it, you know? My family ain't good for me, even when they're here for me, but you and Chit, at least you got normal families and all, even if, you know, it's hard times with everything right now."

"I got a letter from Kim." The words rush out like they've been waiting for this moment. "Well, Proctor did. You know, Kim writes to him." I take the letter out of my breast pocket, put it on the table, and push it her way.

She unfolds it slowly, like it might rip or crumble if she's not careful. She reads. First, there's Kim's report on how she got another golden egg in *Angry Birds*, written mostly in capital letters. Then there are a few lines about listening all the way through an Earth, Wind & Fire album she and Proctor apparently talked about and that she doesn't like as much as he does. She writes about going to see the One Direction movie again with Baby Vi even though, and she double underlines this, boy bands are not her thing. She tells Proctor how much she hates school and everybody there because they're fake, which is also double underlined. She says she can't see how Baby Vi does it, but then she remembers Baby Vi is just "that way," which is all right and maybe even good. She tells Proctor how she went back to our empty house the other day and sat in her room for no reason and how she went and threw rocks at the restaurant for obvious reasons. She tells him how much she misses him.

When Mercedes glances up at me, then back down at the letter, I know she's gotten to the part that says:

> *Daddy, you know you and her are different, right? She plays favorites and you don't. But maybe I am sorry for telling. I just get so mad sometimes especially at her. It's like I want to explode all the time and I think that time I just did. You remember how she was that day I did the call, don't you? All kicking me off the cash register because I made one little mistake with somebody's change, just one little thing, then not letting me go to the kitchen to help in there because she said I would mess my diet up. Then just making me sit there with nothing to do and everybody all looking at me*

like I'm stupid and making me just sit in that stupid booth. When you told her you were taking me home, I heard you guys fighting over everything and that's why I didn't want to go for ice cream or anything like you wanted to. I just wanted to go home and to my room and before I knew it I had my phone out and I was calling the police on her but it wasn't even like I thought to do it or anything like that, it wasn't like I planned something, I was just doing it. When I think about it sometimes I think maybe part of me wanted to pay her back for all the times she was the way she was, all yelling at people and expecting people to be little Miss Perfect and everything all the time. I think I just thought that maybe the police would come and scare her or something. I think I was just trying to scare her, that's all, because it would have made her see how it feels to have somebody always all up in your face all the time. But I didn't know everything would turn out so bad and I didn't know you would get in trouble. I think about going back to the jail to see her sometimes and maybe I would go if she wanted me to but she doesn't want me to, does she? How could she kick us out like that when we came there that time???? Even Baby Vi???? It was because of me I know it. She's never been good to me. She's always been different with me my whole life so maybe I'm not sorry I called the police on her. I don't know.

"She's just a kid," Mercedes says, folding the letter back up. I notice she's not looking at me. "Kids say shit like this all the time. Hell, just about every kid thinks they're getting a raw deal from somebody, especially their friggin' parents."

I nod. Baby Vi was always easy, but Kim? From day one, she was a colicky baby, and it went on from there. When she started talking, she had a smart mouth. She's a know-it-all. And I don't care if everybody says she looks fine, she doesn't. She's too big, and she needs to hear it. It had to be tough love with her, which is what Proctor doesn't understand. I was tough because *life* is tough. That's what you do. And her saying she's not sorry? See, that's just like Kim. Her attitude. That's the reason she *always* needed a strong hand. But Proctor wanted to be a buddy, a friend, and, obviously, their favorite. I'd hear them laughing and having fun without me. I'm the one who always had to do what needed to be done. While he had his dreams of RVs and the rest, I was making a real life for us.

"She's just a kid," Mercedes says again, sliding the carefully folded letter back to me. But she's still not looking at me. She's fingering the colored pencils, like she's trying to decide which one to use. But I don't think she is. I think she's hiding her eyes and what she's thinking. I bet she believes what's in this letter because it occurs to me that, just like I heard all about her Kick Me–sign life on the news, she's read or heard reports about my life, too, including Kim's testimony. Mercedes believes her. So does Proctor.

She's never been good to me. She's always been different with me.

I stuff the letter back in my breast pocket, my hand shaking.

"I got to go," I say, standing up as bubbly laughter floats over from Adira's table. It's louder than it should be. It's like everything's turned up: talk from the other tables, Mercedes's pencil marking the paper.

I feel shaky legged. Sweat's pinging out on my upper lip.

"I got to go," I say again to Mercedes.

Mercedes gathers up the art supplies.

I put a hand on her inked-up forearm to stop her.

"You all right?" C.O. Jordan calls out from the guard station.

I nod. I tell Mercedes, "I need to go."

She frowns but says, "Okay, sis."

* * *

I stop at the top of the stairs, pressing a shaking hand over my heart, which is thumping fast under Kim's note in my breast pocket.

What's wrong with me?

I hear somebody asking if I'm okay. I don't recognize her. "You don't look good," she says, pausing on her way past me down the stairs.

"I'm fine." But my voice sounds breathless and far away.

"If you say so," she says, as she goes on down to the dayroom.

My heart beats faster.

Is this a heart attack? Am I dying?

Get a grip. This is kind of what you felt like in the courtroom on sentencing day, I tell myself, *when you collapsed. Or before that, like when you were listening to Kim's testimony.*

How could she? We lost it all because of that phone call. After everything I've done. Everything I've sacrificed for her and everybody else? I sat in that courtroom listening to Kim speak, with my eyes dry, my mouth parched, and my lips chapped. It was like everything in me was draining away with every word she spoke: breath, blood, life, love.

Here's Gale, heading up the steps in my direction. Her meds must not've kicked in yet because she's limping fast. Her mouth's moving, but all I hear is rushing and roaring in my ears and the thumping of my heart. My tongue's stuck to the roof of my mouth. Dry mouth. Dry bones.

Our bones are dried up and our hope is gone; we are cut off . . .

Those words. I know them. The valley of dry bones.

"Hey! You okay?" Gale's face is so close, I smell the stink of her breath. I see the delicate, serrated skin of that smile-scar on one side of her face, closer than I ever have before. On the other side of her face, her nicotine-browned lips are frowning. She pats my face. Other women are coming over; somebody's yelling, "Get help!"

And I think, *Just a drink, please. Just something to unstick the tongue.* Or maybe just somebody to say, "It's going to be all right, Althea." Then you can tell everybody how you were only doing what you had to do to stay above water, like you've always done. Tell them how you can't help it, but Kim's name feels like sand in your mouth, and every motherly word you'd say about her tastes like grit.

And all of a sudden I hear it. This whisper that comes to my mind from time to time: *You know, as a mother, you are your father's daughter.*

My breath's coming fast and ragged. The hallway's rotating. And there's the scuffed green-and-white-checkerboard floor, folding up *smack* against my face. But it's like some part of me keeps right on sinking. Right out of my body, right through the floor into a pit that's deeper than any valley of dry bones.

Everything goes quiet.

Except for: *Our bones are dried up and our hope is gone; we are cut off*. . . And I remember where I was when I read that scripture for the very first time. Sitting there at my mother's bedside. Ezekiel 37:11. I see the note in the margin above that scripture in my mother's Bible, written in her cramped but careful hand: *Dry bones. Read Revelation? (Then the angel showed me the river of the water of life.)*

I remember asking her what she meant by what she wrote.

She was quiet for so long that I thought she'd drifted off to sleep again, but then she said, "Sometimes life can pull a lot out of you, Althea. Just squeeze you dry. And if you don't have a way to get back whatever's good and precious to you, it's like losing your soul." She smiled and breathed, "I've lived long enough to see that much."

She was only thirty-two.

I've outlived her by sixteen years, and all I can see is a whole lot of nothing.

DRINK IT IN

Viola

"All right, ladies. What will it be?"

There's silence from my sullen companions. Maybe because it's a little hard to hear with the *thump-thump-thump* of music, the *rumble* and *crash* of bowling pins, and the *pop-pop-pop* of video game gunshots. Maybe I should talk louder. "LOOK, WE CAN GO OVER TO THE ARCADE." I make a big, loud gesture in the direction of the *Big Buck Hunter* game over in the arcade area. "I'M UP FOR ANYTHING."

Baby Vi shrugs.

Kim mumbles something that doesn't sound like English. Which seems about right. I feel like I'm in a foreign land. Or a forgotten one. Bowling alleys, arcades overrun with children and overly loud adults? This is, in no way, my scene. I haven't been around a crowd like this in a place like this, this particular place, no less, since I was a teenager. Based on how crowded it is, this is still the place to be on a Saturday night.

I see Mr. and Ms. Pac-Man over in the corner, sitting alongside their highly evolved descendants. I bet the aging Mr. and Ms. over there are the very same couple that gobbled up countless tokens when David, Lillian, and I used to come here after school. Hard-earned coinage from David's lawn mowing, my babysitting, and our joint snow-shoveling venture. Our high scores must be long gone by now. But I smile because the feeling from those days, the sense of escape, is coming back to me, carried on the aroma of nachos and beer.

I smile a little wider as I say, "THEY HAVE GLOW BOWLING. I'M UP FOR TRYING IT IF YOU GUYS ARE!"

"You don't have to talk so loud, Aunt Viola," Baby Vi says, speaking a little louder than she usually does. "We can hear you okay."

The three of us stand, quiet, the sounds around us seeming to amplify the silence between us. I can't quite find the best place to put my hands. The girls seem to be having the same problem with their shuffling feet. We haven't been out alone together since they were little, and I'm realizing they're almost as foreign to me as everyone else here. Their likes and dislikes as forgotten as this place.

"Anyway, what do you guys think? You want to bowl? Play some games?"

They exchange a look.

"Hey," I say, gently. "We're all trying our best here." There's the rumble of balls, the clatter of pins dropping, a big cheer going up. Strike in lane two. High-fives, fist pumps, hugs. This isn't the time for talking about best efforts, but I've already started. I guide the girls out the door we just came through, so I can finish.

Outside in the parking lot, in the cold and relative quiet, I say, in my clinical therapist's voice, "Look, I know what a difficult time this is. No one expects anyone to pretend to be happy, okay?"

Baby Vi looks down at her shoes, but Kim holds my gaze. We bunch up, hugging ourselves against a coat-shredding gust of wind. I pull up my scarf to protect my face. The girls burrow deeper into their coats.

"I just think it might help if we give ourselves something else to focus on," I continue, "if only for a little while."

Still nothing, but Baby Vi is at least peering up through her long eyelashes at me.

"What's happening is real," I go on. "We can't minimize it, but it's important we don't let ourselves be consumed by it every second of every day."

Kim's eyes, the same big, brown eyes as her sister's and her mother's, remain steady, but there are tears now. She looks down. Unsnaps then resnaps a closure on her black puffer coat that's already straining against the great expanse of her. *Snap-snap-snap.* Repeatedly. I resist the urge to ask her to stop. I say instead, "I know it's tough, but we have to try, okay?" The *snap-snap-snap* and the muffled noise from the bowling alley behind me are the only replies. I clench and unclench my gloved fingers, trying to work up some warmth. "You don't deserve this. But we'll get through it. In time—" The basic bullshit, clichéd sound of what I'm saying stops me midsentence. How does time heal the *want* of time, such *crucial* time, with someone you miss? You learn to get by with a loss like that, but something is always off. I wish I could at least tell them they'll get to see Althea soon. That Lillian and I will see to it when we visit her. But what if Lillian is right?

Ice crunches and cracks under the girls' shuffling feet.

"Maybe let's just go back home?" Baby Vi says, quietly.

"We told you, they don't want us here," Kim says. She has stopped her snapping and unsnapping, but her mittened hand is still hovering there at her coat closures. "Can't you see how they look at us? They don't want us in there."

"I noticed a couple of glances, but"—I shrug—"that's nothing."

"They don't like us," Baby Vi puts in.

"That's not true."

"How would you know?" Kim says, shoving her hands in her coat pockets, giving me a glacial look that says, *How could you know anything about us?*

"Fair enough," I say, gazing back at the street and passing car lights, thinking of yesterday afternoon in the principal's office and what it must be like to be Kim and Baby Vi at school and everywhere else, in a town where their parents are pariahs. "I'm not going to pretend to know what you're going through," I say, "but I *do* know you haven't done anything wrong. I *do* know this isn't your fault and you have just as much right as anyone else to go where you want to go and do what you want to do."

Kim rolls her eyes and looks off in the direction of my car.

Baby Vi keeps staring at her shoes.

"Girls, look at me."

A side-eye and a hard stare.

"You guys didn't do anything wrong here," I say. "Your mother and father—"

"Not my father." Kim's voice is sharp as she cuts me off. She crosses her arms in defense.

"All I'm saying is, this isn't your doing. Please don't punish yourselves for it by hiding in the house." I point in the direction of the bowling alley. "And you can't let them punish you for it either."

Silence, but the girls seem to shift, standing a little closer together.

"Why don't we go in and bowl a game? Do you really want to just sit around the house watching movies?" I smile. "Or playing with the cat and the grandmother?"

The girls glance at each other. Baby Vi looks at me and cocks her head to the side. "Why do you call her that? 'The grandmother'? It sounds"—she frowns—"not very nice."

"I don't know. That's the translation, right? Grandmother?" Do I need a reason? "Anyway, sitting at home is really what you guys want to do?"

"Yeah," Kim says. "Didn't you hear us?"

"Pizza and Nai Nai and movies are all right." Baby Vi looks at Kim and smiles. "Except I think it's her pick."

Kim winces. "Another old-timey, bad one. Sometimes I wish I was the one who couldn't hardly see. Or hear. Maybe she won't remember it's her turn."

"*We* remember," Baby Vi says.

"Look, I have the keys." I dangle them out in front of me. "And I don't want to go home. What do you say you humor me and bowl one game? Just one. Please?" I bring my hands together in mock prayer. But it's a more serious supplication than they know. I truly don't want to be at home.

Baby Vi makes a face but asks her sister, "One game?"

Kim shrugs.

"Thank you." I give them a big smile.

Baby Vi returns a half smile.

Kim offers something less than that, but it's better than nothing.

"It was like some kind of after-school special gone horribly, horribly wrong," I say, collapsing into the deep comfort of a leather armchair. "Not backing down? Exercising your right to go bowling?" I shake my head and murmur, "Best when scripted."

Lillian is sitting to my right in an armchair that matches mine, with Thelonious resting on her lap. The cat eyes me with vague interest. Lillian's best friend, Elaine, and my friend, David, co-opted by Lillian, are opposite us on the couch. We're all enveloped in the warmth of the library. Orange flames writhe and rise in the stacked stone fireplace, and there's the smell of cherrywood. The three of them were laughing and just starting in on their second bottle of wine before my buzz-killing "horribly, horribly wrong" pronouncement.

"What happened?" Lillian asks, leaning forward, cradling her cat. "And does it have anything to do with that?"

She points to the small, pizza-box-sized square of wood on my lap that I finally brought in from my car. I think about how the wood chunk and the car itself, impulse the driving force behind both, feel more and more like regrets.

"No," I say, looking down at the wood square. "This and the horribly, horribly wrong thing are separate incidents." I help myself to a supersized glass of their wine.

"Pace yourself," cautions Elaine. Her concerned smile is set against rich, caramel skin. Elaine, Lillian's best friend since they were in middle school and mother to Kim's boyfriend, Junior, is a round, plush type with a serious senior citizen streak. Always issuing cautions or giving you one of her *there-there*s or *oh, dear*s.

I take a deep, restorative swallow from my glass, trying to decide whether to talk about the chainsawed chunk of the bar or what happened at the bowling alley first. I hold up the chunk. "This is part of the bar from the restaurant," I say. Elaine and Lillian both look perplexed. "David and I, um, procured it when I got into town."

I look at him as if to say, *Can you help a sister out, here?*

"Yes," he says. Then he gazes off at the closed door of the library, as if to distance himself from the whole affair.

"Thank you," I say to the side of his face. "That was helpful." To Elaine and Lillian I explain, "The plan is to make it into a going-away gift for Proctor. I thought we could have it whittled down to something."

"I'm sorry," says Elaine, twirling a finger in the air, "but can we rewind? What do you mean by 'this is part of the bar'?"

"David sawed it off." I run my fingers along the square's jagged edge while looking at the distanced David, who shrugs and says, "She made me."

Lillian looks from David to me. "You want to have it whittled down to what, exactly?"

"Still trying to figure that out." I turn the wood chunk over, considering what it could become. "Any suggestions would be appreciated. It's crazy, I know that, but I do think it could be a good keepsake. Proctor made that bar with his own hands."

Lillian, David, and Elaine exchange a look, and Lillian says, without much conviction, "I'll have to think about it." She strokes Thelonious's back and looks up at the ceiling where floorboards are creaking and groaning under the girls' feet. "I'm scared to ask, but what went 'horribly wrong' at the bowling alley?"

Right. That. When we got in from the bowling alley and I stupidly tried to revive the movie-and-pizza-night idea, Kim rounded on me and said, "You think you can show up out of nowhere, like, *I got this*, and force us to do stuff we tell you we don't wanna do? I see why you and Mama are sisters. Go back to Chicago."

"We tried to tell you," Baby Vi added, sounding like she'd have me gone, too.

And I stood there at the foot of the stairs trying to apologize while they ignored me, slowly hauling themselves up the stairs like overburdened, stiff-jointed old women.

"Well," I say, "we weren't chased out of the bowling alley with pitchforks and torches or beaten up in the parking lot or anything."

Elaine, Lillian, and David exchange mildly horrified glances, and Elaine murmurs, "Oh, dear."

"It was just . . ." I pause, trying to find the right words. "The people. Some of them, not all of them, but . . . some of them were very cold. Very, well, angry."

Elaine reaches over and pats my leg, like, *there-there*.

Lillian nods, knowingly. She told me not to go.

"Kim and Baby Vi didn't want to go in," I say, "but I made them. I shouldn't have done that."

We had suffered through about half of a game under the cold stares and sideways glances of a few people in the bowling alley when an old woman came and stood near our lane. I didn't notice her at first. It was Baby Vi who gave me a poke in the arm while pointing at the lady. I gave the woman a *Can I help you?* smile, but she just stood there, looking at us with unsteady, milky eyes. When I asked her if there was something I could do for her, her eyes went from Baby Vi to Kim, and she said, "Do you know how much we gave the Cochrans?" There was a pause that went on for so long I half expected she actually wanted me to take a guess. But then she spoke again in her high, thin voice: "And not only my family, but the people in this community. Do you know how much we got took for? These folks in here may not have it in them to say it"—she flung open her arms to indicate the bowlers and gamers for whom she was speaking—"but I'll say it. You have a lot of nerve going around here laughing it up like nothing's happened!"

There hadn't been much laughter in our bowling threesome, but, clearly, there was no point in telling her that. Baby Vi was shrinking beside me, as if trying to disappear into the bench we shared. She tucked in close to my side, shielding herself. But Kim was standing, fully exposed. She'd been staring down the lane at the spare she was about to pick up. She looked like a statue now, bowling ball still held up close to her shoulder, ready to roll.

My eyes shifted back to the old woman. A middle-aged couple sidled up beside her. "Come on, Mom," the man in the couple said, grabbing the old woman's elbow, pointedly *not* looking at the girls and me. The old woman shook him off and looked around the bowling alley, her arms out crucifixion-style. "Am I the only one mad here? Was my family the only ones that got fleeced by these Bernie Madoffs?"

The Bernie Madoff comparison seems a bit extreme and not at all related, I wanted to say, but at that moment, it was as if the whole bowling alley, once a cacophony of sound, fell silent. Falling pins suspended in air, the *pop-pop-pop* of video game gunshots stopped, games gone dark. I felt like every eye in the place was on us. A few were mildly sympathetic, but none of them were what I'd call friendly.

An old man doddered over to the woman. "You're causing a scene, honey," he said. The younger man gave him a helpless, palms-up gesture, then aimed a disdainful look at me.

"Ma'am, I," I started, then stopped because I realized there was nothing I could say. No defense, no explanation, no apology. I realized that for me, Althea and Proctor's crimes had been distant, deniable things seen from some far-off, isolated place. Chicago. But as I slowly brought myself to my feet there in that bowling alley, I felt like some stooped-over, squint-eyed creature dragged from its hiding place, blinking and adjusting to the nearness and brightness of reality. It was more vivid than the prosecutor's staged, parking lot press conference or the news reports or any of Lillian's warnings.

"You know," the old man said in a quavering voice, "we went to the fund-raisers and wrote checks because we knew Althea and Proctor personally. Ate at their restaurant—"

"Every Sunday after church!" the old woman cut in.

"We're on a fixed income," the man said, "but we dug deep to help the flood victims. For what? So they could line their pockets while the rest of us suffered through hard times!"

I pulled Baby Vi to her feet and put an arm around Kim, who was by then blank faced. The lack of expression was somehow worse than her usual variation of shell shock and do-not-fuck-with-me defensiveness. But there was this look in her eyes: something dark, something distant, something desperate.

"Let's go," I whispered.

A few people started clapping. They actually *clapped* as we left. The clapping was backed up by the music, bowling, and arcade sounds that had before seemed to fall silent. All of it somehow amped up, as if in celebration of our retreat.

Having recounted everything to Lillian, David, and Elaine, I watch varying degrees of concern cross their faces, but they don't seem as shocked as I am.

Lillian says simply, "I tried to tell you. It can be bad out there."

What I saw, out there, was such a contradiction, such a contrast to the story I want to believe. Althea's story. That it didn't happen the way the prosecutor said. That they borrowed small sums that built into something bigger, but it was all in good faith. That they used the money to pay workers, to meet the mortgage, to stay in business to pay it all back. That it wasn't about greed. That nobody really got hurt.

After a silence, Lillian clears her throat and says diplomatically, "Well, I can understand why you wanted to go to the bowling alley. I mean, we all have our I-won't-back-down things, right? You guys know mine."

I think for a second. "This house?"

I look around the room, but the beauty of everything suddenly strikes me as unseemly in light of those old people on a fixed income. My guilt or distaste or something must show on my face, because Lillian tilts her head to the side and looks troubled.

"Nooo," she says, drawing out the word.

"You know there's been talk about the house," Elaine notes. "You know how people can be."

"There's been more than talk," Lillian says, looking around the room.

I'm reminded that during the trial, people threw rocks through newly replaced windows, sprayed graffiti on the outside walls of the house, which had to be painted over repeatedly, and indeed Lillian did not back down. Occasionally, she still finds small mounds of feces left on her porch. But Lillian waves her hand, apparently dismissing it all. "No, my I-won't-back-down thing was Let's Mingle," she says. "You remember my singles' meetup?"

David clears his throat loudly and pushes up his glasses.

Elaine gives me a quick glance, then looks down in her wineglass.

Those gatherings never drew in anyone beyond the grandmother and two weird guys, once. David and Elaine, both of whom are married, put in pity/protection appearances.

"That was my stand," Lillian says. "I was like: I want to meet somebody, just like anybody else in this town, so I'm putting it out there." She frowns. "But things didn't go my way, and I took it as a message from the Universe to keep working on myself after, you know."

"You have to stop with that, Lillian," Elaine cautions quietly. "You made a mistake."

"Yeah," Lillian says. "A mistake." She looks at me. "Anyway, you see what I mean now, right? About what it's like for them?"

"I promised them we'd do something fun," I say. "That's all I was trying to do."

"There's nothing *fun* you can do for them, Viola. Not here anyway. I told you that. And you know what? I think Joe's right. They *do* need to get out of here. They need a fresh start."

"With him?"

"I didn't say that."

"Then what the hell are you saying?"

"Okay, you two," Elaine chastises. "Enough."

Lillian turns away, frustrated. In profile, her plain features are distorted, set aglow by the flames from the fireplace.

David stands. "Guys, look, it's been a long night." He glances down at his watch, confirming that, in point of fact, it has not been a long night at all.

Elaine is on her feet, too. "David and I should probably get home to the hubbies." She clasps her hands together in front of her, like a kindergarten teacher. "But please, you two, talk to each other. Get yourselves in a good place before you see Althea, okay?" Elaine gives Lillian a firm look. "You need to say what's on your mind."

Lillian regards Elaine as if to say, *You've said enough.* Her hand goes up to her ear, but she sees me watching her and the hand returns to her lap. She nudges Thelonious off and gets up from her chair. "I think everybody's had enough for one night," she says and shows David and Elaine out.

I take a sip of my wine. Gulp it, really, as I look into the fire. The fireplace, a massive stone mosaic commissioned by Lillian, was small and unobtrusive when we were children. But she has made the fireplace into the focal point of the room.

"You can't make over everything, Lillian," I say, as I get up and wander over to the bookcase, stopping at the *World Book* encyclopedias. She kept the whole set. I touch the faded green and yellowing-white spine of one book. Our father gave us these. He was so proud. I go over and pick up the picture of him Lillian keeps on one of the shelves, a man in a dark suit and tie. There's his perfect, square-toothed smile and his almond eyes. This man could tease or pull a ponytail or do his funny George Jefferson walk just to make you laugh when you least expected it. He could take you to Burger King for lunch, when you just knew you were going to get a whipping for ending up in the principal's office. He could do those things. This is the man—the fishing partner, the cheering parent in the bleachers, the made-over man—Lillian came to know. But the man I knew was someone else. His worst self, on the very last day I saw him alive.

I take a sip of my wine, and by some strange alchemy, it's transformed into syrupy sweetness in my mouth. I examine the glass of cherry-red liquid. It's undrinkable. But I take another sip anyway. Then another.

I put the picture back.

"You just never knew with you, did you?" I say to my handsome, smiling father.

I used to think it might be easier if he were like the father of my forced friends, the Ketchum twins. If Mr. Ketchum came in scowling and staggering and stinking of liquor, you knew to get out of the way. But what do you do with someone who wouldn't touch a drop of "the devil's tonic," as my father called liquor, but who could raise hell like a man under the influence? What do you do with a man who disappeared for weeks at a time like an alcoholic on a binge, when he went out on the road to evangelize, leaving little money but all of the responsibility to Althea? What do you do with a man who, when he was home and not trying to make you smile, would berate you over the smallest things, like forgetting to put toilet paper on the roll or being a second late when he was ready to go? Or a man who would, worse, whip you over those small things until red, tender welts rose on your bare arms and legs and back? And what do you do with a man who, like a drunk after a blackout, acted as if nothing at all had even happened?

I recall him once, right here in this room, kicking Althea in the back for telling a lie about Joe's whereabouts. And another time out there on the front porch, backhanding her across the face after she told him she was leaving to marry Proctor.

"You think you got everything all figured out, don't you?" he yelled at her. "Don't come running back here when you find yourself starving, out on them streets!" Then he reared back and swung down with so much force, he knocked Althea off her feet. I was watching from the other side of the screen door. I pushed it open, stepped outside, yelling at him to stop, but Althea, sprawled out on the porch floor, caught my eye. She shook her head: *Get back.*

And I did. Especially when our father turned and yelled at me to do the same.

Althea bore the mark he made on her face for days, but to him, it was as if nothing at all ever happened. He would go on to pack up what little Joe, Lillian, and I had—clothes, the *World Book* encyclopedias, Lillian's toys—put them all in his white Chrysler New Yorker and take us Butler kids to live with the newlyweds in their one-bedroom apartment. He would go back out on the road.

What do you do with a man like that?

You make something of yourself, just like he told you to. Even as you're made to be on guard and always a little afraid.

I sip my syrupy wine and wander along the bookcase to the classics: Jane Austen, Charles Dickens, Robert Frost, Langston Hughes, Zora Neale Hurston, and so on. They're lined up perfectly, about a quarter inch from the edge. I suspect it's precisely a quarter inch, knowing Lillian. The books are all similarly bound. Beautiful. I wonder if Lillian has read any of them. I run my finger over the books' spines, imagining the weight of them, remembering the words in some of them, stopping to linger for a moment at *Every Tongue Got to Confess.*

"One way or another, right, Zora?" I ask.

I top off my glass with what's left in the wine bottle and sit down in my chair again. I hear the distant thump of a closing door, the give of floorboards underfoot upstairs. Sounds from real people. Not the apparitions I feel creeping out of these walls, rising up through the floors, crowding in around me in this room. Memories. These are the things that remain in this house, despite all of Lillian's changes.

This very room, the library, didn't use to exist. It never had a place in this house when I lived here. No one was into books, except for me. If it were up to me, this is the one room that would have stayed exactly as it was. And in my memory, it has.

So much of what I can recall of the past involving my mother is what Althea heard and saw and told me: *Oh, you remember* . . . But I have my own memory from a time in this room. When it was the living room. It's my clearest memory of my mother. It's just the two of us, and her Tupperware friends are coming.

This memory lives in a burst of color: green plastic bowls, pink plastic pitchers, orange plastic cups; gold couch, gold chains, gold charms; Mama's white dress; her lotioned, light brown skin.

I remember: I'm helping her arrange the buffet of sandwiches cut in the shape of triangles, the chips-and-dip plate, the platter of deviled eggs, red punch in a big glass bowl with its ladle and tiny cups.

I remember: her hands on mine as we put the punch bowl in place. "You're a good helper, Viola."

I remember: her smile with the little gap between her front teeth that she worried with her tongue.

This memory is suffused with scent: the sweetness of Mama's Juicy Fruit gum; the aroma of her Jean Naté perfume; the sour smell of vomit; the sharp, nose-tingling fizz of ginger ale.

I remember: her cool hands on my hot face; my hot face pressed into the warmth of her neck; my whole body cradled in her arms. "Didn't I tell you not to eat so many deviled eggs? Just chicken soup for you tomorrow. Double noodles. You'll feel better."

But that's all there is of that memory.

I squeeze my eyes shut, trying with everything in me to see more. To inhabit a place that no longer exists. I open my eyes and take a sip of my wine. Then another. Drain the glass. I look at the bookcase again. Get up. Go past the books to the pictures again. Graduations, weddings. Our smiles are practiced, posed, perfected for those milestones.

I pick up the picture of Eva and me. The two of us, on our wedding day in Canada, wearing off-white and the biggest smiles. Maybe the happiest day of my life, apart from the day I met her, which was on a terrible double date—both of us with other people—at a Kenny G concert. We both hate Kenny G, but we liked each other quite a bit. We secretly exchanged numbers and talked on the phone that whole night. To this day, we listen to something from Kenny G on our anniversary as a kind of torturous tribute. We used to. I take my phone out of my back pocket. *Don't do it. You've been drinking. You'll say something stupid to her.*

"And I've said and done enough stupid things tonight," I say to myself. I put the picture down and slide my phone back in my pocket.

There's the picture of all of us together. We four Butler kids on Easter Sunday in our Easter best. We're standing outside of our father's church. Our Easter baskets are at our feet. Althea is holding Lillian, squinting down at her, frowning. Lillian is a bundled blur of movement. Joe is in a casual lean against Althea's side in a little pinstripe suit. I'm next to him, arms ramrod straight at my sides with an overeager smile in the pink and purple dress that I'd wear in a few months' time to my mother's funeral. My gaze is steady, concentrated on something in the distance. Our father is in the background on the front stairs of the church shaking hands with somebody, but he's looking off in another direction, his mouth open like he's saying something to someone.

I can't recall anything from that day, but I remember Althea telling me about it. Pointing to this picture, saying, "Oh, you remember . . ."

I take the picture and settle back in my chair, check the wine bottle. Empty. I look down at the picture cradled in my lap, but it's not what's in the picture that I'm straining to see. What I want is some time-bending, view-shifting lens that will bring my mother into focus on the other side of that camera because she was the one, back then, looking at the little, overeager girl. A helpful little girl, when she knew me last.

I look up, startled, at the sound of the door. It's Lillian.

"What?" I say. "I'm not doing anything. I was finishing my wine. That's all. Can you stop spying on me, please?"

"I'm not spying!"

But Lillian has been watching me closely, trying to make sure I'm eating "normally." She doesn't understand, though. It's not as easy as surveilling someone as they successfully keep down a carefully considered sandwich. It's not as easy as eating when you're hungry and stopping when you've had enough. Sometimes there's never enough.

Lillian is looking past me. Panicked.

"What's wrong?" I say.

Her eyes dart around the room, searching. "Kim's not in her room."

I stand.

"I was doing my rounds. I didn't hear anything when I was outside Kim's door, which, I mean, is strange. She usually goes to sleep to music. So I knocked and went in and she wasn't there. I've looked all around the house. She's not in Nai Nai's room. I checked with Baby Vi. This is the last place to look, and she's not in here with you?"

I find myself looking around at impossible hiding places: by the chairs, in the corners of the room, in the fireplace. "Okay," I say. "What did Baby Vi say?"

"Well, I didn't really *ask* ask."

"I'm not sure what that means," I snap, putting the picture of my siblings and me, the helpful little girl, back on the shelf. I look at a distressed Lillian. "Don't worry, it'll be fine," I say, feeling bad about being short with her about not *ask* asking, and about being defensive when she came in. And about being all of the things I am right now.

* * *

Baby Vi sits in the center of her bed, with Lillian and me standing on either side. I don't hesitate to *ask* ask:

"Are you sure you didn't hear anything?"

"Yes."

"But her room's right across the hall from you—how do you hear nothing?"

She inclines her head toward the pair of earbuds beside her in bed. "Headphones."

I glance at Lillian. She isn't buying it either.

"Are you sure she didn't say anything?" I press Baby Vi. "Anything at all?"

"About what?"

"Please don't do that. You know what I'm asking. Do you know where she is?"

She shakes her head. Eye contact had already been minimal, but now she's not looking at me at all. She hugs her knees to her chest, rolling in on herself protectively like an armadillo, as Lillian lobs more questions at her.

Baby Vi's responses are, as before, unhelpful.

Lillian and I go to Kim's room. I need to see for myself.

We flip on the light and pick our way around rolling mounds and drifts of clothes, with empty potato chip and candy bar packages and earbuds peeking out of the piles. I make it over to Proctor's stereo system, which sits along the wall opposite the bed. It's a fabulous Frankenstein of a machine that Proctor built from premium parts: turntable, CD player, cassette players, even, and waist-high speakers. Next to one of the speakers, there are milk crates that hold Proctor's albums.

"We took the stereo and everything we could carry," Lillian says, watching me. "You know, before the government could take it. The stereo and the records, it's all they had of home, you know?"

"You don't have to apologize, Lillian." On the turntable, the album *Songs in the Key of Life*, one of Proctor's favorites, sits ready to play. I take in the unmade bed. Shirts and socks, crawling out of the partially open drawers of the antique dresser. It all looks normal, like Kim could come in any second now and command us to leave.

"She can't be gone," Lillian says. "I mean, she's never done anything like this before, you know? She might come home late or whatever, but to just disappear in the middle of the night like this?"

"And wouldn't she at least take her phone?" I say, noticing it there in its turquoise case, plugged in and resting on her bedside table. "Who wouldn't take their phone?"

"Right," Lillian says. "This has to be some crazy game or something."

But I recall that deadly serious look in Kim's eyes at the bowling alley tonight: something dark, something distant, something desperate.

Lillian

My fingers find that delicate skin on my ear, but it doesn't calm me down as we do a slow roll past empty sidewalks and dark storefronts. I glance at the clock on the dash. After one in the morning. Driving around sleeping neighborhoods, practically alone in the world, looking for signs of life, it's clear: This definitely isn't a game.

"I hope she's someplace safe," I say. "And warm." I send that hope out as a prayer to the Universe.

"Me, too," Viola says, looking out her window on the driver's side as we bump along the ruts of yet another snowplow-bitten side street.

"Maybe try Dunkin' Donuts?" Baby Vi says from the backseat. "Sometimes Kim goes there."

Viola makes a right onto one of the main drags, headed for the Dunkin' Donuts a few blocks away. This street is smooth and better lit. We've been driving around for more than an hour on the two main drags and a bunch of side streets, but we've got nothing.

"I think Junior was lying," Viola says, bringing up our earlier stop at Elaine's house. "He has to know where she is."

"Yeah, but it's hard to tell with him," I say. "He's, well, he's Junior." I look in the rearview mirror at Baby Vi. "What do you think?"

"I don't know," she mumbles.

"And you're still sure you don't know where she is?" Viola asks Baby Vi.

"I'm sure."

I give Viola a look: *Stop it.*

"I promise," she goes on, looking in the rearview mirror at Baby Vi, "you won't get in trouble. If you know, please tell us, okay?"

"I don't *know,*" Baby Vi whines.

Aside from suggesting different twenty-four-hour fast-food places we should check (which aren't that many), Baby Vi's been quiet most of the drive. Maybe she really doesn't know. And Junior? When we stopped by Elaine's to talk to him tonight, the first stop on our search, he stood there blinking, saying how crazy this was and shaking his head, promising, "I'll keep an eye out. Most definitely."

We pull up outside of the Dunkin' Donuts and even from here I can see it's not looking good. It's mostly empty. And it's depressing, in a lost-souls kind of way.

"All right," Viola says, turning off the car. "Let's check it out."

Inside, there are a couple of old, hunched-over guys sipping coffee. I nod hello in their direction as they watch us walk in. We go up to the uniformed, half-asleep man sitting behind the counter, who's in mid-yawn.

"Excuse me, sir," Viola says, pulling out her phone. "I'm sorry to bother you, but would you have a moment to look at a picture for us? A missing girl. We're trying to find her, and we'd appreciate any help you can give us."

The man stretches, waking up a little. He puts on the glasses hanging around his neck and motions for the phone.

Viola pulls up the picture of Kim. The man squints at it. "That's the girl that was on the news a while back. Yeah, I've seen her in here before."

"Her name's Kim," I say. "Did she happen to come in tonight?"

He closes his eyes, like he's thinking hard, then shakes his head. "Nah, not tonight. Not since I've been on shift, anyways."

Viola puts her phone away, disappointed.

"Would you mind if we check your bathroom?" I ask. "Just to be sure?"

He nods, and I thank him as I go to do a bathroom check. Both the men's and women's.

We sit out in the parking lot under a floodlight that's blinking like a strobe. As I cradle an unopened box of a dozen doughnuts in my lap, I say, "At least he was nice."

"Sure," Viola says, staring out the window. "But nice isn't what we're looking for."

"I know," I say, thinking about what the man said after I got back from the empty bathrooms. He leaned on the counter, taking off his glasses, and said, "You kind of wonder who could blame her for running off, you know, with all this stuff everybody says about what went down."

Neither of us said anything.

The man didn't really seem interested in a response, because he only paused for, like, a second, before saying, "When I'd see her in here, she was always by herself, just sitting in one of those booths over there"—he waved in the direction of the booths by the window—"stuffing herself with jellies and chugging milk, you know? And I gotta say, I felt sorry for her. I'd usually give her an extra doughnut because, like I said, if you ask me, she did the right thing. I think of her as a, what do you call it? A whistler."

"I'm sorry?" Viola said, impatience in her voice.

"I think he means whistleblower," I said, smiling at the man. "Right?"

He nodded. "Yeah, that. But like I said, I never said anything to her when she came in here, because who am I? And you know, I never gave them people any of my money, but I know people that did. Heck, we had one of their collection jars right here on the counter, and people stuffed that thing full all the time." He pointed to a place where a tip jar with a dollar and three pennies sat. "So, anyways, I'd just let her sit over there at her table and enjoy her doughnuts."

"Thank you," I said, not sure how else to respond.

But he nodded, like he appreciated it. "Look, you might have a long night out there," he said, turning to the doughnut case and packing up a box. "I'll keep a watch for her," he promised, handing us the box and refusing to take our money.

I thanked him again as Viola gave him our contact info.

I glance in the backseat and see Baby Vi curled up with her eyes closed. I doubt she's sleeping.

Viola glances back at her, too, then whispers, "I think we should call the police."

I look out the window, past the parking lot and as far as I can see down the street. It's like, in the blinking floodlight/strobe light, this town is pulsing and bulging out to the size of a megacity with a million blind corners, dark alleys, and dangers.

"We're not far from the police station," I say. "Let's go."

Oldham County Correctional Facility
Proctor Cochran
720 Smith Avenue, NE
Park Point, Michigan

Friday, November 22, 2013

Althea,

You doing okay? Our friend told me you collapsed in the hall and they had to take you to medical. He told me you were with Mercedes before it all happened and that you rushed out the dayroom looking like something was wrong with you. Did she do something to you? Whatever it is, I need you to take care of yourself and like I said, be careful of the company you keep.

It's hard, all of it is. With all the time I've been spending out there in Darth Vader Space, I've been trying to do this kind of "self-help" thing, trying to focus on what I'm grateful for. I got a new cellmate. A real Zen brother with a bad dope habit, and he told me about this "gratitude exchange" he used to do with his recovery group. The past couple of mornings I've been trying it by myself because I don't know what else to do. I write down one thing I'm grateful for and carry it around with me. I don't know, it's not a magic bullet or anything, but when I take out that piece of paper and hold it in my hand and look at what I wrote, it's like it keeps me hooked in to something good in this world.

Sometimes it makes me think about what I saw that day when I was in the darkest of the dark after the sentencing. You know, when I saw that deer out there, lit up by the sun. I was telling my cellmate about it and he told me this story about how the Buddha came back in one of his lives as this golden deer and saved this man who was drowning. All the deer wanted in return was for the man not to tell anybody, because they'd want his golden hide. But the man sold the deer out. Get this, though: The king the man sold the deer out to was ready to kill the man for breaking his promise not to tell. Then, the deer begged the king to have mercy on the man.

My cellmate had a lot to say about the deer/Buddha's compassion in protecting somebody who sold him out. I talked to Lillian about it, and she was all about our "capacity for forgiveness and compassion," just like my cellmate. That was all good, but I couldn't help thinking about how the man who sold out the deer/Buddha sold himself out, too, because, from what my cellmate said, the man did mean to keep his promise. I keep wondering how you find compassion for your own self when you go against what's good in you.

I'm getting heavier than I should. I was writing to see how you were doing. On that song hint I sent you, you're still guessing wrong. "I'll Be Loving You Always" isn't it (but it's true). Here's another hint: think FLACK not Wonder. In the meantime, I do have a song for you this week, but you don't even have to try and guess this one because you never could. It's something another guy taught me the other day when we were just riffing a cappella style. It's country rock. Not really my thing, but hang with your boy on this one. It's about a girl named Daisy Mae. Stop laughing (I hope you're laughing), that's what a lot of the country ladies are named, isn't it?

Anyway, some of the lyrics made me think about a girl named Althea and how hard it is right now and how hard it's going to be for a good long while. These words right here stayed with me:

> You and I are charged with this, to hold the essence of a kiss.
> To take these broken plans and make them rhyme.

Hard as it is, we can, can't we? That's why we got to take care of ourselves, so please do whatever the doctor tells you to do, okay? And enjoy your sisters when they come. That will make you feel better. I know I'm looking forward to seeing Viola after so long, too.

As for me and you, we'll see each other when we do.

All my love,
Proctor

P.S. I miss you.

P.P.S. Remember, we got Thanksgiving. Talk about something to be grateful for.

Lillian

"What do you think Althea'll do?"

"There's nothing she can do, Lillian." Viola tightens her grip on the steering wheel, at ten and two. We're just clearing the two-lane bridge over the Saint Joseph. Still miles out from the jail, driving under a pale, gray sky. "Maybe we shouldn't tell her," Viola goes on. "She and Proctor are even more powerless to do anything than we are."

"I can't believe Kim slipped out of the house, right under my nose."

"Under *both* our noses," Viola says. "She'll come home. Or the police will bring her home. Soon."

"We hope. I wonder how hard they're looking."

When we walked into the police station the other night, I just knew they'd rush to set up one of those big searches you see on TV or in movies when a kid disappears. I pictured police out with dogs, the community coming together to help, all of that. But as we sat across the desk from the officer, who took a while to see us in the first place, he rolled through questions in a half-sympathetic, half–"I've seen this before" kind of way: *How old is she again? Has she ever run away before?*

Viola, frustrated, kept cutting in: "We've told you everything we know! Aren't you going to issue an alert or something? Like, now?"

The officer tried to calm her down, explaining, "I'm just trying to get a better picture of what we're dealing with, ma'am. We have our proced—"

"I don't care about your fucking procedures!" Viola pointed to the black abyss out the window behind us. "She's out there. In the dark. In the cold! What if it were your kid?"

Another officer approached cautiously. Shaggy haired and Paul Bunyan big, he introduced himself as Officer Hopkins. In a quiet voice, he asked if there was anything he could do to help. "I heard you mention Proctor and Althea. Proctor's a friend of mine," he explained, "from way back."

He took over from the other officer, filing the missing persons report and explaining what they'd do next: "We'll just want to have a look around the house first, make sure we don't see signs of a break-in, that kind of thing. We'll also get a BOLO out—sorry, that's a 'be on the lookout'—to our officers in the area, that kind of thing." Watching him type things up, looking intense and determined as he stared at his computer, I had some hope. I even saw Kim's picture on one of the local stations the next morning—"Daughter of disgraced restaurateurs and charity leaders missing"—along with the police tip line. Viola, Baby Vi, and I have been expecting the police to show up at the door with Kim at any minute. But a whole weekend's worth of minutes have now gone by.

"You're probably right, Viola," I say. "We shouldn't say anything. There's nothing Althea and Proctor can do but sit and worry."

Viola's quiet for a moment. "You know," she says gently, glancing at me from her place behind the steering wheel, "I think we do have to talk to them. About Joe. And his 'next steps.'" She pauses. "Lillian, you've never said anything. And I guess I've never pressed the point, not like I should have . . . But this thing with Joe. I want to . . ."

She takes another pause.

My stomach flutters.

"So, okay," she goes on. "Is there something Althea should know? In case Joe really does or has asked about taking the girls? Isn't it relevant? Please think about it."

Out the window, strip malls and fast-food restaurants and filling stations whip by. I breathe in, trying to get myself centered. "You should take them, Viola."

"What?"

"The other night, when I said Joe was right about the girls needing a new start? That's what I meant. I didn't mean we should let them go with him. I was trying to say they should go with you."

There's a quick eye dart in my direction. "Are you out of your mind?"

"I talked to Elaine and David about it. I really do think it's the best option."

"*You're* the best option, Lillian."

"But maybe we won't have to get into *anything* about Joe if you step up and volunteer. She'll choose you. Trust me. She always has. And you know how she is. She probably won't even believe me anyway. Not over Joe. She's never listened or paid any attention to me. She literally gave me away and never looked back until she went to jail and needed me to take the girls."

I wait for Viola to defend Althea (like she always does). When she doesn't say anything, I go on: "I just . . . Look . . . I just feel like, for me, I have to try to forgive and move on. Understand?"

Viola glances at me, then back at the road. "Tell me this: Did he ever ask you to forgive him?"

"Yeah," I say. "Pretty much every time."

Viola's grip tightens around the steering wheel. "I'm sorry," she says, her voice breaking.

Quiet settles in like a fog. "But that's not what we're talking about right now," I say, finally. "What I want to say is that I wish you'd at least think about it." I look out my window again, taking in the flat, endless road in front of us. As we pass a Walmart, floating in a full parking lot like an island, the car picks up speed.

"Slow down," I say.

She eases up on the accelerator, and after a beat or two of silence, she says, "I have thought about it, Lillian. Of course I have." She pauses. "Look, it's been a hard few weeks. We're going through a rough patch. Eva and I. We're separated, whatever that means."

"I'm so sorr—"

"Anyway," Viola interrupts, "it's been hard. I moved out. I'm in a studio with a futon. It's bad, Lilly."

No. Not a breakup. Not with Eva the ballast, the best thing that ever happened to her. No wonder Viola's flailing. "When did this happen?"

"About a month ago. But it's been bad for a while. We're still talking, but . . . I don't know."

"Why are you just now saying something?"

"Embarrassed? Stupid? I haven't even told David yet." Viola shrugs. "Fifteen years together, and then *bam*. It just unravels. She says I'm working too much. I'm distant. I'm this. I'm that." Viola glances around in disgust. "And this stupid car."

I look around, too. The car's a little showy and not what I'd expect for her, but it's beautiful. All premium leather with that new-car smell. I look back at Viola and think, *Not to take sides, but knowing Eva (sensitive, even-tempered, patient to a fault) and knowing you (lovable but difficult), I can't help but think the breakup is probably your fault, Viola.*

"I'm a mess, Lilly. I can't take them, but I'll do a much better job helping you. I promise."

I touch her arm. "But maybe it could help you. Maybe it could be centering, a kind of stabilizing force, having the girls."

"Were you not listening?" The car picks up speed again. "What part of *separated* and *personal crisis* and *studio apartment with futon* did you not understand?"

Viola looks at me (too long!), and the car swerves. "Pull over!"

"What do you expect me to do with them?" Viola asks.

"I mean it! Pull the car over!"

She lets out an irritated hiss and pulls the car to the shoulder, like I asked. We're past the Walmart and the stretch of strip malls now, with nothing but hibernating, brown farmland as far as I can see. Viola cuts the engine.

"You know I can help," I say. "You know I have money from Daddy's life insurance." I pause, not wanting to think about it, let alone say it. But I do: "And Sam's." Sam, always so focused and meticulous when it came to dreaming up new ideas for cloud storage systems, but not interested at all in updating beneficiaries or changing anything after our divorce. "And, you know, I haven't sold our apartment yet," I add, quietly.

"That's because you can't sell it, Lillian. You can't even bring yourself to rent it out. Have you packed up Sam's effects yet?"

That's not a question (she knows the answer). "They're not 'effects.' They're his things, from his *life*. Some of them from *our* life."

"Okay," Viola says, her voice softer but stiff. "So, even if you could pack up Sam's things and sell the apartment, and even if that resulted in some actual rooms for me to put the girls in, I'm obviously not my 'best self' right now. Remember the relapse?" She leans in my direction, as much as the seat belt she's still wearing will let her. Her throat is working, her eyes watering. "When I was supposed to be at the sentencing and here with you and the girls, I was engaging in some, let's just say, less-than-healthy behavior, binging on, on"—she looks around the car wildly, then back at me—"binging on vending machine any fucking thing and delivery . . . and, and convenience store crap and . . . you get the picture, right?"

"I understand, Viola."

"No, I don't think you do. Do you know what it's like to be that out of control? Then actually finding *peace* and quiet and calm when you're crouched over the toilet heaving your guts out, promising yourself this is it. The last time. But of course, you're a liar." Viola jabs a finger in the direction of her healing eye. "You think a popped capillary is the worst of it? Try living in my head right now. Try knowing you can't be trusted with your own well-being, let alone someone else's."

I reach for her arm. She jerks away and hunches over the steering wheel. As we listen to the hum of passing cars and the whisper of the wind at the windows, I try to think of the right thing to say, but now Viola's pounding the steering wheel. "After all these years! God damn it! 'Physician, heal thyself.'" Her voice is mocking. "Oh, right. I have a PhD, maybe that's my problem." She gazes up through the windshield, laughing. Sobbing. "I've done so much work, and these past weeks I've been trying, *really trying*, you know? Talking to my own therapist. Telling myself everything I tell patients. But there's this . . . this thing that takes over my brain. Renegotiating every rational thought, every reasonable plan."

Viola sits back and puts her hands on either side of her head like a vise grip, like she's trying to keep her head from splitting in two.

I think back to when Viola was concentration-camp wasted in college, all sunken cheeks, deep-set eyes, and sharp angles. Back when I decided to do as I was asked and not to tell her (or anybody) about Joe. I said only that he was "gone." Not that he'd been sent away.

Viola's face looks a little gaunt now, but I've been keeping a close eye on her. She did a run this morning, but it was pretty short. I know because I timed her. And she ate breakfast before leaving the house. A measured-out bowl of cereal and milk, and we've been together ever since without so much as a bathroom break, so she kept it down. "You can absolutely do this," I insist, raising my own hand to her head to join her hands, like I might be able to help hold everything together.

She stares out at the road, tears dropping and darkening into black dots on her navy blue sweater. I dig through my feed bag of a purse for tissues and push the whole mini package into her hand.

She wipes her eyes and blows her nose. "This place does something to me, but home doesn't feel like home without Eva." I know "this place" means the house in New River Junction. "I feel like a refugee."

She looks at me.

"What?"

"Yes, I know I shouldn't compare myself to literal refugees."

"I wasn't even going there."

"You were thinking it, Human Rights Watch."

I was, kind of.

Viola gives me a sad smile and rests her forehead on the steering wheel.

An eighteen-wheeler rumbles by, kicking up salt and sand. There was freezing rain and ice last night. The pale sky's deep gray now. Snow's coming.

I rub Viola's back, her vertebrae rising like a row of small cobblestones under my fingertips. We sit this way for a few seconds, with the sound of passing cars and her quiet sobs. But then Viola sits up and wipes her face with a soggy, wadded-up tissue. She slumps back in her seat, her head against the headrest. "Aren't we a pair?"

"Yeah," I say. "We are. Always."

"We better get going," she says, sounding weary.

We're sitting in a depressing cinder-block holding area, waiting to go back to see Althea. They don't even try to make it feel less stigmatizing. There's the wall-mounted TV up there, I guess to take our attention away from the fact that somebody we know and love is in jail.

Across from me, there's an older woman, hugging her purse. Somebody's grandmother? She catches me looking. I smile and she looks away, like she's embarrassed to be seen here. There's a young, dark-skinned guy in a blue suit. He's been shuffling through papers the whole time. And there are two withdrawn-looking teenagers, a girl and a boy, with a breakable-looking woman I take to be their mom.

"I don't know," I say. "Maybe Althea and Proctor have the right to know."

Viola sighs. "This has been decided, remember?"

I don't answer.

Viola looks down at her left hand, rubbing her fingers (a nervous tic of hers) and turning her wedding ring, a thin gold band. I see a little hope in the fact that she hasn't stopped wearing it. She checks her watch, which she's been doing off and on every few minutes. I look at her watch, too. It's nine fifteen. Our appointment was at nine.

Viola's terrible at waiting. So am I, so I talk. "You know what's weird?"

She blows her nose into one of the tissues I gave her. "No, Lillian. What's weird?"

"Every time I come here, I have this flashback to when I was in elementary school."

She raises an eyebrow.

"It's the phones back there in the visitors' room," I say, waving my hand toward the door we'll be going through soon. "I always remember this lesson I had on two-way communication. My teacher did the two-cups-connected-by-a-string thing."

Viola smiles. "Mrs. Livengood."

"You guys did it, too?"

She nods. "But that's about all I remember."

"Okay, so Mrs. Livengood told us about sound waves from our voices becoming vibrations going across the string, et cetera, and about our phones at home using an electric current instead of a string so we could talk to anybody in the world." I point to the door to the visitors' room. "So, whenever I'm back there, with the phones on either side of that glass separator, and I pick up the phone on my side to talk to Althea on hers, I think how weird it is, using something that can connect you to anybody anywhere in the world to talk to somebody who's right there in front of you. It seems like a waste."

Tears well up in Viola's eyes. She blinks and looks away. "Yes," she says in a quiet voice. "A waste."

I reach for the sleeve of her sweater to pat her arm. Then I hold on and take a deep breath to draw in some positive energy. I think about what Viola expects me to say when I pick up that phone today to talk to Althea. That's something else we ended up deciding. It's okay, isn't it? I whisper a mantra in my head: *Everything works out for the highest good.*

"You know," Viola says, "when we were together in that principal's office, and then again when I had the girls at the bowling alley, I realized I don't really know them."

"I've had them for almost two years, and I wonder how much *I* know them, which is probably why things have gone off the rails." I glance down at Viola's watch again, suddenly wanting to run away myself. "They've never been this late bringing Althea out. I'll see what's taking so long."

At the reception desk they tell me, "Any minute now." I feel like I might be sick. Part of me hopes they'll cancel. It's bad enough seeing Althea when I'm on my own. There's too much distance between us. We're not natural with each other. And now . . .

I tell Viola, "Any minute," as I sit down again. I stare up at the TV on the wall. A news show is on. The headline: *Jury set to decide fate of accused boyfriend killer Shannon "Mercedes" Sullivan* pops up on the bottom of the screen. They show a tall, skinny, washed-out blond woman being walked into court, and a flashy graphic promises: *Channel 2 Team 2 coverage tonight at 6.*

Another crime story flashes by: *Dispute over leaning on car sparks deadly shootout*. People. Unbelievable.

Fire guts crime spot, Althea's Kitchen and Grocery, appears on the screen. It takes a second for it to register. I slap Viola on the leg. "Look!" I point to the TV and shoot up out of my chair. Viola rises, slowly, at my side. There's no sound, but there's a nighttime picture of the restaurant with blackened walls. A fire truck is hosing the place down. The words on the screen: *Was overnight blaze arson?*

Viola and I look at each other, both of us in saucer-eyed shock. We inch closer together.

"You don't think . . . ?" I whisper, shaking my head, denying my own thoughts.

Viola shakes her head, too, whispering, "No, there's no way."

On the TV, there are pictures of the gutted, charred insides of the restaurant. I can make out a few wrecked booths and the bar, which makes me think of Viola and David chainsawing the thing to get Proctor's keepsake.

I whisper, "Well, on the upside—"

"*Up*side?" Viola looks horrified.

"No, listen. I mean, if it *was* her, at least we know one place she was last night, right?"

"Ladies," a disembodied voice interrupts.

We jump, startled out of our whispering huddle. We look to see where the voice is coming from. It's the officer, standing by the door to the visiting room.

"You can come back now," he says. "They're bringing her out."

Viola

The sight of Althea extinguishes all thoughts of the fire. She's heavier than the last time I saw her, in an unhealthy, bloated way. And her face. There's a bandage above her right eye.

What the hell happened?

When I last saw her, a few months ago, on the day Kim took the stand, Althea had her familiar fierce look when her eyes locked with mine in that courtroom. Having chosen a trial over a plea deal she didn't like, Althea was a woman always ready for a fight, even as Kim sat down to testify. Kim, who knew only about the food stamp fraud, had no knowledge of the crimes involving the charities (there were other witnesses and evidence for that). No, Kim's testimony, ultimately, put Althea, the mother, on trial:

Prosecutor: Would you say you're close to your parents?

Kim: Um . . . [Pauses to look at Proctor.] Yeah. I mean no, sir. I mean, my dad I am.

Prosecutor: What about your mother?

Kim: [Looks down, shaking her head.]

Prosecutor: No? You weren't close?

Kim: [A furtive glance at Althea.] She was mostly, um, away. She didn't have time.

Prosecutor: No time for you and your sister?

Kim: [Tears up, moves her lips, but only makes little squeaking sounds.]

Prosecutor: It's okay. Take your time.

[The bailiff points to the box of tissues sitting on the railing of the witness box. We wait for Kim to take some and wipe her face. Lillian and I cry, too.]

Prosecutor: You okay?

Kim: [A small nod.]

Prosecutor: You said your mom was busy a lot. No time for you and the rest of your family?

Kim: [Another small nod.] Work.

Prosecutor: I see. And what went on at work in the restaurant's market, when customers came in with their food stamps?

Kim: [Silence, stares off straight ahead, not at Althea, not at Proctor, tears spilling over. The prosecutor nods toward the box of tissues. We wait while Kim pulls out more tissues and presses them to her face. Lillian and I cry again.]

Prosecutor: You okay to keep going?

Kim: [Nods, but, clearly, she's not okay to keep going.]

Prosecutor: Okay. Good. So, you told the court you knew what your parents were up to for a long time, buying food stamps and using them themselves to buy items for the restaurant. They didn't shield you and your sister. Didn't protect you girls from any of that. But did something change that day, to make you pick up the phone and report it when you did?

Kim: [Long pause; a wad of tissues still pressed to her eyes; her round brown cheeks shining with unwiped tears; Kim shakes her head and whispers.] I was just mad . . . she . . . nothing ever changed.

But sitting in front of me now, Althea is greatly altered. Starved of whatever source of confidence she had in the courtroom that day.

Lillian and I exchange a glance, and I get the sense that even she thinks Althea looks different. Worse than when Lillian last saw her, which was last week, right before I came to town. As Althea picks up her phone across the partition from us, I notice the bandage above her eye again, and my stomach seizes up. Just like it did when I stood at the screen door, watching our father smack her across the face. I remember how terrified Althea was. But there was also defiance in her eyes as she looked up at me from the floor of the porch, shaking her head when she saw me ready to run to her: *Get back*. And what she said later, to calm me down: "It'll heal, Viola. Don't worry about me. Just make sure you stay out of trouble."

Althea looks at me through the glass and, suddenly, there it is: the self-assured, *assuring* smile of my big sister. The afroed, bell-bottomed, boogie-down big sister who was mother, friend, teacher, all the world to me.

Althea waves.

I wave back.

But as she turns to look at Lillian, it's as if Althea time-lapses back to the slow-moving, enfeebled old woman the guard led out.

I move to grab the phone—but stop. Lillian's right. This is weird. I signal for her to pick up and talk first. It's been a long time, but I need a little more.

"Hey, are you okay?" Lillian says to Althea. "What's going on with . . ." She motions toward Althea's bandage.

Althea points to her face, apparently explaining.

Lillian nods like she understands.

Althea waves her hand dismissively.

"Well, just as long as you're okay," Lillian says. She tells Althea about the girls. "They're doing great," she lies, speaking generally about school, leaving out, thankfully, the fact that Kim's missing. "The girls definitely miss you," she says, with strained lightness in her voice. The lying is getting to her. Apart from cheating on Sam, I've never known Lillian to be false, and even then, she confessed to sleeping with a design client in short order and immediately commenced on self-improvement.

Lillian's voice relaxes as she tells Althea how good Proctor looked the last time she saw him and how we're looking forward to seeing him today.

Tears well up in Althea's eyes. I've never seen Althea cry, and she doesn't now. She blinks her eyes clear and speaks.

Lillian clears her throat and says, "That's great. Looks like you guys will definitely have something to be thankful for on Thanksgiving." Althea smiles and Lillian says, "Let me pass the phone to Viola."

I put the phone to my ear. Althea says, "It's so good to see you. You look good, girl." She leans in, examining my face. "A little on the skinny side, but good."

"It's good to see you, too," I say. "You getting along okay?"

"When I'm not being clumsy." She laughs and points to her bandage. I laugh, too, stiffly, wondering whether it's fair to bring up Joe. I glance beside me. Lillian's nervously fidgeting with her ear.

Althea's talking about Thanksgiving now and how she'll get to see Proctor.

"That's great. That's going to be really special." I glance at Lillian again. Her smile is rigid. She's gripping the arms of the chair, as if on a roller coaster trying to keep from flying off.

This needs to be done, doesn't it? Won't we be better for it? "Look,

Althea," I say. "I know we have a lot of catching up to do, and I can't wait to, but there's something . . . Has Joe been to see you? About the girls?"

Althea sits back, her eyes moving from me to Lillian, who's looking down at the counter, grimacing. "What's going on?"

I swallow, weighing how best to do this. "Well," I say, "we think . . . Lillian and I . . . we think there's something, while you consider the girls' future and everything, we think there's something you should know." I touch Lillian's shoulder. "I'm going to give the phone back to Lillian."

Lillian holds the receiver to her ear, still staring down at the counter. "Well," she says quietly, "it's about . . ."

A second or two tick by.

Lillian turns to me. "But I don't even know how . . . what should I say?"

Althea leans in. She says something I can't make out.

I put my arm around Lillian and move in close to speak into the receiver. "Joe. He used to . . ." Then I remember that I don't really know, for sure. There are only the questions I should have asked but never could. "He hurt her."

"Yeah," Lillian says, nodding.

Althea looks from Lillian to me. With my head still close to Lillian's and the phone between us tilted so we can share it, I hear Althea say: "What's she talking about?"

"I can't . . . That's for Lillian."

Althea's eyes dart back to Lillian.

"I . . . he used to . . . he'd always get so mad. He was always just—" She cuts herself off. "I never did anything," she says, as if we might think otherwise.

"Of course not," I say.

"He was mean," Lillian says. "And it didn't matter if you were extra nice to him. It made things worse if you showed you understood things were a little harder for him, you know? Anytime Daddy would leave, it was like it was his chance to take everything out on me. I was right there. By myself a lot. And he was always telling me I'd done something wrong." She stops, her lip trembling. "I never did, though. But he had his punishments, anyway." Her fingers tighten on the receiver, held awkwardly between us. "Sometimes he wouldn't let me eat, he wouldn't—"

"Why are you telling me this?" Althea cuts in.

Lillian stiffens.

"Why didn't you say something before?" Althea goes on. "Why're you doing this now?"

"I didn't know how. I still—"

"And what do you want me to do with this, from in here?"

"Althea!" I say into the receiver. "What's wrong with you?"

Lillian blinks. "To know. For the girls."

"Don't worry about them. I got that."

"You *got* that?" I say. "What does that mean?"

"See, I knew it," Lillian says to me, her voice thick. "She doesn't care. She wouldn't have, even if I'd told her right when it was happening." Lillian leans in toward Althea, taking the phone with her. "You were right there in town. Just a couple of blocks away, but you hardly ever came to see about me. You'd show up for Joe. And Viola, too, all the way in college. But not me, and you were right there the whole time he was taunting me and trying to control me and keeping me—"

Lillian suddenly jerks back and shoves the receiver at me.

"You had a father!" Althea's saying. "A halfway decent one, it turned out. More than I ever had." She stops, apparently realizing she's talking to me now. "Why didn't she tell him? I had to work. I had my own—why is everything my fault?"

"Jesus, Althea. This wasn't meant to be an indictment of you."

"Forget it, Viola," Lillian says.

"I did my best," Althea says, as she leans in and smacks the glass, her palm frozen in front of me. For a second, it could be mistaken for an anguished goodbye. An agonized *I'm sorry*. But then she gets up, the move jarringly swift.

She leaves us.

I pull up my collar against icy, lacerating winds as we weave our way through the nearly full parking lot. We canceled the visit with Proctor. We haven't spoken a word to each other since leaving the jail complex. "Hey." I put a gloved hand on Lillian's arm to slow her pace. "You all right?"

She makes a failed attempt at a smile. "Just what you'd expect, right?"

"I'm sorry," I say, for the millionth time.

Lillian looks past me to the boxy jail complex, frowning, like the building itself is the cause of our problems. "But I told her," Lillian says, her voice breathless with surprise. "I mean, what I could. What she'd hear. And that's something, I guess."

"It is."

What did I expect? Not that, but there it was, laid bare. All I've refused to see in Althea: her neglect of Lillian, from the time we were children; her jealousy over the fact that our father wanted Lillian home, because weren't we all jealous, in our way? Joe, perhaps, in the worst way.

I think back to Althea telling me she was "leaving Lillian to Daddy," since he favored her so much. "Let that man raise somebody for once," she said. I never challenged Althea on it, because she favored me.

I pull Lillian into a hug. "You did great. And look, if you ever need to share more or talk things through, you can."

She pulls away. "I know. Thank you." An unusually quick cutoff for Lillian. "What do you think Althea meant? About the girls? She's 'got this'?"

I shake my head. "I have no idea. I bet she has no idea either."

I feel moisture on my face. Snow. It's falling as light as talcum powder, sifting through tree branches, dusting the asphalt, swirling up around us. I look up at a sky thick with clouds.

"We should get on the road," I say.

"Yeah, but look, I want you to go home, okay? To Chicago. I want you to deal with your situation and see Eva. If there's something left, something worth saving, you have to try. Not everybody gets a second chance, Viola." Lillian's breath condenses and curls up around her face.

"You're right," I say.

"Good, because there's not a lot you can do with the search, except sit with me, waiting and worrying."

I look over at the silver Lexus. The Midlife-Crisis-Mobile, Eva calls it. It wasn't time for a new car, but I wanted it. Had to have it. Bought it despite her objections and our financial limitations. My "reward" for making the last payment on my student loans. The last straw for Eva. The last big argument for us. I hate that car. I hate myself, too. I hate Althea. I hate not knowing what to do. I imagine myself going home to my sad little studio with its beige walls, beige carpet, and unpacked boxes. Crawling off into a corner of sugar-rushed, salt-spiked, binged-out oblivion.

But.

"I can't right now, Lilly," I say.

Because I'm recalling that video of the gutted-out, charred remains of the restaurant. I remember Kim crying up there on that witness stand. Kim, witness for the prosecution, has a motive for arson. Kim, herself, is a walking conflagration.

Althea

She's going to be living with strangers for the holidays, but there she is, dancing it up as "Celebration" hisses and buzzes out of the chaplain's beat-up boom box over on the table in the corner. It's like the room, even with its dingy white walls and little bitty windows, is lit up. It's one of those rare Splenda moments in here. Little imitations of life that, depending on your tastes, can be a kind of substitute for what you're missing on the outside, like real friends, real family, and something really worth celebrating.

"That Chit's got some moves," Mercedes says, leaning back in her chair across the table from me, watching Chit shimmy and twist with a bouncing knot of women over in the boom box corner, under the watchful eye of the chaplain and a guard.

"Yeah, she got that going for her," Gale murmurs, digging into a bag of Fritos, part of the commissary some of us agreed to share. "But I tell you what. You can turn Bible study into a party for her all you want to, but mark my words, she gone be back in the drunk tank by Christmas. Watch."

Mercedes drops her smile. "Don't speak that shit on her, just because you can't stay clean."

"Don't *want* to," Gale corrects, her voice rattling with phlegm. "My first day out, you best believe my people's gone be waiting for me with a goody bag." She closes her eyes like she's already in ecstasy. "And I'mma be gone baby gone."

"Dead baby dead is more like it," Mercedes says. "By the grace of God, you're about to see sixty. You need to retire from that shit."

"I ain't the retiring kind." Gale smiles, showing off the postprison bridge she got a few years back from some life-rebuilding charity. The bridge is the only perfect thing in her face. She looked close to death when I met her nine months ago, brought in on prostitution and drug charges. Her face was a Halloween horror mask. They called her Freddy Krueger. A couple people still do. "You've gotten clean in here," I say. "You're going to throw that away?"

Gale stares at me like I'm retarded. "Ain't nothing to keep." She shoves a couple of Fritos in her mouth and chews. "They forcing sobriety on me." She leans forward and taps her chest. "But see, I got the heart and soul of an addict. I made peace with that a long time ago."

"That's *bull*shit," Mercedes snaps. "And you know it."

"What I know is me," Gale says. "What's wrong with knowing what makes you—"

"Weak!" Mercedes cuts in.

"Weak? What about you?" Gale's words come out wet, and she pauses to clear her throat. "What you gone do if you get out?"

Mercedes's sharp face pinches up. It's day two of deliberations in her trial. She's more on edge than usual, but Gale just keeps pushing, asking Mercedes, "You mean to tell me you really gone be free if they turn yo' ass loose? All yo' cravings and shit gone, poof"—she snaps her bony fingers—"disappear if you get back out there on them streets?"

At times like this, Gale reminds me of the hyenas I used to see on *Wild Kingdom* when I was growing up. I bet that's exactly how she is out on the streets. A scavenger with an eye for weaknesses like what you see, if you look close enough, in Mercedes. You probably wouldn't want to meet Gale on the streets.

"Leave her alone, Gale," I say.

"Hold up, let me finish right quick." The hyena turns back to Mercedes, digging in. "Okay, you found Jesus. I get that. You got Him living all up in here now"—she taps her chest—"but that ain't got shit to do with nothing. If you get out, what's yo' soul, hell, what's everything in you gone crave? I bet it damn sure ain't gone be no Jesus. You might need to call on Him sometimes, Lord knows I do. But it ain't enough."

She tosses back a Frito, still looking at Mercedes, whose eyes are fixed on a stain on the table. After a moment, Mercedes looks up. "Don't worry about me and what I might do, Gale," she says. "Just don't speak your negative shit on Chit. She wants to stay clean. She's about family, and she's got a shot at it." Mercedes gazes down at the table again and goes silent. We're all quiet. But now, Mercedes's head snaps around in my direction. "Will you eat something, please?"

It takes a second or two to catch up with the turn of the conversation toward me.

"You're gonna mess around and faint again," she says.

"I didn't faint, Mercedes." I touch the bandage above my eye. No, I didn't faint. I was conscious in ways I've never been before, there on the floor the other day, just steps away from my cell. "Just mind your business, please," I say, looking at the unopened bag of potato chips I've had in front of me since I sat down.

"You're my business right now." Mercedes leans in across the table to get a closer look at the bandaged cut above my right eye. "Whether you fainted or whatever the hell, if you don't take care of yourself, Althea, you might find yourself in a health crisis."

"Mercedes right," Gale cosigns.

It was Gale who hurried over to help me, holding me to her bony chest, looking down on me like some gruesome guardian angel, saying,

"It's all right now, Gale got you. Gale got you." But what had me was fear. I was scared I was having a heart attack. I thought I was dying. And I had that voice in my head whispering louder than ever before, *As a mother, you are your father's daughter.* And I hate everything about him.

"Here!" Mercedes huffs. A Snickers bar swishes across the table and stops at the edge of my tray.

I look at it. I look at her. "Thanks, but I'm not hungry." I slide the candy bar back to her.

She pushes it back and crosses her tattooed arms, like she's daring me to reject it again. When I move to push the candy back, she leans forward and holds the bar in place on the table.

"You need to eat something." She points at my cup of watery, light purple "fruit" punch. "And drink that! Hydrate!"

We stare each other down.

After a few seconds, I say, "Fine."

I'm tired and, truth be told, I'm hungry. And thirsty, too. Probably dehydrated. I pick up the candy bar. "I'll have it if it'll stop you from mother-henning people." Pecky, prickly mother hen that she is.

I unwrap the candy bar and take a bite, and it's like a tasteless glob of wax in my mouth.

"You might not be crying, but I can see it in you," Mercedes says, narrowing her eyes on me. "Everything's gonna work out about your sisters." She looks at Gale and explains: "The sister who don't come came with the other one yesterday, and it wasn't good."

That's all the detail I gave her. I never said what made it so bad.

"Rich White Girl came?" Gale asks, jerking forward in her chair. "Why didn't you say something?"

"Don't call her that!" I snap.

Mercedes shoots Gale a look. "Don't you ever get tired of saying inappropriate shit?"

Gale waves a dismissive hand at Mercedes and apologizes to me.

"Whatever, Gale," I say.

"What? You wasn't bothered by it before," Gale says, sounding confused by the change in me.

Mercedes glares at her.

Gale shrugs. "What? She wasn't."

They go back to their snacks without another word but keep sneaking glances at me.

Rich White Girl. I should've said more than I did when the Bible studiers called Viola that. It was my second time with them, and I was telling them I hadn't seen her in a long time, and when I said something about Viola's work, they all started talking about how crazy it was for somebody to starve themselves or stuff themselves then throw it all up. Somebody said, "Those girls'll eat if they get hungry enough." And we all laughed because we all knew that commissary is both a commodity and a currency in here. A comfort, too, which is why hardly anybody's sharing any of theirs for this thing.

I look down at the bite-marked Snickers bar on the table. Snickers bars are Mercedes's favorite. Commissary doesn't always have them, so she keeps a stash. She didn't pitch in any Snickers for the "party."

I force myself to take another bite.

"You can talk about what happened," Gale says, I guess seeing the fact that I opened my mouth to take a bite as a sign I might keep it open to talk. "You know, with yo' sisters and everything. I really am sorry for calling the one, you know, that name."

I glance over to the boom box corner. "Why don't you go keep Chit company?" I say, even though Chit's already in good company, shimmying her way down a short, scraggly *Soul Train* line.

Gale coughs and gets to her feet. "I'mma go on ahead and see if it's some other goodies around here, right quick, but think on what I said. Holding shit in ain't healthy."

Me and Mercedes trade looks.

"Y'all can think what you want to, but I'm telling you something real." Gale's eyes move from me to Mercedes. "You know *The Color Purple*? That part when Celie and Nettie get separated? Where Mister's evil ass kicked Nettie out?"

Mercedes shakes her head.

"What's that got to do with anything?" I say.

"It got *everything* to do with everything for me," Gale says, pausing for a second to cough and pat her chest. "See, I can't cry for nothing, but when I put that DVD in and play that part with them two hanging on to one another with everything they got, and then you got Mister's ass"—she looks disgusted and moves her hands like she's prying apart two balls—"that motherfucker straight up pull 'em apart. Whenever I watch that, I cry like a baby. It's like a crying enema or something."

"Jesus, Gale," Mercedes says. "I was actually with you, but enema? Why'd you have to go there?"

"You know what I mean. All I'm saying is it ain't healthy holding shit in. I always feel better after I get a *Color Purple* cry on."

"Ain't too much you can say to that," Mercedes says, standing up as Gale makes her cough-shuddering way around the room. She points to the Snickers on the table. "Finish that. I mean it. And stop worrying so much." She taps my cup of "fruit" punch. "And drink up!"

But as I watch her go, I'm thinking about my sisters. I'm still thinking about Viola and Rich White Girl and what I did and didn't do about it. *Who came up with that name for her?* When the Bible studiers were going on about Viola's job, somebody said, "Eating disorders are a white girl thing," which made the white girls mad, especially Mercedes. They said it was a *rich* white girl thing, which was something everybody got behind: the white girls, the black girls, the Hispanics, the two Vietnamese chicks, and a girl nobody could ever figure out race-wise.

I thought about telling them Viola had been a poor, black girl with a problem, but I was embarrassed. And truth be told, she's always been kind of an Oreo, hanging around with that faggy David and the whole lesbian thing and Eva. I didn't say anything in Viola's defense. She wasn't showing up for me, so why should I defend her? But I should've.

If, as a mother, I am my father's daughter, and I hate everything about him, what am I as a sister, who was all the mother they had?

I pick up the candy bar again and hold it for a second, looking at it. I take another bite, chewing slowly, tasting nothing.

He hurt her.

I close my eyes to block out Viola's and Lillian's faces. I put my hands over my ears to block out their voices. If I could've, this is what I would've done as I sat on the other side of the glass from them, but I had that phone up to my ear with the words oozing into my skull like something putrid and poisonous, contaminating every one of my thoughts and every minute ever since.

There's a rush of wind on my cheeks. When I open my eyes, I see a bony, brown hand waving in front of my face.

"You good?" Gale's holding half of a granola bar in her free hand.

"I'm fine."

She sits down, staring at me the whole time. "Don't look fine to me." She puts her elbows on the table and leans in. "I meant what I said, Althea. I know I talk a lotta shit, but I can listen."

She looks like she means it.

I start to speak, but the room erupts around us with voices, some high-pitched or mannishly low or way off tune, singing "Do You Love What You Feel?" I look over to the boom box corner and see Adira smiling and bopping up and down next to her friend, Tina the Talker. Adira waves. I wave back.

She's always smiling and waving like she knows me. Something in me feels like I know her.

Mercedes is taking a turn down the *Soul Train* line, doing some kind of boot-scooting thing with her thumbs hooked around the elastic waistband of her jumper.

"Watch yo'self now, girl!" Gale hollers out to Mercedes, clapping her hands, just tickled. Gale looks around the room at the other women, smiling, then she looks at me. "Hate you can't let it go and enjoy."

"I hate it, too." My words are muffled under the singing and clapping and laughing, but something about that makes it easier to speak, so I keep going. "My sisters. My sister. The younger one who comes to see me sometimes. Lillian."

Gale leans in and cocks her ear in my direction. "Go on 'head. I'm listening."

How do I . . . ? I lick my lips, which are all of a sudden dry and stiff. "Lillian told me some, um, family business that has me, well, that's making it hard. And I don't even know if I believe it."

Gale sits back in her chair and looks me up and down. "Look like you believe something, and it ain't good."

I take a breath. "She said my brother used to hurt her. When she was younger."

"Baby boy who comes to see 'bout you?"

I nod. "But he was a good boy," I say, trying to put what I know up against what Lillian said. "He got in trouble sometimes when he was young. Smoking weed. Stuff like that. He did have a temper, always kind of on a low boil. But me, him, and my sister Viola"—I cut my eyes at Gale, like, *Don't call her what you're probably thinking*—"for us it wasn't good with our father. I never wanted to make it harder than it already was for Joe, you know, because it's like that rejection feeling hollowed something out of him. So, maybe I didn't discipline him like I should've. But he did settle down. He's a good man. He doesn't miss a visit. He brings his kids to see me. He's a good brother and a good father. I truly believe that."

But now I'm remembering the calls from Tanya, Joe's wife. Early in their marriage, with Joe just back from the military all short fused and silent, she'd call, speaking in a shaky, teary voice, asking me to talk Joe down from some threat or other he was making. But just as quickly she'd tell me everything was fine with Joe and anything that wasn't fine could be worked out. "Can you just talk to him, Althea? Get him to calm down?" Other times, it was Joe calling. Talking about the weight of being the head of his family, his struggles keeping everybody in line, and the problems that came from sparing the rod and spoiling the child. He never sounded overboard or abusive, but still I hear myself asking, like Gale might be able to tell me, "Why didn't Lillian say something? How was I supposed to know? Nobody said anything to me about it."

Gale shrugs. "Now, you know I can't speak on that. But I'll tell you this. I didn't have no brothers and sisters coming up, right? I come up with my cousins. My Big Mama raised us. She'd tell me and my two girl cousins every time we left the house, 'Y'all be careful. It's dangerous being a girl out there.'" Gale lets out a hard, sharp laugh that turns into a wet cough. "What I found out was the danger wasn't always *out there*, if you get what I'm saying. But it was like I just knew not to say a word 'bout nothing 'cause people don't wanna know that shit."

"What're you trying to say? It was up to me? Through some miracle to somehow see?"

"Nigga like me ain't trying to say nothing but what she said, Althea, which is if anybody cared enough to look, they could've saw my dangers." She stops, like she just hit on something. "You know, maybe it'd be easier if they was just straight-up monsters, right? Walking 'round with horns like the devil, so everybody could see 'em real easy." She raises her hands to her head and makes horns with her fingers, then laughs. "I'll tell you, this old girl's seen a lot in this raggedy-ass life of mine, but I still can't monsterfy somebody that mean something to me, even when I been gutted by their horns. Now, that right there's what really fucks with you." She scratches at her smile-scar as her words disappear into a rush of whoops and laughing. And just like that, Gale's on her feet, smiling as we watch Chit and Mercedes and even the chaplain join a gliding, bopping group of women starting in on the electric slide.

Gale looks at me. "That's my jam right there. You sure you don't wanna get on out there and slide it up? Let this shit go for a minute?"

"You go ahead."

She winks. "I'll hit some moves for you, girl."

As I watch Gale limp away, my chest all of a sudden feels tight, just like it did the day I went down in the hallway and she found me. I put my hand to my heart and take some deep breaths, like they told me to in medical that day. Anxiety attack, they said. I close my eyes, feeling my lungs expand as I take in air. "Try taking deep breaths from here," the woman in medical said, touching my belly. "Just drink it in."

I touch my belly and feel it rise and fall.

I remember falling.

I remember my head slamming into the green-and-white linoleum floor.

I remember lying against Gale in the grip of my fears, feeling empty and dried out: *Our bones are dried up and our hope is gone; we are cut off.*

But then, something moved in me, didn't it? Words, rising up to the surface of my mind like through mist or muddy water. The words my mother wrote in the margins of her Bible above that scripture from Ezekiel: *Dry bones. Read Revelation? (Then the angel showed me the river of the water of life.)*

When I got out of medical that day, I went straight to my cell, unlocked the cabinet near the head of the bed, got out my mother's Bible, and flipped through the Book of Revelation with nothing but her words, if not her voice, as a guide. Like looking for some message in a bottle. Some help tossed my way from another shore, because I need to know, *How would she deal with Joe?* He's her son, even though he was left mostly to me. *And how do I deal with her daughters and my own?*

I look over at Adira and the Talker. They're laughing like they're not in jail. Splenda.

I get up and wave goodbye to everybody. I need to get back to my cell. I'm almost through my reading of Revelation, and I mean to pick up where I left off searching.

As I push my chair under the table, Mercedes yells, "Hey, you all right?"

I hold up my empty Snickers bar wrapper. I pick up my cup of punch and drink it down.

She gives me a thumbs-up and goes back to doing the electric slide, a beat or two off from everybody else.

I head out the door and in the direction of my cell.

"You ready for Thanksgiving?" It's C.O. Jordan. I walked right by without seeing him. "I talked to your boy today," he says. "I know he's looking forward to it."

I smile. "I'm looking forward to it, too. Thank you again for your help setting up the visit."

He lowers his voice and whispers, "And hey, you got something special delivery." He lowers his voice even more. "In your cell, under your pillow, from your boy." C.O. Jordan looks more serious than I've ever seen him. "About your daughter."

My chest constricts again.

"Why don't you head on back to your bunk," he says.

"I am," I whisper, rushing off. "Thank you."

When I get to my cell, I scramble up to my bunk as fast as I can, not even worried about disturbing Crazy-quiet, the lump in the bottom bunk, who does nothing but sleep between meals. I reach under my pillow. It's a letter from Proctor. He's never, *never* sent anything "special delivery."

Althea,

Junior drove Kim up here to see me this morning, which was crazy because both of them should have been in school. She gave me some nonsense about school being out today and Lillian and Baby Vi being off somewhere. Junior has brought her here before, when Lillian couldn't, but Baby Vi is always with them. When I told her I thought she wasn't telling the truth, she tried to play it off, and I let it go because I could tell things weren't right. She said she was here because she just wanted to see me. We talked about the usual things, but like I said, I could see things weren't right. She looked rough. I wouldn't say dirty, but like she wasn't really keeping herself up. Her hair was all over the place, like she hadn't combed it, and her coat was all wrinkled up like she's been keeping it balled up or something.

She's too much my child for me not to see the bad parts of myself in her, like in the way she sat there looking like she was having to concentrate so hard to stay focused on our conversation and the way she just trailed off sometimes into nothing. I could see that same darkness that gets hold of me. I kept trying to get her to tell me what was up, but she wouldn't. And Junior wasn't any help. He was just sitting there. I still can't believe he qualifies as an adult, allowed to bring them here. When I kept pressing Kim about what was going on, she just said she loved me and they had to go.

You better believe the first chance I got, I called Lillian and, sure enough, she told me Kim had run off. Lillian said she didn't say anything because she didn't want to worry us and they thought they'd have Kim back soon. Didn't want to worry us??? What the hell is that???? Where could she be for three days? Lillian said they filed a report with the police and they have a BOLO and everything. But I bet it didn't go out past the New River Junction Police. And I guess they didn't have a reason to run her name through here anyway.

If I would have known about her running off, I could have at least tried to have the deputies hold her here until somebody could come and get her. But all I did was just sit there with that bad feeling and stand up, pressing on the glass, dumb to everything, watching her go. I'm not going to lie, I straight up went off on Lillian. Viola, too, when she got on the phone, trying to "explain." None of this had to happen. Kim was right there in front of me. She was right there, and I just let her go.

You see what I mean, now? All you had to do was reach out like I asked you to, but you wouldn't do that, would you? Now look at where we are. I swear to God, if something happens to that girl, it's on you. You know that, right? I'm tired of trying to referee and this and that. This is flat-out on you.

Viola

"Is this a good spot, Aunt Viola?"

Baby Vi holds her flyer up to a light pole like she's trying it for size. I give her a thumbs-up, and she tapes it on. I move to affix my flyer to a willing storeowner's window. Kim's smiling face stares back at me. It's the same smile from the same picture that ran on the local news, briefly, the day after she disappeared. But instead of MISSING stamped above her head, it's: HAVE YOU SEEN ME? Below the picture, our plea—ANYONE WITH ANY INFORMATION PLEASE CONTACT—and information for the police department's hotline.

"Okay," I say, smoothing and taping my flyer to the window, "let's go across the street to that coffee shop. See if they'll let us put one of these up inside."

"Sure," she says, glancing over her shoulder at the Solid Grounds and rubbing her ungloved hands together for some heat.

"And maybe we'll have a warm-up, too. Good?"

"Good." She follows me across the street and along the shoveled, salted pathway to the door. Inside, the warmth is welcoming and so are the two workers behind the counter. With permission granted to tack up the flyer, I offer to buy Baby Vi a hot chocolate.

She scrunches up her nose and requests tea.

"Is tea the thing now?" I ask. "Seems a very adult choice." We settle in at a table by the window. Tea for her, black coffee for me.

"It's just what I like," she says, shrugging and looking around. Two girls, who appear to be high school age, are sitting a couple of tables over with whipped-cream-topped drinks. A middle-aged man is on the other side of the room in a comfortable-looking chair, pecking at his computer, nursing something in a large silver thermos. Baby Vi hunches over her tea, steam rising as she blows to cool it. "Mama liked this place," she says. "We stopped sometimes on the way to work at the restaurant on Saturdays."

"You like this place, too?"

She nods. "We had fun, sometimes. Especially when it was just me and her. She always wanted to know about school and whatever I was up to. She was all serious a lot, but she could be funny. She could still be fun, talking about boys and movies and stuff."

"I miss her, too," I say.

Baby Vi gives me a sad smile. "Even with Kim, sometimes. We could have fun. All of us together. But then Mama was stressed out and depressed a lot with work and stuff. And Kim was all touchy about everything. Anytime you said something to try and calm stuff down, it made it worse with both of them." She looks out the window at the empty sidewalk. Across the street, the tape on the lower corner of the flyer she hung has come undone. Part of the paper is flapping in the breeze. She looks at me again. "What did she say?"

I'm not sure what she's asking.

"Mama. When you and Aunt Lillian talked to her about us going to see her? You never said. When're we going?"

I'm briefly at a loss. "Look," I start. But I'm not sure where to go from here. How do I tell her we never got a chance to ask? And Althea, most certainly, never brought it up. "We're still working things out," I offer.

Baby Vi's face falls in a mix of confusion and disappointment. "Kim's right," she says slowly, as if coming to an understanding. As if resigning herself to a fundamental truth. "I didn't . . . I wasn't . . . but she's right. Mama doesn't care."

"You know that's not true."

She stares at me, pain the main feature on her face now.

"Kim is angry," I say. "She's hurt. She's pushing people away and—"

"At least she's doing something. Not just sitting around." She looks around the coffee shop, angrily. "She's not sitting here like an idiot, waiting for Mama for nothing. I keep telling her she's wrong and to come back, but she's right."

It takes a beat for the words to register. "Wait. You *keep telling her to come back*?"

Baby Vi blinks, startled.

"You've been talking to her."

Her eyes dart away.

I lean in toward her, trying and failing to hold her gaze. "Baby Vi, I'm going to ask you again, and tell me the truth: Where is she?"

"I told you. I don't know." She looks down in her teacup and starts stirring fast, for no apparent reason. She hasn't added sugar or lemon or milk or anything.

"Kim could be in serious trouble," I say. "I can't stress this enough. This thing with her going to the jail to see your father? You were in school, where you belonged, when Junior came by this afternoon, but maybe if you could have seen him for yourself, telling us what happened, you'd see how serious things are." Junior stood in Lillian's kitchen, rattled and dazed, after confessing to chauffeuring Kim to the jail to see Proctor. His mother, Elaine, had brought him over to tell us he'd been lying. He'd been helping Kim hide. But she'd given him the slip at the jail, for reasons he was too overwrought to even consider. "After we saw Mr. Cochran, she told me she was going to the bathroom, but she never came back. I sat there for like an hour, man, waiting for her," he said. "But she just, I don't know. She was all zero dark thirty. But she'd never just disappear on me like that! Never!"

Panic and fear rise afresh at the thought of Junior's words and the freaked-out sight of him, and I try to impress upon Baby Vi the seriousness of the situation again.

"I know it's serious," she says.

"But you don't seem worried at all. That she's out there all by herself. Or is that not the situation?"

"I don't know what the situation is!"

I'm this close to reaching across the table and shaking the truth out of her. "Give me your phone."

Her face twitches with a brief flash of panic. "I don't have it."

"You don't go anywhere without your phone."

"I forgot it."

Do I frisk her? What the hell? "Damn it, Baby Vi, I mean it. Give it."

She stands up, quickly and conspicuously, and pats her pockets. "I *told* you. I don't have it!" She flings her arms open and turns around, as if aggressively modeling an outfit. "See?"

The guy with the thermos glances over. The girls with the whipped-cream-topped drinks turn around to look. The counter guy is eyeing us, too, along with the customer he's helping.

"All right, all right. Sit down."

She sits, arms crossed and defiant.

I lean in. "You're not helping her, not at all, by hiding what you know."

"What I know is she's at least doing something. That's what I know."

"No, you and Kim are—"

"Kim's stronger than you think!" She sets her jaw as her lips tremble. "And so am I. I'm stronger, too!"

Dial back, Viola. You're not helping matters. "Look, Baby Vi, I didn't mean—"

"I don't care what you mean," she interrupts. "I want to go home." She pushes her barely touched cup of tea back on the table and stands. "Please," she adds. But not politely.

I can't resist the call of home. My round trip to Chicago will be quick, though, picking up a few things, checking on the apartment, getting a bit of distance from the day's failures and fruitless searches.

As I move to turn up the car radio, my phone rings. I answer.

"Hello?"

"Viola?"

"Althea?"

"Yes, it's me." The words are fired out fast. "What's going on there? I got word. From Proctor. About Kim. You couldn't have told me when you were here?"

"It's not like we had a chance, did we?" I catch myself. Now's not the time to deal with her walkout. "Sorry. Yes, we should have told you. I apologize for that." Althea lets out a weary breath. I picture her there on the other end of the phone line, looking like she did when the officer led her out. An old, beaten woman. "I didn't mean for it to go this way," I say. "We didn't want to worry you."

"Is she back?"

"No. Not yet." I weigh whether to tell Althea about Baby Vi and the phone she mysteriously "couldn't find" when we got back to the house. How inept will I sound when I tell Althea that Lillian and I couldn't find the phone either, when we rummaged through drawers in Baby Vi's room, rooted through her closet, turned up her book bag, looked everywhere, stopping short of a cavity search? How idiotic will I sound if I tell Althea that while watching an impassive Baby Vi watch Lillian and me search, I was weirdly impressed with how Baby Vi was playing things in service of her sister, while, at the same time, roundly pissed about being played?

"Baby Vi and I went out and hung more flyers after school today," I say, deciding to stick to what Lillian and I agreed: Let Proctor try to get Baby Vi to talk. "We're out looking every day, and the police are doing what they can."

"Doesn't seem like they're doing much."

"I guess there's only so much they can do."

There's a silence.

"Althea?"

"Yes," she says, her voice suddenly hard to hear. "Proctor says it's my fault."

"Whoa!"

"What does that mean?"

I tap the brakes. Cars are slowing down ahead of me, and I'm way too close to the minivan in front of me. "I'm sorry. I'm driving. There's some kind of backup up ahead. Sorry." But there's still the question of blame. "Althea," I say, "about whether this is your fault or not, I don't think anyone should be laying blame."

There's the muffled sound of a phone shuffling around. Women's voices echo in the background.

"Althea?"

"Yes," she says, "I'm here."

"Look, don't—" I'm in the middle of saying, "do this to yourself," when her words overtake mine: "I never should've had them, Viola."

"Excuse me?"

"The girls," she says impatiently, like how could I not know? "Proctor's the one who wanted kids, and I owed him. He got us out of our father's house, didn't he? Proctor's a good man." She pauses. "I need to say this. So, give me a minute, okay?" She whispers fast, like she shouldn't be speaking, but the words can't wait. "I need you to take them, Viola. Once Kim comes back, and she will. She's just out there being hard-headed, trying to prove something. She'll be back. And I need you to take them. It's what I was thinking about when I wrote that letter, telling you we needed to talk. My lawyer, everybody, they kept saying they weren't going to send us away for this long, but I just had this bad feeling. And I thought about you. Remember how you always used to say you were meant to help girls like you? Remember that?"

A fine helper I am now.

"They're like you now," Althea rushes on. "Like *us*, Viola. Practically no parents. And Kim—" She stops. She's quiet for a moment before whispering, "I do love them, you know that, right?"

"Of course I do."

"But something isn't what it should be. Not with me," she says, still whispering. "I'm not like Mama or other mothers I know. I see that now. I used to watch other women with their kids. Isn't that crazy? They always seemed so . . . I don't know. Right. So natural." She pauses. "But not me, Viola. I don't think I feel what I'm supposed to feel. And Kim's so hardheaded and so . . . I don't know. I couldn't ever get it right or do enough for her."

I want to say, *And a lot of what you did do was in excess: nonstop criticism of her weight, her clothes, her "attitude," her grades. When you were around, that is.* And there was Baby Vi, sitting there quietly with her special burden of being the favored child, even if she never benefited. Was never fawned over or coddled or regularly hugged. Not by her mother.

"Kim wrote me a letter," Althea says. "Well, she wrote it to Proctor, and he sent it to me. Look, maybe I wasn't everything I should've been, but all I ever wanted was for them to see that life isn't easy, you know? I only wanted to get them ready for life and the fact that nobody's going to give you anything, just like I used to tell you and Lillian and Joe." She sucks in a breath, as if something has startled her. As if she's pulling back from something hot.

"Are you okay?"

"No." She pauses. "I mean, I'm sorry, Viola. About what happened when you and Lillian were here."

"Shouldn't you be apologizing to her?"

"Viola—" She stops. "Look, I wish it was different, okay? I wish I'd been different that day. I wish I'd been different most days before all of this. I wish we'd all had better."

"Did you know? About Joe? Do you know what he did?" The questions come out barely above a whisper, with the reluctance of someone who, to this day, doesn't want to know the answer.

"How would I know something like that, Viola? I wasn't there. I wasn't in that house."

"But you were right there in town, Althea. You saw Lillian."

"Not enough, I guess. I don't know."

"Does any of this even bother you?"

"Of course it bothers me!"

"Have you talked to him?"

"He's been here—look, Viola, he's my baby brother." Her voice catches, and in its place is a silence so strained, I imagine it stretching out in the air, pulled from cell tower to cell tower into something brittle and fragile. Something breakable. Like everything about us. "I know what you want from me, Viola," she says finally, "but this is all I've got right now." There's a quaver in her voice, the big sister who used to be so steady.

This unnerves me, and suddenly I'm reassuring her. I'm telling her I wish we'd had better, too. I tell her this is hard, all of it, and it's going to take time. I tell her she's right, Kim will turn up, and when she does, I'll bring her and Baby Vi to the jail to say goodbye.

Althea cuts in: "*No.* Don't bring them here."

"But I think it will help." I think of Baby Vi, sipping her tea at the coffee shop Althea used to take her to, trying to convince me she's strong. "I don't know that you appreciate how difficult this is for them."

"Seeing me won't help them, trust me." Her voice is low and quavery again. "I can't pretend like I'm not still having a hard time with what Kim did to me and Proctor. Daughters carry the hopes and promises of their mothers, Viola. And my hope was . . . See, so much turned on what Kim did. I could hardly look at her when Lillian brought them here to see me. I wanted to talk to Baby Vi, but not Kim, sitting there with her arms folded like she does, with that *look* she gets."

"I'm sure she was just defensive and nervous."

"And always trying me, Viola." Her voice is still shaking, but that's not crying. I think that's rage. "Looking at her that day, I just felt something rising up in me and then guilt over it all. I have this crazy mix of everything," she says. "I'm like him, Viola."

"Him? Who?"

"Him. Our *father*." She spits out *father* like it's something bitter in her mouth.

"No, you're not." I start to say more, but I see the truth of it. No, I heard it. In Kim's eyewitness testimony: *She was mostly away.*

"This is a mess," Althea says, sounding flat and resigned. "I know that, and I'm the one who made it, okay? I'm sorry you're part of the cleanup, but I need you to let me know you'll take them. Get them out of New River Junction. Out of Michigan. I'll handle Joe."

To my silence, she says, "I remember how you were with Lillian. You'll be good with them, Viola. Will you at least think about it? You know, you and, um, you and Eva?"

The overly nice, forced mention of Eva. The sugarcoated disapproval, even after all these years. It's not a phase, Althea. But I don't get into that or the fact that we're not together anymore.

"Can I have some time?" I say.

"Yes, but time's not our friend right now."

"I know."

"Speaking of, I'm burning through my debit account, so I'd better go."

I'm suddenly seized by the thought that there's more I should say before she hangs up. I search my mind for the most pressing, most important thing, and I hear myself say, "I love you, Althea, okay? We have some things to work through, but I love you."

"Me, too," she says.

As I get ready to hang up, I hear: "Hey! Viola!"

"Yes?"

"You take care of yourself. Do you hear me?"

"Sure."

"No. Do you *understand* me?" There's a pause, as if she's giving me a second to think. "You were too skinny when you were here."

I feel this rush of emotion. This intense missing.

"All right," she says, as I have yet to respond. "You know what I'm talking about, then. Get some happy, Viola, okay? At least one of us Butler kids should have it."

The line goes dead.

The glowing exit signs, the L tracks crossing the highway, the cars and trucks zipping by, the streaks of head- and taillights. They're all rippled and wavy through tears. I wipe my eyes, then click on my hazards and get myself to the relative safety of the highway shoulder. As everyone whizzes by me on the Dan Ryan, I look up at the jagged skyline, alight in the night. The steel, the glass, the concrete, the cranes, the antennas. I imagine Chicagoans rushing through the streets, unaware of the conversations, the consequential information moving above their heads into the ether. I imagine what Althea and I said and see our words as digital dust, raining down in want of fertile ground.

Her last words take hold, and I wonder: *What's my best avenue to happy?*

I consider the exit in front of me, even though it's not the one I mean to take. Even though I told Lillian I'd be back tonight.

* * *

It's strange, knocking on your own door. Or what used to be yours.

Eva answers, still in her work clothes—a blue sweater dress with gold flecks, a lot like the ones in her eyes. Her feet are bare, and she looks relaxed.

"Hey," I say.

"Hey."

The smell of garlic wafts out, chased closely by tomatoes.

"Spaghetti," she says.

I glance over her shoulder to the family room. Looks like she dropped her briefcase in the usual spot by the breakfast bar and got right to the business of dinner. She leans casually against the door frame, her expression soft but not yielding.

What did I expect? I ended it, so it's done. *She's* done. I step back and jam my hands into my coat pockets, because I don't know what else to do with them.

"How are you, Viola?"

"I've been better." I look off down the hall, toward the elevator. "I just, I wanted . . . I thought maybe I left some shoes here or something?"

I glance at her. She rolls her eyes, but there's a small smile there. A small chance?

"Look, I, um . . ." I burrow my hands deeper into my coat pockets, my nails digging into my palms. "I'm sorry. I haven't . . . I've been distant and selfish and not well. But I want to be better. I want us to . . . What do I need to do?"

Eva regards me, as if assembling an exhaustive list in her head. She closes her eyes and exhales heavily, as if it is too much to contemplate.

Got it. I turn toward the elevator. "Okay, I understand. I'll just—"

"No, Viola." She reaches for me. "I was . . . What you're doing right now is good. Let's talk. Come back."

Althea

"You wanna talk about it?"

"No."

Mercedes leans back in her chair, staring at the gray-streaked and yellow-stained wall across from us. We're the only ones left, sitting side by side in the Bible study sharing circle. Everybody else left a few minutes ago, but I'm not in a hurry to get to the kitchen for work.

"Why don't you go on," I say. "I'll put the chairs back before I go. I just need a few."

"Fine. Take 'em, Althea, but the room's my responsibility." Said like the trusted, model inmate she's known to be.

We both go quiet for a good minute, the echoing voices out in the dayroom coming through the open door.

"She'll come home," Mercedes says, finally.

There goes that tightness in my chest and a twist in my empty, rumbly stomach. I haven't had much of an appetite.

"Hey," Mercedes says, her voice kind, "I'd bet you money she's gonna turn up by tomorrow."

It sounds so much like a Hail Mary, last-hope kind of thing to say that I don't even bother saying anything back.

"No, I mean it," Mercedes says. "Tomorrow's Thanksgiving. She wouldn't wanna be out there on her own. She'll wanna be with her family, don't you think?"

I shrug. "I don't know what she wants. I don't know what to think. And I'm supposed to be her mother."

"You are her mother, Althea."

"I don't know what I'm going to say when I see Proctor tomorrow," I whisper. "That is, if he still wants to see me. I don't even know if we're still doing this, after his 'special delivery.'" I sent my question about that back to him through C.O. Jordan, and I haven't heard anything yet.

"You two got some shit to deal with, that's for sure," Mercedes says. "Can't really get around that."

I look up at the little frosted rectangular windows, wishing I could see at least a piece of the sky. But all I get is that glow that lets me know it's daylight.

Mercedes reaches into her breast pocket and glances at me, looking shy. "I was gonna wait to give you this, I don't know, later, I guess. Before your transfer. But hell, now seems like as good a time as any." She pulls a wadded-up ball of toilet paper from her pocket. "Here." She shoves it at me. "It's nothing. Just, you know, I've been doing my sculptures."

"Didn't they tell you to stop that?"

"Whatever," she says, waving my words away. "Unsanitary, my ass. It's art. Besides, people still bring me their leftover soap. I can't just let it go to waste, can I?"

"Yes. You can." But I go ahead and unwrap the ball of paper to find a little soap carving of a man about the size of my index finger in flowing robes with a disk sprouting up around his head. I turn it over, amazed at what can be made from all those little pieces of soap that would've just dissolved down the drain or been thrown away.

Mercedes leans in, smiling a big, gray-toothed smile. She taps the sculpture with a long index finger and says, "That's Saint Joseph right there." She smiles bigger. "Or *Soap* Joseph."

"Funny."

"Whatever, buzzkill. Anyways, remember when I did that picture of you and you told me about your river, the Saint Joseph, and everything like that?"

I nod.

"Well, that whole thing sounded like it was important to you." She shrugs.

Looking down at the grayish-white carving in the palm of my hand, I think of *P+A* carved into the tree by my river. "One river for each of my girls," is what my mama said after Viola was born. The Saint Joseph for me and the Portage, its tributary, for Viola. Me and Viola, we're always supposed to run together. And Mama told me, "You girls, us women, we're water." Strong stuff. A force of nature. A source of life.

Dry bones. Read Revelation? (Then the angel showed me the river of the water of life.)

I think of my reading, my searching of the last book of her Bible. I believe I found the right part: "The angel shewed me a pure river of water of life, clear as crystal . . . and on either side of the river, was there the tree of life." I stopped cold when my eyes landed on those words. And my mama's words, written next to them, in the margin: *Show me the way.*

She was searching, too.

But if there's more for me to see or learn, my chance is gone. I've sent the Bible on to what should be its final destination. It's wrapped up kind of like a present, but it's more of an apology.

"You all right?" Mercedes asks, calling me back.

"Sorry. Drifted for a minute."

"Yeah, I know. Look, I get that you don't believe in any of this, but see, Saint Joseph is the patron saint of travelers. Hell, patron for a lot of shit, if you wanna know. But anyways, he's supposed to help you on your way. And families, too, Althea. He's the patron of families, and, you know, you got a lot going on with yours." She looks down and shrugs as she wipes at something on her pants. "Anyways, it's nothing. It can be something, you know, to keep in your new place if you want to or whatever."

"This is nice, Mercedes," I say. "Thank you." I touch the little disk that I guess is a halo around his head. I look at her. "Why are you—" My voice catches in my throat.

"What?"

"Why did you do this for me?"

She blinks. "I don't know. You're my friend, I guess."

Have I ever had any friends outside of Proctor and Viola and Joe? Since they're family, do they even count as friends? There were a couple of kids I hung around with growing up, but I didn't have time for kid stuff. And yes, I know just about everybody in New River Junction. But most of them weren't friends, were they? Yes, there were hugs and parties and all kinds of fun. They looked up to me and respected me. I did what I could to keep it, but it wasn't enough.

"I don't have anything for you," I say, and my words hit my own ear like a warning: Don't expect anything from me.

Mercedes draws back. "Do I look like I'm asking for something?"

"Well, this *is* jail," I mumble.

She cocks her head to the side and says, "Maybe I already got something from you."

I raise an eyebrow.

She laughs and looks up at the frosted, chicken-wired window.

"What I mean is that you never seemed scared of me. I guess maybe you were just scared off your ass in general, so I didn't take it personal or something. I don't know." She shoves her dirty blond bangs back out of her face. "Anyways, I mean, just like Chit, I feel like you don't look at me like some kind of crazy, battered-ass bitch who cut out her boyfriend's tongue." Her head snaps around in my direction, and she points to me. "Which, by the way, I didn't. The fucking media put that shit out, but they never fixed it when it came out he bit the damn thing himself! And he didn't even bite it all the way off! Do you think they'd let me in here around normal people if I was some Hannibal Lecter or some shit?"

She's glaring at me, like I'm the one who reported it all wrong.

I raise my hands, like, *It wasn't me.*

She says quietly, "But I did, you know, hurt him when he couldn't fight back. I did do that. And I did shoot him. And like I told you, I meant to do it." She shakes her head, like, *Why?* "If he would've just kept his mouth shut, you know? Stopped calling me names and talking shit about me. I know I'm not the best, but I'm not all them things he said I am." She rubs her face, practically scrubbing it, then glances at me. "I got so high after I did what I did that I don't even remember the police showing up. I couldn't tell you what happened between the last time I got high and finding myself in here. I was that far gone, and I didn't wanna come back."

Assuming the media got at least something right, the police brought Mercedes back from a food-and-bodily-fluid-stained hotel room that most people rented by the hour. Back from the corner of that room where she was nodded out beside a dresser flipped on its side, with blood drying in her hair and a baseball bat by her dirt-caked, bare feet. Back from where her boyfriend sat across the room from her in another corner, with blood smudges and spatter decorating the wall behind him. He had three bullet wounds that the medical experts said he could've survived because, apparently, Mercedes was such a hand-shaking, bad shot that she didn't hit anything vital. No, it was the "blunt force trauma to the head" that killed him. And he'd been dead for days. It was the smell of his rotting body sitting in that corner across the room from Mercedes that brought the police to that hotel room to bring Mercedes back.

I tell Mercedes, "I was scared of you."

She turns to me, eyebrows raised in surprise. "You're not still scared, are you?"

I look at her pockmarked skin and in her anemic blue eyes, wondering what all she's seen and done. "Sometimes," I say. "But these days, I got to tell you, I'm mostly just scared for you."

She lets out a laugh, but it's like acid on the ear. "I am, too." And she looks scared. "If they let me out, Althea—I mean, that jury's been at it for, like, three days, and my lawyer thinks the longer it goes, the better it looks for me. Fucking lawyer should've let me testify. There wouldn't be no question about them sending my ass up. But if they let me out . . ." She shakes her head. "I don't know. Sometimes I think Gale's crazy ass might be right. I know what's waiting for me out there at home with my family, and Gale said it: It damn sure ain't Jesus."

"Don't listen to Gale. Either way it goes, you're going to be fine."

She looks down and traces one of the tattooed vines snaking up her forearm. "That's what people say, ain't it? Everything's gonna be just fine. People always say shit like that. Hell, I just said it to you about your kid." She starts to say more but stops. She looks down at her arm, then up at me again and says, "You remember that time we were talking about confession? We were talking about that shit people say about confession being good for the soul and everything like that?"

I nod.

Mercedes stares off at the wall across from us and says, "Something about that ate at me, and I started thinking about this whole confession thing, and you know what I thought? I thought, maybe it's just about having a come-to-Jesus with your own ass." She looks at me and cracks a sad, mangled smile. "Maybe that's the soul saver or soul crusher, depending on what you got to say, right?"

I think about that for a second. "Yeah, I guess."

Mercedes's eyes, pale like always, are all of a sudden penetrating as she leans in and says, "I ain't got much to say for myself, Althea. My family screwed the pooch so bad with me and my brother that—look at us." She opens her arms wide, like, *Behold*. "Me and my brother ain't good for much more than killing ourselves or somebody else. So far, Bobby's only going after himself. See"—she points up to the window—"that's the truth about what's waiting out there at home for my ass if they say I'm innocent. That and then some. So, as much shit as I say in here about miracles and salvation, that's my come-to-Jesus truth I been telling myself lately. I got nothing good. And I tell you what, that's a soul crusher right there."

She shoves her hair back with both hands and slumps forward with her elbows on her knees, staring at the floor between her legs.

I gaze down at the tiny sculpture in the palm of my hand and close my fingers around it. "If there's ever anything I can do for you, Mercedes, I will," I say. "Wherever you end up, okay?"

"Yep." She nods, but she doesn't look up.

I stand. "I'd better get on to work. And look, Mercedes." I wait for her to glance up at me through her shaggy bangs. "Thank you for the sculpture. It means something to me."

She stands, tall and gangly, giving me an embarrassed smile. She adjusts her baggy jumper in an unnecessary and nervous way and turns, without a word, to take apart our Bible study sharing circle.

Very carefully, I slide the tiny Saint Joseph into my breast pocket and help her, going over to the wall to take down the sign that says SPIRITUAL SAFE HAVEN.

"Hey!"

Me and Mercedes look over to where the *Hey* came from to see Gale at the door, breathing hard like she's been running, which I know she hasn't been. It doesn't take more than a few quick steps to pull the wind out of her ruined lungs.

"I thought y'all might still be in here—" She cuts herself off, coughing and hawking up phlegm into a tissue.

"What's up?" Mercedes says to Gale, then she looks at me. "She's about to actually cough up a lung this time, I think."

"Shut the hell up," Gale coughs out, pounding her chest. "Whew!" She leans against the door frame, trying to get her breath. Finally, she gets out, "Guess who I saw?"

Mercedes freezes with her hands on the back of a chair she's pushed about halfway under a table.

Gale nods. "Yep. Chit. They just brought her up. I know I said she'd be back, but damn!" Gale looks shocked and even a little disturbed. I guess she'd hoped for something good for Chit, too. "And homegirl look like hell," Gale says. "Got a big ol' knot upside her forehead and a busted-up mouth. Arm all jacked up and in a sling." Gale cradles her own arm, looking even more disturbed. "She won't talk either. I hear it's real bad, what she did."

Mercedes looks confused. "What did she do?"

"My people say it's a DUI." Gale looks from me to Mercedes. "They say she hit somebody. And I tell you, I'd like to see who let her behind the wheel, 'cause that's a stone fool right there."

"I'm sure everything's going to be all—" I stop myself.

CARE AND FEEDING

Althea,

I hope this makes it to you okay. I got word on what you said, and yes, I still want to see you. It's our last chance for a good long while. We shouldn't throw it away.

I was going to wait to tell you when I saw you, but I think I should go ahead and do it now. Hop is running point on Kim's case, and he drove up this morning to see me. He apologized for how things are going. He said with them thinking Kim's a runaway and probably not in danger, the department just isn't putting a lot of resources on it, not that they have a lot to start with. I think he honestly feels bad.

They've had some calls to the tip line, but they've been slow running them down. The tips they have looked into have been dead ends. Somebody called about a girl wandering around Riverside Park, but it wasn't Kim. Didn't even look like her. There was a girl sleeping in the library. From the description, Hop thought it could have been her, but when he got there whoever it was was gone.

He's going over to talk to Junior at some point today. He said the boy was so upset yesterday, after Kim ran off, he couldn't get much out of him, except that he didn't know where she was. I know how much she likes that boy. I'm worried about what her running off from him says. It's been four days. It's like she's vapor out there. What if she really left town? Where to? We'll talk more when I see you.

Love,
Proctor

Viola

"You good, Viola?" David asks, crunching through ankle-deep snow to meet Eva and me on the sidewalk.

"I think so." I glance up at the church, which is small and modest compared to the stone and stained-glass edifice Eva and I attended in Chicago. This church, where I spent so much time as a child—reading on back pews, resting my head on lumpy prayer pillows—is red wood and brick with clear glass panes. The most striking thing about it is the tall but simple cross that stands like a steeple against what is, today, a sky the color of cement. With the weight of everything, the day feels quite nearly as heavy.

"It's a thoughtful thing for Joe to do," Eva says. "Let's just try to keep that in mind."

She tugs me forward, but I feel rooted to the ground. "I never thought I'd have a reason to come back here. After my father's funeral."

"Well, this is a good reason," David says, looking over at the half-full parking lot. "It would've been nice, though, if there was time to make a big thing of it. Get some more people here. Maybe the media."

"I doubt they'd come," I say.

Kim's disappearance isn't news. The big story today? Black Friday shopping strategies. How to cook and carve your turkey, complete with a phone number to call or text for your culinary emergencies. And, of course, advice on avoiding family conflicts at the Thanksgiving table.

I look at the steps leading up to the wooden double doors, and part of me goes back to my conflicted feelings about certain members of *my* family.

The heavy double doors open, and someone peeks out.

"It's time," I say, leading Eva and David toward the stairs.

Lillian called last night to tell me about the pre-Thanksgiving prayer service for Kim.

"It's Joe's regular Wednesday afternoon prayer," Lillian explained. "But he wants to focus on Kim. One of us should be there, don't you think?" She paused. "And one of us should stay at the house, I mean, just in case Kim comes back." There was a certain quality to the quietness in Lillian's voice. Not necessarily a turning down of volume, but a kind of muting of that Lillianesque positivity. A modulation of her internal voice. She's been that way since telling Althea all Althea would let her say about Joe.

"Eva and I will drive in for it," I said. "You keep the vigil at home. Keep an eye on Baby Vi." We've been watching Baby Vi closely, ever on the lookout for her now-elusive phone, after even Proctor failed to get anything out of her. Indeed, Baby Vi is proving stronger than any of us thought. Stronger willed, at the worst possible time.

And here I am, powerless. Sitting between Eva and David, inside a church not much changed from when I was a child. There are the same dark wood pews, the stain worn lighter in spots by time and so many bodies. There are the same four steps leading to the raised platform where the altar sits, painted white and dressed in purple linens. Behind the altar and to the left, there is a large, half-moon pulpit and the seats for Joe and his ministers. On the right, a small lectern and the chairs for Joe's wife and other elect ladies who aren't allowed near the pulpit, a male-only space.

Behind the chairs, three steps up, there are the organ, piano, and drums, as before, and the choir, robed in purple with white sashes. The large movie screen hanging above the center aisle near the front of the church is new, though. It shows the day's scriptures or the action in the pulpit or the choir box. The kind of thing you see in megachurches, but this church is quite small by comparison. We're in a seat down front with the screen overhead, so we can't see what's on it.

If Joe is surprised to see us among the handful of people in the pews, he doesn't show it. In point of fact, during the part of the service where they welcome visitors with a song, handshakes, and hugs, Joe calls out David, Eva, and me, and we are embraced by everyone who files by, including Joe, though Joe is noticeably stiff. So many of the old ones tell me, "It's been too long! Why don't you get yourself home more?" And, "We're praying for your family, for God to lead Kim home."

In my father's absence, when I was a child, these people would pray for us. Provide for my sisters, my brother, and me. They would sometimes have all kinds of things waiting at the church for us: clothes their children had outgrown; a plate of crunchy, salty fried fish or fried chicken; chocolate sheet cake; and rhubarb pie. Always something good from the church's busy kitchen. And concern. They'd have that here for us, too, with the church sisters almost always looking at us with sad smiles, asking, "Y'all getting along okay? Where's your daddy preaching this week?"

Althea hated them for it. She hated God for it, too.

As members of the congregation move on from shaking our hands and hugging us, Joe stands there behind the pulpit, watchful. So at ease in black jeans and a black turtleneck. He's telling an old deacon in the front row he's glad to see him back after his shoulder surgery and joking about when they're going to play him on the church basketball team. He's telling a woman he's praying for her mother and her, too. He's thanking everyone for their prayers for his family and for Kim.

Joe's smiles seem sincere, his jokes are funny, his worry looks genuine, especially when he calls people by their names. They love him here.

"I'd like to invite you to read with me," he says.

Amid the breathy whisper of flipping pages, I imagine the scripture floating above my head on that screen. Joe looks to his left, my right, at the women sitting in the rows of chairs reserved for the elect ladies. At Joe's command, a woman stands and steps up to the small lectern and reads in a loud, firm voice: "But let him ask in faith, nothing wavering. For he that wavereth is like a wave of the sea driven with the wind and tossed."

"Thank you, sister," Joe says. He launches into a sermon about faith, hope, and God's power to "bring the lost back home."

I find that even I'm drawn in. Even I have tears in my eyes.

Everyone is getting out of their seats. A woman in a pew across from me mouths: "I'm praying for you." And I think, This is the thing I miss about Pentecostal churches. You can cry your eyes out, run up and down the aisles, sing or scream at the top of your lungs. They'll only encourage you or join you or gather around and pray with you. You don't feel so alone. There isn't just safety in numbers like that; there's grace.

Joe comes down from the raised platform. Stands in the center aisle with his arms outstretched to the ceiling, singing about new life. Everyone sways with him. Everyone sings. Everyone prays for Kim. Then everyone files out, until it's just David, Eva, and me standing a pew apart from Joe. David says to me, glancing at Eva, "Why don't Eva and I wait outside?"

Eva squeezes my hand, and she and David go.

Joe and I face each other, separated by the pew. He's wiping his bald head with a soggy handkerchief, saying, "Look at me." His shirt is soaked through with sweat from the rigors of delivering his sermon. "I'm a mess."

"Thank you for holding the service," I say. "It was a kind thing to do."

He nods reverently, still in minister mode. "The old-timers looked happy to see you."

Are you? Apart from the time we spent in the kitchen waiting for Lillian, I can't remember the last time I was alone with Joe. I don't know when I will be again, so I ask: "Do you ever think about what you did? To Lillian?" I pause, for a second. "What did you do?"

He leans heavily on the pew behind him, like every ounce of strength and divinity he displayed is ebbing away. Was it as illusory as one of his old magic shows? "I'm not gonna talk about this with you," he says. "Why can't you leave it alone, Viola?"

"Because I can't." Because I left my little sister alone with you. "So, what was it, Joe?"

"Not that." His jaw is working, knotting up. The vein in his forehead is rising. "I wasn't the best brother to her, all right? It got tense in that house sometimes, okay? Is that what you wanna hear?"

"Yes, for starters. What do you mean by 'tense'?"

"Viola, when you ask for forgiveness, God throws your sins in the sea of forgetfulness."

"Well, I don't. And Lillian can't either." I think of how she sounded on the phone last night, that muted quality. "Call her. Go to the house. Make it right—hell, I don't know if it can be made right, but at the very least, apologize and mean it!"

"I have!" He pitches forward and grabs the top of the pew, his fingers practically digging into the wood. "And I paid for it, too, okay? I got sent away. What else do you want from me? You don't got enough?

You got Althea on your side. And I let you have that, all right? I didn't push. I said, fine, if you and Lillian are gonna act like this about Baby Vi and Kim, when I'm trying to do something good, when I'm trying to do something right for my family? Fine. I went up to see Althea. She brought it up, you and Lillian going there, saying this and that about me, and I didn't fight it, all right? I left it alone."

"Well, you can't really fight what's true, Joe."

"I've put this to rest, Viola. Lillian did, too. I love my family."

"Do you even—" I stop at the sight of his trembling jaw. The raised vein in his forehead, where his pulse ticks. A good therapist might see him empathetically: What was it like to be you, Joe? With your extension cord beatings, your losses, and your jealousy? What is your idea of love and family? But not me. I can't stop thinking about what it was like to be Lillian, after I left her behind.

"Look," Joe says, "you can stay here as long as you want to, but I'm gone. It don't matter what you can and can't forgive. I know what's what."

He turns and goes.

Suddenly, fatigue pulls at every part of me. I sink down in the pew and find myself observing another church service. This one in my mind, yet unfolding as if before my very eyes. Was it Easter Sunday? *That* Easter Sunday? The day my mother took that picture? I'm in my pink and purple Easter dress, so surely it was. But I feel somehow dislodged, discarnate, far removed from that girl. Watching her rather than being her. And my mother is up there with the other elect ladies to the right of the pulpit. She stoops down, and there I am, sitting in a chair near hers. She puts Lillian in my lap. She rubs my head, then Lillian's delicate baby head, saying, "Careful, hold her head," or, "Careful, hold her, don't drop her," or maybe, "Careful, Viola."

Then she stands up straight and reads for my father. Words I can't recall.

"I haven't been very careful, have I?" I say aloud, to nothing and no one.

David, Eva, and I are at a red light, a few blocks away from Lillian's. David eyes me in the rearview mirror from the driver's seat. "You okay back there?"

"Yes, just thinking," I say, as I look out my window at the passing yards covered in snow. At snow, windblown into waves.

"If you want to talk . . ." Eva says quietly from the passenger's seat, letting the words hang there.

I don't know what to say about Joe because I don't quite know how I feel about him. I'm somewhere between wanting to be empathetic and remaining on guard. And how do I tell Eva and David what happened after Joe left? How do I say I just had a moment that felt less like a memory than a vision? A visitation? They'll think I'm nuts. Maybe I am nuts, with everything—

My phone pings. I dig it out of my purse.

"It's Lillian," I say, scooting forward quickly and holding my phone so David and Eva can see the text: Need you at the house ASAP. News on Kim.

"I hope—" But a horn blast drowns out Eva's words. We all jump and look back to see the driver in the car behind us making threatening hand gestures. We have a green light now.

David mutters something about rudeness and pulls off. "We'd better get to the house."

"Once more unto the breach, dear friend?" I say, trying to tamp down a rising panic.

"Once more," David says, driving considerably faster than the speed limit.

Lillian

I pace the kitchen as I press the phone to my ear.

"Lillian?"

"Thank you, Officer Hopkins. For calling back, I mean."

"What happened? Your message was a little . . . What's going on there?"

"Texts," I say. "From Kim."

"Any idea where she is?"

I scroll through my memory hunting for clues, like I've done over and over. "She doesn't sound good. I have the phone." I hold up Baby Vi's phone like he can see it. "She texted her. Baby Vi. Kim texted Baby Vi."

"Okay, good," Officer Hopkins says. "We should be able to track whatever phone Kim's on. This is just what we needed. I'll be over as soon as I can. Just, okay, hang tight."

I stand in the middle of the kitchen, holding Baby Vi's phone in one hand and my phone in the other, like their weight's the only thing keeping me balanced. I have my coat on because I was about to run out the door to the police station when Officer Hopkins finally called me back. Over on the breakfast nook table, there's Baby Vi's abandoned pile of synthetic berries on a paper towel and one lonely berry shunted off to the side. I hear soft, shuffling feet and the sound of rolling wheels. I look over toward the entrance to the kitchen.

Nai Nai stops. "What wrong with you?"

"We heard from Kim. Officer Hopkins is coming. I just texted Viola. She's on her way, too."

Nai Nai puts her weight on her walker as she stares, trying to read me. "Sit down," she says.

I take my coat off and sit at the breakfast nook table, but with my back to her. I don't want her to see that I'm starting to cry.

She rolls up behind me. I feel a trembling hand on my shoulder.

I touch her bony hand.

"I make tea," she says.

I nod because I'll probably just start sobbing if I say something. Anyway, for someone who doesn't hear the greatest, Nai Nai manages to hear what she needs to. I'm guessing she's overheard enough of the conversation between Baby Vi and me to know things are bad. I feel her trembling hand lift a little, hover over my shoulder, then pull away.

"No worry," she says, firmly. "We have some tea. We wait for everybody."

I should've known something was wrong when she came down. When Baby Vi walked in on me, I was in front of the pantry, staring at a half-eaten bag of potato chips, last seen cradled in Kim's arms one day after school.

"What're you doing?" she asked, startling me out of my trance.

I closed the pantry door. "Nothing, just . . ." Just what? Just stuck. Too agitated to sit down. Too exhausted and distracted to do much more than stand there, staring. "Just thinking about lunch," I lied. I looked down at Thelonious. "Isn't it good to see Baby Vi, Mr. T.?"

He blinked as she bent down to pet him.

"What draws you out of your lair on this fine Wednesday afternoon?" I asked, moving over to the refrigerator, trying to put some distance between me and the pantry and this helpless feeling that, let's face it, stalks me everywhere I go.

Baby Vi stood hugging herself, rubbing her twiggy arms.

"You all right?"

She hugged herself tighter.

"You want to go out? Grab some lunch?" Out the kitchen window, the world had gone white and bright and as pretty as a picture. We'd been cooped up all day, keeping watch for Kim. And in my case, avoiding Joe's church service and Joe himself. "Just a quick lunch run," I said. "Maybe it'll give you a reason to get out of your pajamas?" I smiled, trying to lighten the mood.

"If you want to," she mumbled, dragging her feet as she moved over to the place in front of the pantry that I'd just vacated.

"Really, Baby Vi, it might be nice to get out for a little bit."

She looked over her shoulder at me, biting her lip. "Can we stay here?"

"Definitely."

She grabbed the Crunch Berries out of the pantry and went over to the breakfast nook table and took a seat. Reaching into the box, she pulled out a couple handfuls of cereal and made a pile. "Didn't Aunt Viola and Aunt Eva go to church?"

"Yeah," I said. "Why?"

"Their car's still out front," she said, picking out the "berries." It's something she does all the time, but it was a sad reminder of what Kim used to do, too. Baby Vi always took the "berries" and Kim went for whatever you call the other sugar bombs. The crunch, I guess.

"They're with David. They're coming back and staying over for Thanksgiving tomorrow."

I got up, went over to rip off a sheet of paper towel, and took it back to the table. "Remember the crumb problem?" Kim left crumbs everywhere, making an endless trail for Thelonious to follow, which isn't good for him. I handed Baby Vi the paper towel and took a seat next to her, helping myself to a couple of the square sugar bombs in her reject pile.

"Is Uncle Joe coming, too?" she asked, sorting some more and building a small pile of synthetic berries.

"No."

She looked at me, her hand still hovering above her tiny pile. I said that too fast and maybe with too much force. I was about to try again, but she was opening her mouth like she was about to say something. Then she closed it.

"What's wrong?"

Baby Vi shook her head.

"Look—" But I stopped myself. "Okay. No pressure. But I'm here. You know you can talk to me, right?"

She nodded and went back to sorting her cereal pile, plucking out one fake berry and looking at it like she was checking for defects. She put the berry down on the edge of the paper towel and stared at the cereal box. "If I tell you something, do you promise not to be mad at me?"

A worry knot pulled in my stomach. "Definitely."

She swallowed. "Me and Kim have been texting." She glanced at me, checking for a reaction.

I managed to hold it back.

She reached under the table and pulled out her phone (I guess from some hidden pocket in her boxers?).

I looked at the phone. I looked at her. I couldn't hold back anymore. "I'm glad you were able to *find* it. Where was it?"

"I promised her I wouldn't say anything."

"We lost valuable time with this, Baby Vi. How could you just—?"

"She promised it was only for a little while. But I don't know now."

"Okay. It's all right. Just"—I reached for the phone—"let's see."

She punched in her code and pushed the phone at me like she couldn't wait to get rid of it. In my hand was a string of blue and gray conversation bubbles with smiling, frowning, angry, and sometimes crying emojis:

Saturday, Nov 23, 11:52 PM: Hey V, this Kim, not Junior. Forgot my phone on the charger so using his. Stupid. Anyways. Worst. Night. Ever. Now officially hate everybody in town and scarred for life from bowling. 😭 Need a break and want to teach know-it-all Aunt V a lesson too. When I say I don't want to go bowling, I don't want to do it! I'm with Junior but DON'T TELL ANYBODY WHERE I AM, I MEAN IT!!! 😬 Junior said you guys came by asking about me and he played dumb. They didn't even really look for me right here in the house. I guess they think who would want to hide in that scary-ass basement? Will be back tomorrow so act like normal and like you don't know, right? Remember, I'm two minutes older, so obey your elders! TTYL my nig 😘

Sunday, Nov 24, 9:34 AM: I got the whole house to myself watching Netflix and eating anything I want while they're at church. Elaine brings the deliciousness at all times!

Sunday, Nov 24, 1:07 PM: Guess what???? Me and Junior are going to jail!!! 😈 Mwahahaha!!!!! I'm going to see Mama and Daddy and get this shit right. For real though I been talking to Junior about stuff and you know he's all one love and everything but I think he's right on that. Maybe it's time to try and forgive people even if they don't deserve it. It's like being the bigger person. That's me now. One love my nig.

Sunday, Nov 24, 5:00 PM: I'm not on Mama's list. I was going to try and fix things but look at her! Didn't I tell you about her? I was so mad, I just left. I know I'm on Daddy's list. I bet you're on her list and the aunties too. She got everybody on there but me. 😭😭😭

Sunday, Nov 24, 8:09 PM: Me and Junior are camping at the restaurant tonight. Junior hid me in his room and we almost got caught so we had to move. They think Junior's at his boy's, all-nighting on a school project. It's janky as hell and all haunted feeling out here, but with everything at the jail today, Junior thought it would be good to face the demon, you know? I think so too. In the morning, none of this shit will have power over me. Please keep it hush, V. 🤐

Sunday, Nov 24, 11:55 PM: I did something that's probably going to be on news. Don't be mad, okay 😟? You'll see. OK, we're high and feeling some Boone's Farm but I think it was right to do anyways because that's where everything got started and destroyed everything for us, so your girl said fuck it and destroyed the demon restaurant 🔥 YES! That's how I face it. Maybe it's the ganja and the Boone's running through me but I miss everything, V. I miss home. Me and Junior had to move again obviously and that's where we are. It's like camping, but not like real camping. Remember that time up in the UP camping with Daddy? Roasting marshmallows and telling ghost stories and how fun that was? Right before I started texting you, I closed my eyes for a little bit while me and Junior just snuggled together on the floor in my bedroom smoking and it was like I could pretend nothing bad happened, right? Like my room's not all empty and dead and shit and I got all my stuff around me just the way it was and you're across the hall in your room and Mama and Daddy are in theirs and everything is good. Not like before, but really good and different like a dream family. Do you think we can change like that? I'm high as fuck, I know it, but do you think? I miss you. I burned up the demon. I want things to be good. I want everybody back at home, but different.

I kept reading, and the messages got sadder and darker:

I try and be good but I'm not like you, okay? What I did to the restaurant was stupid stupid stupid stupid. I keep doing stupid stuff.

Baby Vi's texts begged Kim to come home and threatened to tell if she didn't. Then Kim said she needed more time and if Baby Vi told, "something very bad will happen."

Then, nothing. It was hard to take it all in.

"You read the last one?" Baby Vi asked.

"Yeah, I—"

She motioned for me to give the phone back.

"No," I said. "We need it. We have to call the police, like *now.*"

"But there's more. I have to show you!"

I gave her the phone. She thumbed around and handed it back to me. "That's her," Baby Vi said, pointing to the screen. "She's on a different phone."

There was just one text from that number. From last night:

Tuesday, Nov 26, 11:30 PM: I never knew a person could feel so sad but that's me right now. 😥 Junior took me to see Daddy today, and he tried to make me laugh. It didn't work. I saw myself on a sign out by Riverside Park and somebody wrote Good Riddance over my face in big letters. Maybe they didn't like the pic. I don't take good ones, so I guess that's me. Anyways, good riddance to these motherfuckers too. People are mean, V. I got tired of listening to Junior about one love and everything because there's no love out here.

That last text was followed by a bunch from Baby Vi, begging Kim to respond. It had been thirty minutes since Baby Vi's last text, with nothing back from Kim.

"She won't text back," Baby Vi whispered. "I'm scared."

I was scared, too. All I could think was, *It's been four days. How much time have we lost? Phones can be traced. Maybe Kim could've been found.* I closed my eyes and breathed for a second, trying to pull it together.

When I opened my eyes again, Baby Vi was shaking like a puppy waiting for the storm, just like in the courtroom that day. She was hugging her legs to her chest like a barrier. She said in a small voice, "Kim always texts back. *Always.*" She wiped her face with the back of her hand. "Where would she go? She's not—" She stopped and stared hard at me through tears. "Something's not right."

I got up. Pacing. Pulling out my phone. "I'll call the police. Officer Hopkins."

"Call whenever you need to," he'd told me.

I tried his cell. I got his voice mail and left a long, rambling message about texts and not hearing back and being worried.

"Maybe she still has this phone. It's probably one of those disposable ones, right? And maybe she ran out of money. That's all. Or just isn't getting back to you. You know how she can get."

Baby Vi unfolded her long foal's legs and got up, scooping Thelonious up from the floor.

"Everything's going to be fine," I said, finally stopping my pacing and standing still. "Don't worry. Okay?"

She was nodding and blinking fast, tears flowing more with every blink. "Okay," she said, moving toward the archway.

"You don't have to go."

"I know."

But she kept moving.

I watched her leave, not knowing what to say.

I called and left another message for Officer Hopkins.

I read through the texts again, like I could figure things out myself. My eyes fell on the text from Kim that said: I'm so stupid. I should have known I wasn't on her list. Remember what happened when we went to see her?

I remembered. Althea's lips were peeled back in a fake smile and her eyes were sometimes blank, sometimes unblinking and scared, when she looked at the girls. I was the one who thought it was a good idea to take them to see her, not Althea.

On our side of the partition, Kim sat with her arms crossed, looking like she didn't want to be there, but she absolutely did. She never said it, she never would, but she came straight home from school with Baby Vi, seeming happy she'd had a "conflict-free day," and both girls were ready to go when I was. *Before* I was, now that I think of it, because I'd found them sitting downstairs right here in the kitchen, waiting for me.

But in that visitors' room with Althea, Althea told me, "I can't."

I pressed the phone to my ear (practically attaching it) so her words wouldn't leak out to the girls, who sat on either side of me. And I said, "Sure you can."

"I can't," she said again. "I don't know what I might say. I'm scared of what I might say. Unless I tell you, don't bring them back here. I mean it."

I got up, touched the girls' shoulders, and said, "Your mom's not feeling well." Both of them looked at me, then at their mother, like they didn't know whether to go with me or keep sitting there across the partition from her. They were still used to her telling them what to do, not me. "Come on," I said quietly. "She can't talk right now. They're going to take her back." And slowly, the girls got up as Althea waved goodbye.

Althea took Baby Vi and Kim off her list after that.

I sat there in the breakfast nook for a minute, staring at Baby Vi's phone, rubbing my ear. Trying to center myself. It didn't work. I texted Viola: Need you at the house ASAP. News on Kim.

I got up and touched Baby Vi's chair. "Safe," I whispered as I pushed it back under the table.

Viola

We're all being uncomfortably polite.

"Did you get enough sweet potatoes? No, no, pass me your plate again. Please."

Down at the end of the table, Lillian is speaking to Elaine in a sugar-coated voice that's at least half an octave higher than normal. Elaine, meanwhile, is piling extra helpings on her two boys' plates. The younger boy, who looks to be about nine or ten, keeps saying he's fine, while Junior sits there looking shattered.

The grandmother, down at the corner of the table to Lillian's left, is about to fall asleep. And God knows, I'm not far from doing the same thing as I sit here listening to Elaine's husband, Big Ed, give a lesson on home brewing.

Whenever he, mercifully, turns to someone else, my attention gravitates to what's happening around the table: Lillian's adjusting and re-adjusting some of the baby pumpkins, pinecones, and pine leaves she decorated her "Harvest Table" with; on my left, Eva's giving me copious, comforting knee pats under the table, and it's like she's *pat-pat-*

*patt*ing out a Morse code message: *Steady as she goes*; Elaine, next to Big Ed, looks at me apologetically while he talks to someone else. Eva, this time.

"What you're going for is a balance of flavor, right?" Big Ed explains to Eva. "Getting those different elements to come together for you in your brew."

Eva, who hates beer, nods as if transfixed.

"This is really some Thanksgiving," I mumble, louder than I meant because all eyes shift to me, saying, *Don't you know we're trying not to talk about that?*

Lillian raises an eyebrow, and I suspect she's saying something else: *Who would've thought we could have something worse than that* other *Thanksgiving?*

Who would have thought.

I look out one of the floor-to-ceiling windows, darkness just now settling in on the day. "Where the hell is she?"

The police had indeed been able to track Kim's phone, but the last ping they got was around Riverside Park from the other day. The phone hasn't been active since. "That could just mean the power's off or something," Officer Hopkins told us. "So, don't worry. If we get another ping, we're on it. And we're keeping an eye on the park as best we can."

It could also mean she disposed of her disposable phone.

Everyone shifts to look out the nearest window like they might catch a glimpse of her. But there's only the scattered glow of streetlights and fresh snow. We were supposed to be at Elaine's this evening, but we decided to move the feast here in case Kim comes home. Elaine brought over the full spread: turkey, dressing, ham, sweet potatoes, mashed potatoes, deviled eggs, collard greens, green beans, creamed corn, corn bread, assorted desserts, and some of Big Ed's "Private Label," which, to be fair, does demonstrate his home-brewing prowess.

Lillian did her table decorations, and they're perfect. The table, the conversations, the whole gathering is the picture of a kind of normalcy it's impossible to feel.

"We'll go out looking for her again after dinner," Elaine says, still gazing out the window nearest her. "That's that. We'll just get right back out there and maybe get some more signs up."

"Absolutely," says Eva, patting my knee more emphatically: *Steady as she goes.*

She reaches out on the other side of her and gives Baby Vi's shoulder a gentle squeeze.

Baby Vi nods but otherwise looks desolate. On her plate, even the small, perfectly spaced dots of collard greens, green beans, corn bread, and the sliver of turkey she's cast off to the rim of the plate look forlorn.

"We'll find her," Lillian says, trying to reassure, but her voice falters.

As I watch Lillian start in on what's on her plate, I struggle to fill mine. In my current state, the consumption calculus required for this task can be debilitating, particularly when faced with such abundance. I scan the table like a calorie-seeking cyborg. A serving of that turkey is one hundred and sixty calories or more and four grams of fat. Those sweet potatoes with all that butter pooling around them? A couple hundred calories, easily. The creamed corn can't even be considered because of the cream, and on and on down the table until my brain locks up from all the addition and subtraction. Not to mention the anxiety, which is multiplied exponentially by the knowledge that I can't and *won't* excuse myself to go to the bathroom to "take a little off the top." There's also no way I can disappear on a three-hour run.

Just relax, I tell myself.

But they're noticing, now.

"Go ahead, sweetheart," Eva says in a low voice.

Lillian's giving me an encouraging smile.

It breaks up the mental gridlock just enough for me to put a few things on my plate, telling myself: *You will get better.*

I squeeze Eva's knee under the table. Checking that she's really here? That we're getting better, too?

She smiles.

We are getting better.

Now, time to be mindful of the taste and texture of my turkey.

But my mind moves on to something else entirely. To that *other* Thanksgiving. It was the very last time all of us were here as a family. That was, what, four years ago? Kim and Baby Vi were at a card table in the corner with Joe's kids. At the adult table, there sat Althea and Proctor, who, unbeknownst to us, were starting to skim money from their charities. Lillian, the grandmother, and Sam were together but fracturing in a way I couldn't yet see, with Lillian secretly sleeping with one of her design clients. There was Joe and his wife and our father, with Joe talking up some new church outreach program in his never-ending efforts to hold our father's attention and win his approval. All of us, sitting around another beautiful table, styled by Lillian. There was to be a family picture on that Thanksgiving.

"I want all my kids and their families together," my father said, smiling his perfect, square-toothed smile. Althea's smile.

When we moved to gather around him, with the self-timer set, he looked at Eva, his face twisted in disgust, and said, "Not *her*. She's not family." Over the years, he'd mellowed enough to "tolerate" having her at the Thanksgiving table, but, apparently, not anything more.

Eva and I sank back to our seats, even as I made it clear she was, in point of fact, my family. He advanced on me, voice raised, spit flying, accusing me of choosing "that bitch" over him.

I'd seen my father explode plenty of times. Once, while looking up something in the *Diagnostic and Statistical Manual of Mental Disorders*, I'd come across a condition called intermittent explosive disorder, or IED, and thought immediately of my father: outbursts way out of proportion with whatever set off the explosion. It was always Althea and, to a lesser extent, Joe who, like human shields, absorbed the emotional shrapnel. But now it was aimed directly at me. Eva was grabbing and patting my knee frantically under the table. A Morse code SOS.

Althea mumbled feebly, "Nobody's choosing anything over anything." Then she sat there with this distant, defeated look she would get sometimes when we were younger. As we Butler kids sat concussed into silence, Proctor stood. He turned to Eva and me and said, "We're going." He lifted his hand and rallied the girls. Then he touched Althea's shoulder lightly, as if gently nudging a sleepwalker prone to lashing out when awakened.

We left Lillian and Sam and Joe and his family and my still-ranting father. We went to the restaurant, where we had a Thanksgiving that felt as sad and abnormal as this one.

I think of Kim and Baby Vi, huddled together in their own booth, whispering softly, because even they could feel things were wrong.

I think of the beautiful mahogany bar, which was where we adults were sitting, with Proctor acting as our heavy-pouring, easy-to-talk-to bartender.

I think about when Lillian and I visited Proctor at the jail yesterday and were telling him the latest on Kim. Recounting some of her texts and what happened when Officer Hopkins arrived, which wasn't much except for promises to trace the phone. Proctor sat there with his head in his hands, his broad shoulders heaving.

And I think of Althea. How when we told her the same about Kim on that same day, she sat dazed, saying nothing, looking a lot like she did on that Thanksgiving when she was being buffeted by blowback from our father.

I say to no one in particular, "I still have to make something special for Proctor from that piece of the bar. I promised. And I have to find something for Althea, too. For them both to have with them."

"Sure," Lillian says, sounding vague and distracted.

Baby Vi gets up, twisting her napkin in her hands. "May I be excused?"

There's a chorus of Sure! Absolutely! Of course! from every part of the table except the space where Elaine's overstuffed boys are sitting in a food stupor. I focus in on Baby Vi's still-full plate. Women like me pay attention to very thin girls like her who leave full or overly messy or manipulated plates. I've been watching Baby Vi for some time—claiming to prefer plain tea; rearranging food but not eating it; pleading "I'm not hungry" when she should be—and I don't like what I'm seeing.

Baby Vi steps back from the table, and Junior gets up and starts to speak, but a small, thin voice rises: "Wait!"

Baby Vi and Junior pause.

We all look at the grandmother, a little knot of a woman in a pink cashmere sweater, sitting low in her chair. "Let's watch movie," she says to Baby Vi. "You pick."

You can tell Baby Vi doesn't want to, but she's the kind of girl who doesn't like to disappoint, and she had disappointed so recently with her act of phone rebellion. An act she now deeply regrets. She goes over to retrieve the grandmother's walker from where it's parked against the dining room wall.

"I'm gonna go, too," Junior mumbles, head down. Reminding me of the last time I saw him. He was in the kitchen, trembling, telling us how Kim had gone "all zero dark thirty."

"How've you been, Junior?" I ask.

"Making it," he says, fiddling with a dreadlock that has escaped the massive bun piled atop his head. "Making it."

"I understand," I say, as he lopes off behind the grandmother, who's pushing her walker, and Baby Vi, who's gazing out the window, ever watchful.

* * *

We all go back to our plates and our quiet, careful conversations. I glance to my right at Elaine's husband, sitting at the head of the table where my father used to sit, and I think again of that other Thanksgiving. That was the last time I saw my father alive. It was the last time Althea laid eyes on him at all.

"I just want some peace," Althea said, not long after that Thanksgiving.

At least I went to his funeral.

But Althea? No.

I asked her once, before all of this with the arrest, if she'd found the peace she wanted. She told me she had everything she needed and most of what she wanted. She said, in her unequivocal way, that she didn't want to talk about him anymore. And, aside from an occasional reference, she never did, not until that day she called while I was driving to Chicago and said, "I'm like him, Viola."

Lillian stoops down in front of the fireplace. "Pay attention," she says. "There's an art to building a good fire."

"Really? Seems anyone can do it."

She casts a glance over her shoulder to where I'm sitting Indian-style on the floor.

"I know," I say. "That was bad."

Lillian stares into the empty firebox. "But it's hard not to think about Kim torching the place." Lillian, snug in her housecoat, sits back on her heels and looks over at me again.

"Clearly," I say, sipping the tea Lillian made after we got in from tonight's search.

"This'll warm you up and help you de-stress," Lillian said to Eva earlier as Eva excused herself and went up to bed with her cup of tea, discouraged. It was Eva's first time seeing what we've been seeing for days: no trace of Kim out there.

All of us—Eva, Lillian, Elaine, Big Ed, David, and me—had been out driving and walking the frigid, lonely streets tonight. Hitting all the spots we've hit before: the Dunkin' Donuts, their abandoned home on the river, Riverside Park where Kim had likely sent her last-known text. All of us feeling more and more defeated as we passed, but never discussed, the signs we posted days ago, showing Kim's smiling face and the question, HAVE YOU SEEN ME?

On we went, past the Burger King, McDonald's, Popeyes, a couple of gas stations, and strip malls. All of them closed tonight so people can be with their families, enjoying Thanksgiving in the many warm, brightly lit houses we also passed in tonight's pointless search.

"Why don't you go ahead with your fire demonstration," I say to Lillian, taking another sip of my tea, wanting to be distracted.

Lillian reaches into a basket for her kindling. "Now pay attention," she instructs. "Maybe it'll make you think about your fossil fuel consumption. Those gas logs of yours."

"Thank you, Greenpeace."

She chuckles, which makes me laugh, something we both need.

Lillian puts out newspaper and twigs again. "You want to be thinking about air circulation when you lay out your tinder and the kindling. Same with the logs." She throws a quick look over her shoulder to make sure I'm paying attention. "The flames have to be able to breathe. And once your fire's going, you don't want to overfeed it. You pile on too much and you can smother it or end up with it burning out of control."

We exchange a look: Kim. Arson.

"At least she and Junior won't be prosecuted," I say, thinking of her texted confession to Baby Vi, now read by Officer Hopkins. He told

Lillian and me, when he came to the house yesterday: "Proctor and Althea screwed up royally, but I have a son about the girls' age, and, I'll tell you what, I'd hate to see what kind of spinout that kid would do if I got myself taken out of the picture. I'd want somebody looking out for him." He stopped, seeming to realize he wasn't talking like a police officer with an arsonist to jail. "I'll just say," he went on, "that the force has limited resources, so the focus has to be on other priorities, which, for me, is finding Kim."

Lillian sets a match to her incendiary pile and comes over and settles on the floor next to me. We sip our tea in silence as the flames slowly lick their way up the paper and logs. With the first fingers of the fire's warmth touching our faces, Lillian takes a deep breath, as if inhaling the heat. Gazing into the flames, she says, "With all this stuff, with Althea and Kim and Joe, I've been thinking a lot about what we do to each other. I've been thinking a lot about Sam." Lillian glances at me, sheepishly. Guiltily. "I mean, it's like, all this time, you've been this person, a complex person, definitely, but this basic person, you know?" She forms a square box in the air with her fingers. "With certain limits. Then all of a sudden, you see yourself being this other person with this other man." She pauses and, looking sheepish again, says, "Men. It wasn't just the one client, Viola. It was two."

I'm shocked, but I try not to show it.

She clears her throat and says quietly, "I didn't love them, though. I loved Sam. But I think I just had to have this . . . this *thing*."

She looks down into her mug of tea, and I'm thinking about having "certain limits." I'm thinking of how limits become limber. Pliable, when pressed with the *thing in you* that cries out, endlessly, *More, please.*

"I was just, I don't know," Lillian says. "So lonely all the time, I think. Even with Sam." She pauses. "Is that crazy?"

"No," I say, imagining a Mama-shaped hollow space. And for me, a father-shaped one, too. "But in the end, Lillian, you made a mistake. That's all."

"Yeah," she says, "tell that to Sam."

Poor, never-saw-it-coming Sam.

Hunched over, staring into her tea, Lillian looks tortured. Shame, wrapped around her like a penitent's hair shirt. I imagine the fine, prickly strands of guilt rubbing right up against her soul. "You know," she says, "there's this Hindu legend that says, once upon a time, all humans were gods. But we screwed up so much that Brahma, the god of creation, said we didn't deserve divinity, so he took it away. Leaving us to our screwups."

"Leaving us human, Lilly."

She looks at me, her eyes shining. "You know what? I moved back home to give Sam his space, the whole time thinking he'd eventually take me back. But he died hating me." The tears spill down her cheeks. "And I've been trying to, I don't know, make up for it ever since. Keeping all of his stuff and our old apartment like a time capsule or something. And this house, I mean, it was supposed to be my refuge. But no matter how I fix it up, there's no changing anything."

"There are too many ghosts here, Lillian," I say. "You don't have to stay tied to this place out of guilt. Or to people. The grandmother—" I stop myself. "I mean, Nai Nai. We've talked about her before. You don't have to keep her. She would be okay in a nice home. You could have a life away from here."

Lillian draws back, incredulous. "I know I took her in out of guilt. And okay, it was one more way to make it up to Sam, but"—she shakes her head, tears rising anew in her eyes—"I'd miss her too much. I mean, I think we're like a horribly matched arranged marriage. Arranged by Sam, of all people; but it actually works. We take care of each other." She wipes her eyes and exhales. "I don't know. We may not be gods anymore, but we do still have to have some power. Over ourselves. To do what's right."

It's a statement, but I hear the faint whisper of a question in it: *Don't we?*

"Of course we do," I say.

There's a silence. "Althea sent me something," Lillian says in a quiet voice.

"What?"

She gets up, goes over, and opens a drawer in the bookcase. She comes back with a battered, leather-bound book. I've never seen it before.

"Althea said it's Mama's Bible," Lillian says. "She sent a note with it." Very delicately, she pulls the note from between the front pages:

We can't go back, but I wanted you to have this, Althea wrote, *for everything. Seen and unseen. I'm sorry.*

"This is good, Lillian."

She nods, holding the Bible to her chest protectively, like something more sacred than scripture. "Having this, it's kind of like a miracle to me," Lillian says. "Kind of a mystery, too." She flips to the end of the Bible. "It's not all here. There's a page missing." She touches the place where the page should be. I touch there, too.

"What do you think?" she asks.

"I don't know. Maybe it said something Mama didn't like. I don't know."

We sit for a moment in silence, contemplating an act of sacrilege. Finally, Lillian stands. "I'm going to go on up," she says. Very carefully, she puts the Bible back in the drawer and pats it, as if to make sure it's secure. She comes back over and pats my head like a dog and tells me not to stay up too late.

As she leaves, I take in the posed family pictures, the perfectly placed books on the bookshelves, the *World Book* encyclopedias, and I feel the ghosts crowding in again. But this time, I see the ghost of that girl, not the oldest or the youngest sister. *Me*. The girl who starved, gorged, purged, overexercised. Excoriated her soul, like Lillian the penitent, but with a very different form of torture.

"You're going to be okay," I say to that ghost girl.

Careful, hold her, don't drop her, said my mother's ghost to me.

I've been working on myself for years. Maybe now, something is working on me.

I stare into flickering flames, burning low. Listen to the cracking and spitting of incinerating logs. I turn and see the flames reflected in the shiny, jagged-edged piece of the bar, which is propped up against the chair opposite me. I go over and pick it up. A keepsake for Proctor? Honestly, what is there to hold on to?

Maybe Kim had at least this much right. Burn it all down. Let it go. I toss the piece of the bar onto the fire. Orange embers rise and swirl like a swarm of fireflies. The dying flames shudder as if smothered.

I hear the door and look up. It's Baby Vi, standing in the open doorway, her eyes wide.

"What—"

She holds up her phone, and I hurry over. There's a text, less than five minutes old:

> **Thursday, Nov 28, 9:03 PM:** Happy Thanksgiving and merry Christmas forever and ever and I love you. Always remember. Y'all can stop looking now 'cause I'm already gone. It's time for me to drift away, V, that's all. Please tell Daddy I love him and I tried. Please tell Mama I never knew what to say to her that wouldn't make her mad.

Althea

Proctor's on the other side of the door. I stop with my hand on the knob.

C.O. Jordan looks down at me. "You straight?"

"I just need a minute."

"Take your time, but you know we're on the clock, right?" He checks his watch. "It's coming up on five, and they want us to keep it tight, so . . ."

"Right, right. I know. I'm ready." My hand still on the knob, I look up at him. "Can I?"

"Most definitely." He smiles. "Go on ahead."

I turn the knob and push the door open, and there's Proctor in the middle of the white-walled, windowless room, sitting in an orange, molded plastic chair that under his tall, broad body looks like it's made for a little kid. He's dressed in a black-and-white-striped jumper that matches mine, and his bald head is shining under the overhead light.

"I'm just gonna be right out here," C.O. Jordan says, nodding toward the door, "but I'll be checking on you."

"Yeah, man," Proctor says. "We appreciate you. Happy Thanksgiving."

The door closes behind me. I stand against it, holding the doorknob behind my back.

Proctor gets up and smiles at me, but it's not his usual, easy smile. He's working for this one. When he moves to close the few feet between us, I put my hand up to stop him.

"What?" he says.

"You're mad at me."

"Come on, now, Althea."

"You blame me."

"Althea, please." His face is tight, and even though he's not moving, except for his jaw as he grinds his teeth, it's like something in him is leaning away from me, just like the day they arrested us. It breaks my heart; it makes me mad . . .

"Stop lying, Proctor!"

He glances at the door behind me. "Keep your voice down."

He moves toward me again.

"No," I say, stopping him. "What did you see in me?"

He furrows his brow. "What?"

"When you met me. When we met."

"I don't know." He looks around the room like he's searching for a window into another time. "That was a long time ago. We were kids. You were nice. You were pretty." He shrugs and says again, "We were young."

"And look *now*," I say.

He shakes his head in confusion. "What are you doing?"

"I let them put the blame on you. I—"

"Althea, I've told you. I don't want to talk about this stuff."

"And Kim. I've got no idea where she is, and something in me—"

The look on his face stops me. That look says he knows. "I told you,

I don't want to talk about this, Althea," he says, in a slow, warning voice.

"You were more than happy to talk about it in your letter. You were more than happy to let me know this is on me. Now here I am. Right in front of you. So go ahead, give it to me."

He just stands there.

"Come on!" I pound my chest with my fist. "Why don't you ever get mad? Don't you have anything, *anything*, in you?"

"I *am* mad!" He finally sounds like it. "I've been mad for a long time."

"Then show it. Come on!"

His eyes dart toward the door, and he hisses, "Keep your voice down!"

Just then, there's a knock. The door pushes open against my back, and I move with it. C.O. Jordan peeks his head in. "Everything all right in here?"

Me and Proctor say, "Yes," at the same time.

C.O. Jordan looks from one of us to the other. "All right, then. I'm just right out here."

It sounds more like a warning than a reminder. The door closes, and I stand with my back against it again, holding the doorknob like it's an anchor.

"How do you need me to show you I'm mad, huh?" Proctor says. "You want me to hit you or talk hard to you?" He cocks his head to the side and studies me. "You're gonna have to find somebody else to make you suffer like that." He backs away and sits down again. "We had a good life, Althea, you know that? But it was like you could never be content in it, could you?"

On the other side of the wall, the sound of voices echoes off cinder block and stainless steel. There's the *bang-bang* of metal on metal and the clanging and creaking of heavy locks catching and holding. When I don't answer, Proctor says, "When this all started, with the food stamp stuff, I bought it, you know? This whole thing about it being a 'victimless crime.'"

"That's what it felt like."

"I know. But what about the rest, Althea? We knew it was real people involved, expecting something from us."

"You spent that money the same as me."

"I know that, too. So, you didn't *let* me take the blame. I just took it. And I got some extra time for it." He pauses, his throat working as he looks down. "Even now, I don't think there's anything in this world I wouldn't do for you, but I let the blame fall on me for myself, too." He looks at me again. "I should've pulled you back. I should've pulled us both back. But once I realized you were dipping into the charity money, I knew we were too far gone. I knew there was no turning back for you because I know you."

"What do you think you know, Proctor?"

"I know that you saw yourself as the real victim."

"Me? Proctor, please."

"Please? You put your whole life into our business, into being something in that community. You used to tell me, when business was bad, 'They're not taking this away from us.' Remember?"

"I'm not going to apologize for building something and wanting to hold on to it."

"And I'm not asking you to apologize. What I'm asking you to do is see yourself, for once. You made the business and your reputation everything, Althea. Think about it. Where were you all the time? The restaurant. What were you thinking about and talking about all the time? The restaurant or whatever charity gig you had going."

"Because somebody had to look out for us while you were being the music man, the favorite parent, the—"

He raises an impatient hand and waves my words away. "No, you fed off that stuff, Althea. And the thought of going without, the thought of—"

"So I'm supposed to feel guilty for building a business? For having something that meant something to me?"

"Come on, now. You know that's not what I'm saying. What I'm telling you is you didn't have much of nothing else. When that one thing is everything, it gets easier and easier to do whatever you got to do to keep it. And that was you, Althea, with my dumb ass along for the ride."

I'm ready to fire back, but his words are tugging on a line, pulling up something from the depths of me. I think about sitting with Mercedes the other day, coming to see that I've never had any real friends. But I had respect, didn't I? I had a kind of love from the people who reached out for hugs or handshakes or just a word everywhere I went. Who I was to them, that was something to me, wasn't it? And what I wouldn't do to keep it.

"It never felt like stealing, Proctor," I say, tears rising. I blink them back, like a reflex.

He doesn't say anything.

I'm silent, too.

"You wanted to know what I saw, when I first saw you?" he says finally. "I'm thinking now, and what I saw was a girl grieving. And over the years, I'd see you just never stop. And I think I watched you grow into a woman who was always reaching, trying to fill a need that was outside anything I could ever satisfy."

My eyes slip from his face to the bare walls. I'm reminded of my meetings with the chaplain in that small, white-walled office with a window looking out on the world. Trying to get him to say who I am and how I compare to these drug runners and boyfriend killers and prostitutes and whatever else.

"Look at me, Althea," Proctor says. When my eyes meet his, he says: "Stay with me. I can't lose any more, okay? And neither can you."

I nod, but it's like I'm a robot. No feeling behind it at all.

"And the girls," he says, pausing, his eyes glittering with tears. "I see what you're doing there, too. But you can't afford that loss. Believe me. And they can't either."

I'm giving another empty-headed nod.

"Handing them off to Viola and disappearing in your cell because you think you've lost yourself along with everything else"—he shakes his head—"that's almost easy. Showing up, when it's everything you can do to crawl and claw your way through this life? That's hard. That much I've done. I'm doing it right now." Worry wrinkles ripple across his brow. He pats the chair next to him. "So there. I'm mad at you. At myself. At the whole damn world. So, will you come here now?"

I slide my sweaty fingers off the doorknob and move toward him, taking the seat next to him.

Proctor stares at me and leans in closer, touching the scar forming above my right eye. That part of my face is still tender and a little swollen from my fall. "That's where you hit your head when you fell?"

I can't speak. I can't cry. I can't do anything, so I nod again.

"That's not that bad. Did you bust up the floor?"

It's an old joke about my hardheadedness. About me always having to have things my way. But the old joke cuts too close. Still, I go along, smacking his arm, like I always do. But then I find myself grabbing at his sleeve and holding on in a desperate way. There's tapping at the door, and we jump like kids caught in the act. We've been warned about "getting physical." When the door cracks open, both of us sit up perfect-posture straight.

"Just checking in," C.O. Jordan says, peeking around the door. "Y'all still got a few minutes, but it's getting close."

"Thank you," I say.

"We'll wrap it up," Proctor adds.

When the door closes, Proctor says, "'The First Time Ever I Saw Your Face.' That's the song."

I shake my head in confusion. "What?"

"The one you couldn't guess: First time, end of time, Flack."

"Right, right," I say. "Okay. I see it."

I hold his hand and close my eyes, thinking back to that day we met. When I was that girl sitting on the steps, grieving but not crying, watching her father say, "It's God's will," waiting for Proctor to bring me a plate overflowing with everything I loved. But I couldn't eat. I think of him squeezing himself in beside me on the narrow stairs. A big fourteen-year-old boy in a too-big mourning suit; me at twelve in my yellow Easter dress. Just the two of us, the sides of our thighs pressed together. I press my thigh against his now, just like that first time. But it's not enough to comfort me.

"Don't just sit there," the chaplain says. "Would anyone else like to share?" He leans into the circle and smiles, looking like he really wants to hear what we've got to say, no matter how crazy it is, and, with Mercedes not here to put the hammer down, there's been some crazy. Across the sharing circle from me, I see a raised hand flapping in the air and think, *And here comes another nut*. Tina the Talker is waving her hand around like she's in a crowd and needs to make herself seen.

"All right, Tina," the chaplain says. "What's on your mind?"

Eyes roll and groans ripple around our sharing circle.

"Ladies, ladies," the chaplain says over the groans, raising his hands for quiet.

The only one who's quiet is Adira, sitting there next to the Talker with a concentrated look in her eye. "Remember, everyone has a voice here," the chaplain says, pointing to the SPIRITUAL SAFE HAVEN sign.

He nods toward the Talker. "Please, go ahead, Tina. Tell us what's on your mind."

"Thank you." She looks around the circle at us, like, *I guess he told you, didn't he?* as she scratches at a dry, ashy spot on her cheek. Eczema, she'll tell you, and that's even if you don't ask. She leans in toward me. "First off, I wanna tell my sister Althea that I'm happy to see her looking better." She points to my face. "I see yo' bandage gone."

For some reason, my hand goes up to my face to confirm what I know to be true. "Can you get on with your own stuff and leave me out of it?" I say.

She does, talking about her back pain and how she's going to see about filing a complaint about the mattresses in here. She tells us how she thinks she has fibromyalgia, but she can't get into medical to see about it. She leans into the circle toward me again and tells me not to let them get away with telling me there's nothing wrong with me because anybody can see there is. "Did they run any tests on you? X-rays?" she asks me.

"What do you think?" I say.

There are giggles all around the sharing circle. Everybody knows that medical is barely in the health care business.

The Talker's attention and this dingy room, it's all irritating me now. If I could just get up and go. But go where? Back to my empty cell? Crazy-quiet's gone, and even though the woman hardly ever said a word and pissed me off every time I saw her lying in that bunk, I guess I liked having her, *somebody*, there.

Adira raises her hand to share.

Gale, who's sitting next to me, says, "Here we go. The angel fighter."

The chaplain nods in Adira's direction, and she scoots to the edge of her orange plastic chair, pressing her legs together and pressing her hands between her closed knees. "I want to ask everybody to pray for me," she says. "I'm gonna be talking to my lawyer about a plea soon."

"Absolutely, absolutely," the chaplain says. "We'll definitely lift you up."

The women around the circle second that:

"Most definitely, sister."

"We got you."

I take in the fifteen or so faces. Square ones, round ones, oval ones made in shades of brown, pink, or just plain pale, with pimples, blotchy scars, or baby-smooth skin. I notice a lot of these faces are new. People just coming in and out, one after the other. For once, I don't care to know what any of them did. Soon enough, I'll be gone. Any day now, I'll be the new face in another lockup with people wondering about me. My stomach tightens and turns.

Adira's saying, "I did a euthanasia." She looks down at the tattoos on her wrist. A fancy green *BO* inked on one and *DED* on the other. She leans into the circle like she's about to share a secret with us. "You know," she says, "when I first heard that word, *euthanasia*, a long time ago, probably on the news or something, I thought they was saying *youth in Asia*, and I didn't understand what they had to do with anything. Isn't that stupid?" She laughs, like, *What a stupid girl.* "I didn't learn what that word meant until after they arrested me. I didn't know nothing about that when I was a kid."

"You're still a kid," I hear myself say. Stupid, stupid girl.

Adira looks offended. "I'm twenty-five."

"Girl, please," Gale laughs. "You ain't been in this world but a hot minute."

Some of the other older women laugh, too. One says, "You still got dew on you, girl."

But I'm not laughing. I'm realizing: I'm years past the age of dew. And look at me.

Adira reaches into her breast pocket. She pulls out a creased picture and passes it around the circle, her face lighting up with a grin. "This is my kid. My daughter. And that's my grandfather with her." The pride and affection in her voice grates on me. It shouldn't, should it? It wouldn't for a normal woman, a true mother, would it?

The picture reaches me, and I see a little girl who looks to be about five or six. She's like a little bitty Adira, all big eyed and birdie looking. She's sitting on the lap of an old man, and both man and child have smiles as big as Adira's is right now.

As I pass the picture to Gale, I ask Adira, "Was it worth it, then? Doing what you did? If this is so important to you?"

Gale cuts her eyes at me: *Have you lost yo' mind?*

Adira blinks. "Well, it was my grandfather. The euthanasia. I promised him when the time came, I would." She looks around the circle for backup, and some of the women are nodding, agreeing with her.

My mind turns off down a lane of memory I hardly ever visit, to the day my father's time came. Lillian called and said, "Daddy died in his sleep last night. Joe and I are here. Viola's coming for the funeral." She paused, and it was like she was saying, *If Viola can come, why can't you?* But what she said was, "Isn't it time to make peace?" And I told her, "What would you know about having to make peace with anybody? He's been dead to me a long time. I don't owe him anything. If anything, he owes me." And I hung up on her.

I look around at the dingy walls and at all of these unfamiliar faces on women in uniforms just like mine. I feel this rush of grief and regret and that ever-present deep, deep rage.

What I saw was a girl grieving . . .

"It was a promise," Adira's saying. "No—a *mercy*. I didn't want to do the euthanasia, but remember I told everybody about the angel? That I wrestled with?"

A bunch of blank looks from the women who weren't there that day. But everybody who was there throws in some *yeah*s, egging her on.

"Well," Adira says, "I didn't want to say too much the last time because, see, people don't understand." She pauses, like maybe she won't say it after all. "Okay, it was kind of like what happened to Jacob. Back when I had to do the euthanasia, that's when the angel came, right? Because at first, I couldn't do it. Then me and that angel started fighting." She grabs at air, like she's trying to get hold of something. "I felt strong for the first time in my life because I wasn't losing, and I was, like, Okay, this is what it's all about. He was showing me I was strong enough, right? And I got up from that fight, I dusted myself off"—she wipes fake dust from her pants—"and I gave my grandfather mercy because that angel showed me my strength. That was a mercy on me, right? Killing off my weakness."

There's a nervous, crazy-girl quality to her. A few women exchange looks.

"Before he left," she says, "that angel said, 'We only got one life.'" She holds up the wrist with *BO* tattooed on it. "That's what this means. Born Once. And the best thing for the one life is to kill off all the bad things that make you weak and sick in your soul." She holds up the wrist that says *DED*. "Die Every Day, like little mercies on yourself. That's what that is." She smiles, satisfied. "And he gave me my name. Adira. It means strong."

"Do you have a good lawyer?" somebody asks, sounding worried for her. "You got a good lawyer putting together that plea for you?"

Another woman mumbles something about an insanity defense.

Adira smiles. "I'm not worried about it, 'cause that's what's true."

"Not worried about it?" I say. "This is your life! If *you* don't worry about you, nobody else will!" How many times have I said that to my kids? These girls, they don't listen, they don't see. "That lawyer working on your deal, he doesn't care anything about you!"

Adira's eyes widen.

"You have no idea what it's all about," I say. "Just another lamb to the slaughter."

That's what Mercedes said, didn't she? Mercedes, who got her verdict yesterday afternoon. Who's already gone.

Gale eyes me, her scarred face crinkling up with worry. I look around the circle and see that everybody's eyes are on me now, concerned and confused, mostly, but some of them laughing. I feel exposed, ripped open, and oozing like a wound.

I open my mouth to ask what the hell they're looking at.

"Sister," the chaplain says before I can speak. "Adira has made the decision that's right for her. We must respect that."

"What would you know?" I say. He didn't have any answers for me all those times I sat there in his office, wondering how I compare, practically begging for his guidance like any other stupid, stupid girl. I should be old enough to know better.

I know that you saw yourself as the real victim . . .

"It's true, Althea, I don't know a whole lot, that's for sure." The chaplain smiles his do-gooder smile. "I'm just feeling my way, like a lot of us." He puts his hands out to the women on either side of him. "Why don't we grab hands and say a prayer before we go? As a group, as a family, here on this Thanksgiving." He looks at Adira. "And let's remember our sister Adira. May God guide her as she takes the next steps." His eyes make their way around the circle, pausing for a second on me before moving on. "And let's lift up any of our other sisters and brothers who could use an extra word, some of whom aren't here with us today."

I think of Kim out there somewhere, and something shifts in me. There's movement in these dry bones, this thumping, empty heart. Kim's hardheaded, that's true. Mad at the world. At me. Too much like me.

Gale takes my hand, whispering, "I got you."

Adira looks at me as she takes the hands of the Talker and a young girl next to her. Adira doesn't smile at me, like she usually does. She doesn't look confused or upset or nervous or crazy either. She's looking at me like she can see straight through to a neon heart, blinking *vacant-vacant* with every beat.

If I were the praying kind, I'd be praying for mercy.

Because Kim *is* too much like me, isn't she? It's like I gave birth to my own misery and grief and primal screams, and I can't stand to look at myself. No matter what Viola says, I *am* too much like him. I always prided myself on never hitting anybody, never raising my hand to my kids. But I've come close. I'm always just as ready. That's what's true for me, isn't it?

The chaplain's deep in his prayer, but I interrupt. "Would you—" Everybody's looking at me. I'm the nut, now. But I keep going, my voice choked with tears: "Would you pray for my daughter, please?" I manage to say. "She's lost."

Lillian

"How do we find you?" I say, my breath fogging up the windowpanes.

I listen, like the Universe might answer me. Like the headlights I've been watching for might all of a sudden light up the driveway. Like Viola might jump out of that car with some good news.

But there's nothing.

I check the front door again (yes, still locked). "Safe," I whisper, my hand on the knob.

I check the time on my phone again: eleven o'clock.

I go from the front door to the closet door and tap the knob, whispering, "Safe." It's a slow walk up the stairs to the hallway, where I step on checkerboard squares of light coming in from the window. At Baby Vi's door, I knock softly while, at the same time, pushing the door open.

"Baby Vi?"

The small, blanket-covered ball in the center of the double bed jerks upright. "She back? Did they get her?"

"No. Sorry. It's just me. Just checking. Try to go to sleep. Sorry. I'll wake you up if there's anything." I close the door softly, touch the cool wood, and whisper, "Safe."

It's like the word's echoing all around me. That's how empty the house feels right now, with Viola and Eva out there searching. Again. And us here waiting. Again.

"We can't just sit here," Viola had said about two hours earlier, after calling Eva and me down to the library, where Baby Vi showed us her phone. While Viola kept frantically calling Kim's number, we passed Baby Vi's phone around, taking turns, trying to find some map to Kim's whereabouts in her words:

> **Thursday, Nov 28, 9:03 PM:** Happy Thanksgiving and merry Christmas forever and ever and I love you. Always remember. Y'all can stop looking now 'cause I'm already gone. It's time for me to drift away, V, that's all. Please tell Daddy I love him and I tried. Please tell Mama I never knew what to say to her that wouldn't make her mad.

"There was no sense of urgency when I called the police," Viola said, walking back and forth in front of the fireplace with its dying embers, constantly glancing at her phone, like Kim or the police might call back. "It's Thanksgiving—who knows when they'll get on this." Officer Hopkins, for one, was out of town with his family for the holiday. Viola looked around the room helplessly. "Okay. All right. Here's what we'll do: Eva and I will go out again. We'll go to the police station. We'll drive around to see what we can see. Maybe we missed something when we went out after dinner. Lillian, you and Baby Vi stay put, okay? Just in case."

A panicked silence passed between us.

Then Baby Vi spoke the words we all had to be thinking. "You're not going to find her," she said, her voice cracking. "I waited too late."

* * *

I move away from Baby Vi's bedroom door, but I don't go to bed. Restless and aimless, I go back downstairs to see if Nai Nai's up. But I get sucked into another round of rounds. Checking the front door (still locked), staring out at the driveway (still dark and empty), stopping at the door of the closet under the stairs, but this time not moving past it. With my fingers lingering on the doorknob, I think about what I told Althea and Viola about Joe, like I do a lot now when I'm by myself and things are quiet:

. . . he had his punishments . . .

His "penalty box."

I turn the knob and open the closet door to a curtain of winter coats and spring jackets. How much time did I spend in here? Hours at a time, usually. On any given day.

I'm in charge now. You do what I say.

I part the coats and jackets and step inside without flipping on the light. It's close in here, but it doesn't feel as small as I remember. As I spread out my arms, touching the walls on either side of me, I feel the past pressing against my back, its breath hot and sour on my neck. I'm what? Thirteen. Fourteen. For two solid years, this was punishment. For what? Being too nice? Making too much noise? Late getting home from school? Too much time over at Elaine's? Not enough time over at Elaine's? Anything.

"You know the drill," I hear Joe say.

"But I didn't even *do* anything!"

"You didn't? You're doing something right now, aren't you? Talking back."

He shoves me back toward the open door of the closet.

I try to stand up to him, but my voice comes out whimpery and thin when I threaten, "I mean it this time, Joe."

"What? You gonna tell?" He shoves me again. I stumble backward. "So he can take your side, like automatic?" He shoves me again, harder, and my back slams into the door frame.

I turn and run. Usually, I go for the front door. If I can make it outside, down to Elaine's or any other hiding place, I can wait for Daddy to come home. Or I can wait until whatever Joe's mad about passes and he apologizes and he's nice and it's like nothing ever happened. But he blocks the way to the front door. I turn and take the stairs, two at a time. When I get to the landing, he's right behind. An inescapable reach. An unbreakable grip around my wrist.

He drags me back down the stairs, my legs kicking at the air, my free hand scratching at his arms, trying with everything in me to get away. But I'm as helpless as a rag doll, flung into the closet—the "penalty box"—falling through the curtain of coats until my back hits the wall. Coughing and crying and trying to breathe, I see Joe backlit in the closet doorway.

"Go ahead and tell him," Joe says.

The door slams, shutting out the light. The padlock clicks closed. Minutes pass. Hours. Then days. I'm hungry, I'm thirsty, I'm sweating, I'm wet with pee. I'm suffocating. I call for Joe to let me out. Sometimes he'll come and open the door, not able to look at me, mumbling about being sorry, saying he gets tired of having to babysit me. The least I can do is act better, and there isn't any reason to go running to Daddy. "Do you wanna get me in more trouble?" he'd say, sounding really scared.

But this time, no matter how loud I yell, Joe doesn't come. It's dead quiet on the other side of the door.

Like tonight.

I surface from memory, that thirteen-, fourteen-year-old girl fully grown. Sitting here on the floor of the closet, a jacket brushing the top of my head, I reach out and touch the door. Of all the things I changed when I renovated this house, I haven't done anything with this closet or this door. My fingers move over the smooth wood and find the deep grooves. It's my name and other little messages I carved into the wood with a hanger, trying to keep myself occupied and calm during all those times I sat waiting for Joe to let me out. In the darkness, I can't see what's under my fingers, but I remember one thing I carved: *Scared.*

And another, as I tried to reassure myself: *Safe.*

My fingers find a rough knot of scratches. I clawed them into the door that last time, probably after a day had passed. After I'd screamed myself hoarse. Curled up on the floor under the cover of a winter coat I'd pulled down, my stomach empty and rumbling, I finally fell asleep.

My father, who'd been gone all weekend, found me. When my eyes adjusted to the light, I saw him hovering over me, stuttering and struggling to find his words, finally saying, simply, "Lillian?" like he needed me to confirm who I was.

I told him what had happened, the words rushing out with no pauses or periods. Crying the whole time, until he stopped me.

"Come on," he said. "Get yourself cleaned up."

I did, while he went to the kitchen to poach eggs, fry some bacon, and make toast—the only meal he knew how to cook at the time. After making sure I'd eaten enough, he sent me on to my room. Later, he came up and sat on the edge of my bed. When I tried to tell him more—how many times Joe had sent me to the "penalty box" and that sometimes he would lock me outside in the cold or he wouldn't let me eat while he sat there eating in front of me and that I didn't understand why—my father stopped me again.

"Some things that happen to you, or the way somebody treat you, sometimes it ain't got nothing to do with you," he said. "That's something it's important to learn. Before you get too old and can't let loose the burden of them things."

Then he got up, said good night, and went to the door. As he closed it behind him, he paused and peeked his head back in. "Joe going to the army," he said. "You big enough to keep an eye on yourself when I'm gone." But he never left after that. He took the lock off the closet door, saying he'd never even noticed it was there. He told me, "Let's keep everything with Joe between us. We don't want this out there on him."

I sit for a second, thinking about that, my back resting against the back wall of the closet. I take my phone out and stare at the screen. The picture of Thelonious greets me. I go past it to my contacts, my hands suddenly hot and clammy as my nerves catch up to what I'm doing. I tighten my grip on the phone and make the call.

"Hey, Lillian. What's up? Y'all got a line on Kim?"

"No." I take a breath. "But that's not what I'm calling about."

"Okay . . ." Joe sounds wary. "What's up?"

"Do you know where I am?"

"Uh, no . . ." He laughs. "Should I?"

What am I doing? What was I thinking?

"You still there?"

I swallow. "I'm in the penalty box, Joe."

There's a sudden, sharp silence. I can almost feel him tensing up on the other end of the line.

"You remember that?"

"Lillian—"

"Why'd you do that to me?"

He's quiet. "I don't know," he says, finally.

"You don't know?"

"That's what I said, isn't it?" He pauses, like he's getting ahold of himself. "Look," he says, a little less hostile, "I had a lot of feelings back then. I had a lot of . . . just stuff. And you happened to be there in the middle of it, okay? Like collateral damage or something. It wasn't—"

"Collateral damage? Are you *serious*?"

"I don't—look, you're taking it wrong. You're asking me something, and I'm trying to tell you, as best I can. But y'all can't hear nothing I say. I said I'm sorry. I don't know what else y'all want from me. I can't go back in time, Lillian, and do things over."

"I can't either. But you know what, Joe? If I could, the first thing I'd do is try not to feel so sorry for you, try not to feel so guilty about the fact that I had something you didn't have. I think I sacrificed my own self because of that, by staying quiet about how you treated me. I was always thinking you'd do better, because you could, Joe. You could be nice sometimes. A lot of times."

"I never asked you to sacrifice nothing for me. I never—"

"Yes, you did!"

He doesn't say anything.

"Look," I say, trying to calm down. "I'm sorry for how unhappy you were. But it's not my fault that—"

"That you got everything?"

"That I got *anything*. I never took anything away from you. I never asked for anything, not even this house." I think for a second. "But this *is* my house, Joe. It's mine, and I don't want you back here. Not unless I say. And probably, Joe, I mean, you should think about getting some help, because who would do what you did to somebody? Would you have ever stopped? On your own, I mean? Would you have done something even worse to me?"

I wait for him to speak. He's still on the line—I can hear him breathing. I'm holding the phone so tight my fingers are cramping. I let up. "Listen, Joe, I'm going to go."

"Okay." His voice is clipped. "If this is what y'all want."

"Not y'all, Joe. *Me*. The one you tormented and abused. *Me!*" I close my eyes and try to calm down again. "Take care of yourself," I manage to say, in an unsteady voice.

"Go, then, Lillian. Just go."

"I think that's best."

I drop my phone on the floor and pull my knees up to my chest, staring off into the darkness. Did I just do that? My hand flies up to cover my mouth because I might cry or scream or make some noise that's not human. I might do anything, if I weren't so drained. I lie down and curl up like I did when I was a girl, resting my head on the floor. The cold feels nice under my burning, wet face.

I sit bolt upright, looking around in confusion. Disoriented. Where am—

I'm still on the closet floor. Did I fall asleep? I push the door open and squint into the foyer.

That sound.

Buzz! Buzz!

My phone! I pat my robe pockets, where my phone is supposed to be. But the vibrating's coming from beside me. Right. Joe. I feel tiny bursts of panic in my chest. I pick up the phone and flip it over. I don't recognize the number.

I answer, cautiously.

"Hey," a voice whispers. "This Lillian?"

"Yes," I say slowly, trying to place the voice.

"Good, good. Look, I got your niece here."

A chill goes through me. "Excuse me?"

"Yeah, we're at Althea's."

"I'm sorry?"

"We're at her house." The whisper's impatient and muffled now. "Look, I don't think I can hold her here for long."

"Wait. What? Who is this?"

"I'm a friend—" Her voice drops off. I hear bumping and rustling. And yelling.

"Come on!" It's the woman again. "I'm trying to help you!"

"Get outta my way!" Kim's voice.

I get to my feet, caught up in the coats and jackets, yelling into the phone. "Kim! Are you okay?"

Nothing. More rustling. And even the yelling's fading.

"Hey, don't do that!" are the last words I hear.

I grab my coat and run through the foyer. "I'm coming!" I yell into the phone, hoping somebody hears me.

I pull up to the curb outside of Althea and Proctor's long brick ranch. I scramble out of my car, suddenly realizing how I'm dressed: my heavy brown coat, blue plaid robe hanging out, polka-dot pajama pants tucked into Uggs. Whatever. I plow through shin-deep snow up the sloping front yard. The streetlights staggered along the road aren't exactly bright, but there's a little help from what there is of the moon. From here, you'd never know this house is abandoned, or, I mean, surrendered. No electricity. No heat. If you didn't know that, you'd think it was like every other house on this street: a dark, peaceful, warm place for a family sleeping inside.

I approach the front door. Every part of me is shaking, terrified. But I can't wait for the police. Viola either.

I knock.

Nothing.

"We'll get somebody to the scene—but don't go in alone if you get there first," I was told, when I called the police on the way here. Viola said pretty much the same thing.

I look in one of the front windows. It's dark. I try the door. Unlocked. I draw in a deep breath and turn the knob. As I walk in, I take my phone from my coat pocket and turn on the flashlight. The beam arcs around the empty entryway and into the empty living room. "Kim?"

Nothing.

In the living room, there's a backpack leaning against the wall. There's a sleeping bag on the other side of the room. A half-empty bag of tortilla chips and a jar of salsa.

Viola and Eva were here earlier, walking around the outside of the house, looking in windows, but they saw nothing and hurried on.

I sweep the room with my flashlight. I call out again. "Kim? Are you here?"

I go into the kitchen and catch movement through the sliding glass doors. In the backyard down on the little boat dock there are two shadows. I recognize the shorter, round one: Kim. But the other one is tall, in a flapping, blowing coat. I have no idea. I shove my phone in my coat pocket and yank open the sliding door. "Get away from her!" I yell, as I run down the long hill to the dock. "Kim, it's me!"

"Go home," she yells back, sounding agonized. I realize she's talking to me. "Just leave me alone!"

"Hang loose, hang loose!" The shadow down on the dock with Kim says. It's the same voice from the phone. She holds up her hand to stop me.

I keep going, stumbling through the snow. "Kim," I shout, my heart hammering in my throat, "are you okay?"

"We're good," the woman says. "Just slow your roll for a minute!"

Kim doesn't say anything.

I keep moving closer, but a little slower.

"You're gonna come on back inside," the woman says to Kim, as she reaches out and touches her shoulder. "Ain't that right?"

I'm on the riverbank now, and Kim looks from me to the woman.

"It's not as bad as all that," the woman says, raising her other hand so she's holding Kim by both of her shoulders. "Let's go inside and jawbone this out. We were getting to know each other real good for a minute there, weren't we?"

Kim shakes her head and says something to the woman in a voice so low that I can't hear. Then, all of a sudden, but like slow motion, Kim pushes against the woman and falls back like a great tree, cut down. There's a loud splash. I reach the dock. The woman crouches down, looking frantically from one side of the narrow dock to the other. "Fuck!" she says. She looks up at me. "You see anything? Bubbles? Fucking splashes? Anything?"

I'm on my knees, scrambling along the edge of the dock, looking into the blackness beneath me, seeing nothing but faint ripples near where Kim went under.

"It's cold as fuck," the woman says. "We gotta get her outta there!"

I pull my coat and robe off, ready to go in. As I stand, scanning the water for signs of life, time warps, and I can't tell how long Kim's been down or how long I've been standing here, shivering, ready to jump. Then, a ways beyond the dock, I see it. A ripple rising, then spreading.

I move to jump in, but the woman pushes me back. "I see it!" she says, going in feet first. She swims out to roughly where the ripple was and dives down. She comes up, whipping her head around, looking all around her. "See anything?" she yells.

"No!" I say, panicked, dropping to my knees again, looking over the edge.

The woman dives again. Stays down.

I crawl to the end of the dock and call out.

Nothing.

I jump in. Ice-tipped knives rip through flesh and press against bone. I'm blind from the shock and the water in my eyes. I hear choking and coughing and, "Help!"

I swim toward the sound. I can make out forms, then the fullness of what's happening: The woman's head is above the water, but she's struggling, going down again and coming back up, choking and spitting out water. As I get closer, I see she's trying to get her arms around Kim. Kim's head is just above water.

I swim over as fast as I can, my arms and legs heavy as lead, my nose stinging from breathing in water, half-blind again. I grab at whatever's in front of me.

"Come on!" the woman chokes out. "Hold on to her, for fuck's sake!"

But Kim's limp and heavy. I'm sinking. Gulping water instead of air. My lungs are knotting up, clotting with every breath I take. I kick heavy legs, fighting to breathe. Fighting to hold on to Kim and keep my head above water.

"Keep a grip on her!" the woman gasps.

"I'm trying!"

We wrestle Kim to the river's edge, dragging her onto the snow.

"Going in," the woman says, her words coming out in choking breaths. "Get something warm for her!" She staggers off in the direction of the house.

As cold drills down to the marrow, I remember my coat on the dock and go back for it. I run back to where Kim is and throw the coat over her. Pull the phone from my coat pocket. With frigid, stiff fingers I punch nine-one-one and beg them to hurry.

"An ambulance," I say, through chattering teeth. "She went in the water. She's cold. I called the police earlier, but they're not here yet!"

I'm asked to check if she's breathing. I hold my hand under her nose. "I don't know! I don't— I can't— I don't know!"

Kneeling over Kim, I try to remember CPR. I'm afraid to touch her. I'm afraid of making it worse.

"Stay with me, ma'am," the lady's saying.

I tilt Kim's head back, like the woman on the phone is telling me to do, and check for breathing again. I give Kim rescue breaths, like I'm told.

"You're doing great," the woman encourages.

With the phone cradled between my shoulder and my ear, I fumble to undo Kim's coat with numb fingers. I put the heel of my hand on her chest, hoping I have the right place, and start the chest compressions, just like the woman tells me to do.

I hear sirens. The sky pulses with red light.

"They're coming," I say to Kim.

"Any response?" the woman on the other end of the line asks.

I gaze down at Kim's face, looking for a response. She's still and peaceful. As peaceful as I've ever seen her.

Viola

There are eyes on me. I force myself off the edge of an uncomfortable slumber and open my own eyes to see Kim sitting up in her hospital bed next to me, staring.

"Good morning," I say.

"Morning," she says, her voice hoarse.

She touches her neck and clears her throat. Looks down at the IV in her arm, then follows the line up to the bag of clear liquid hanging from the metal pole.

"They brought you in last night," I tell her. "It's probably still hazy. You were on oxygen, but that's gone, which is good. There's just that IV now. Hydration. But nothing serious."

She looks around the room. "You been here all night?"

"I have." I stretch and get no give from the stiff faux leather chair I've been trying to sleep in. I sit up taller and rub the kinks out of my neck. "Lillian went home to get Baby Vi and Eva and some clothes for you."

Kim lowers her head. "I keep doing stupid stuff, don't I?"

"Don't say that."

She looks up toward the wall across from the bed, twisting her dimpled fingers with one hand. It's the gesture of a frustrated child.

"You're surrounded by people who love you," I say. "I hope you can see that."

"All I see here is you," she says. "And when're you going back to Chicago?"

"When do you want me to go back?"

"I don't care," she says, her chin set. "Doesn't matter to me what you do."

I scoot to the edge of my chair and reach for her. She flinches away.

"Look, I'm here and Junior's here and Lillian's here and Baby Vi's here and your parents, they may not be *here*—"

A toxic mix of doubt, confusion, and anger twists her features.

"Your mother will show up for you, Kim. I know it." Actually, I *don't* know. But what else can I say?

Her eyes shift, and she looks over my shoulder out the window. I turn to look, too. There are clouds, cottony and gray, ready to deliver fresh snow. In the distance, the Saint Joseph bends out of sight on its run to meet the Portage River.

"When I was up under the water," Kim says, still looking out the window, "it was . . . it was like everything bad just floated right outta my head. I wasn't worried about stuff. It was like being . . ."

It was like being overcome by hypothermia. It was like drowning. It was like dying. Which is probably a lot like that fuzzy, soothing white noise, that sense of peace and calm I feel when I've fed to the point of bursting, purged until I'm flat bellied and empty. Doing it again and again even though I'm dying a little more each time. "Try not to crave that feeling, Kim," I say quietly.

"She used to say it was something special about the water."

"Your mother?"

Kim nods. "That's why she wanted our house there, even though Daddy was worried about another flood. She went back there all the time, to the dock. She'd sit out there staring at the water. I think she was dreaming about sailing away from everything."

"I didn't know she went out there like that," I say.

Kim nods with a faintly proud look. A kind of satisfaction at having this bit of information that belongs to her, not me. "Sometimes," she says, "if you needed to find her, that's where she'd be. Out there by herself."

Kim looks out the window again, and I lean in to touch her leg. She doesn't move. "Can I ask you something?" She shrugs, her face still turned away, a tear trembling on her chin. "I've been thinking, well, Eva and I have been talking, and we would like, if you and your sister want, we would very much like it if you and Baby Vi would come and live with us in Chicago. I know it's a lot to think about, but it could be good for you. Good for all of us, I think."

She doesn't respond.

"And of course, Junior can come visit. Chicago is nowhere from here. You know that."

She looks at me. "Has he been here?" she asks, her voice suddenly whispery and faint. "To see me? Is he mad at me? For leaving him like that?"

"He'll be back. With Lillian, Eva, and Baby Vi."

She turns her face to the window again.

A few silent seconds tick by.

"Give it some thought," I say.

Lillian

I sit in the car in the driveway, the house looming ahead of me. Anybody'd want to raise a family here or even keep it as an empty nest, wouldn't they?

In the shifting light, shadows move past the windows like an answer: Something's wrong here. I blink and hold my eyes shut, trying to work up some positive energy. When I open my eyes, everything looks normal but somehow still wrong.

Viola's right. There *are* ghosts here. Hungry ghosts.

I cut the engine and make myself get out of the car. I Frankenstein-walk through the snow to get to the front door (note: shovel the walkway). Inside, I'm greeted by the sound of the TV going in the family room.

"Hello?" I call out. "It's me. I'm here."

Nai Nai comes around the corner pushing her walker with Thelonious at her heels. "How Kim?"

"She's doing okay, mostly."

Nai Nai nods approval.

I look at the steps. "Is Baby Vi up? And Eva?"

Nai Nai nods. "Getting ready."

"Goo—" I'm interrupted by tapping on glass.

Thelonious squints and meows in the direction of the front door behind me. Nai Nai looks over my shoulder to the door, frowning. "Who that?"

"I don't know. Not expecting anybody."

Through the glass panes, I see a chapped, red-faced woman staring back. She's about, what? Six feet tall? Wearing a skullcap and a dark, greasy, tarp-looking coat that's flapping open. She moves to hold it closed with one hand. In the other hand, she has a blue notebook busting with papers, straining against the rubber bands holding it all together. Kim's notebook. She holds it up.

I open the door, partway, confused.

"Hey," she says, hesitant. "Hi there. Your address is in here." She holds up the book again.

"How did you get that?"

"Sorry," she says. "Let me start over. You're Kim's aunt, right? Lillian?"

"I am," I say slowly, questioning, then suddenly recognizing that voice: "Oh, my God! You were there last night!"

"That's right," the woman says, quickly adding, "I know her. Althea. I was bedding down at her place. That's all."

I'm confused again, even as I remember the sleeping bag and the food and the backpack.

"She said I could. Althea's a friend. She's helping me out. Until I get on my feet."

"Helping you . . . ?"

"Right. Look, is the kid all right?"

"Kim. Yeah, she's good. And thank you. For what you did. I didn't get a chance to say that. I looked up and you were gone."

"Well, it looked like you had it under control, and I heard the cops coming. I'm not that good with"—she does finger quotes—"'authorities.'"

"Right," I say, not really sure how to take that. "What happened? Before I got there? How'd you and Kim end up out there? On the dock?"

She shrugs. "I was settling in for the night, and I heard somebody coming through the front door. Scared me half to death, but I got a look at her before she saw me. Once it hit me who she was, I walked up to her real slow, right? Tried to introduce myself real calm, but I still scared the shit out of her." She pauses, laughing. "I told her a bunch of stuff about Althea, so she could see I wasn't some nut bag. But she wasn't buying it, so I told her some of the things Althea told me about all you guys. That's what got her. She calmed down, and we talked a little bit. Had some of my Thanksgiving chips and salsa. The kid wasn't bad company, if you wanna know the truth. Anyways, she got up and went wandering around, said she needed to see her bedroom. That's when I called you."

"She gave you my number?"

"Oh, God no. Althea did. In case I needed some help on the outside. But I never meant to use it." She looks embarrassed and rubs her skullcap. "Not for myself. I'm getting along good. Anyways, I'm sitting there on the phone with you when she comes back and goes nuts. She took off. I caught her once and held on to her for a little while, but . . ." She shakes her head. "Anyways, we ended up out there on the dock. I thought I was doing a pretty good job of talking her down, then you showed up and things went pretty much tits up from there, as you saw." She pauses, her eyes sad. "You wanna know what? When I was trying to talk her down, telling her how much Althea loved her and her sister and everything like that, it was like she calmed down, but"—the woman shakes her head again—"then she looked at me, I don't know, kind of dead eyed, I guess. She was just standing still, right there with my hands on her shoulders." She raises her hands like they were last night. "And she said, real calm and eerie, 'Let me go.' But I didn't, and then she pushed me and fell back into that fucking ice bath. It was like she wasn't fighting it. You get what I'm saying, here?"

"I think so," I say quietly.

She licks her chapped lips and says, "So, yeah, that's what I meant by 'is she okay.' Okay, you know, in her head." She holds up the notebook. "Anyways, I went back to the house to get some shut-eye once I figured you guys were gone, and I found this." She aims the notebook at the narrow opening between us. I realize I still have the door open only partway. "Kim had this with her. A bunch of trial stuff and whatnots. But everything's in there still, I didn't take nothing."

I open the door wide enough to take the notebook from her, surprised by how heavy it is. All the times I saw Kim carrying it around and imagined what might be in it, I never thought anything about the weight of it. I thank her for dropping it off.

She nods and smiles, and I notice a serious dental situation. I'm looking at her a little closer. I've seen her before. Before Althea's place. "How do you know Althea again?"

"The hoosegow."

I raise an eyebrow.

"County," she says. "We were locked up together."

I hear warning sirens in my head. I want to say thank you and goodbye, but something in her tired, pale blue eyes makes me pause. I mean, Althea trusted her, didn't she? She saved Kim's life, for goodness' sake. It's only right to ask, "Would you like some tea or coffee or something?"

"You don't gotta do that," the woman says.

I hear Nai Nai (I almost forgot she was there) behind me, making this noise with her throat. It's a kind of dry cough/grumble: the sound of disapproval.

I turn and look at her. "Nai Nai, would you mind putting the kettle on?"

She looks at the woman. She looks at me. She looks at the woman again, while giving a tiny shake of the head. Translation: Your do-gooding for this homeless person is going to get us killed.

"Would you, please, Nai Nai?"

She makes that dry cough/grumbling sound again but turns her walker around and heads in the direction of the kitchen, with Thelonious following behind. I turn back to the woman. "I don't have a lot of time. We have to get back to the hospital to check Kim out. She's coming home today."

"That's good," the woman says. "That's real good. I hope she comes out okay." She taps her temple. "You know, up here." She taps her chest, her heart. "And in here, too."

"Same here." I look past the woman to the tracks both of us made in the snow. "I really think you should stay for a warm-up or at least take something with you. Please?"

She looks past me into the house, like she's the one risking something. Then her eyes come back to me, like she's trying to figure me out. She mumbles, "You really are that way."

"What way?"

She makes a face, like she's thinking how best to say it. "Good," she says, nodding like she's satisfied with what she came up with. "You're good. Althea said that when she gave me your number."

She said that about me?

The woman smiles. "My name's Mercedes," she says, putting out her hand for a handshake.

I stiffen like a pointer dog, but my brain is chasing down bits and pieces of memory: She's the one who was on TV. For killing somebody. God, she cut out her boyfriend's tongue, didn't she? The verdict came, what, just the other day? She looks different with her face all red and chapped, but it's her all right. I realize I'm looking at her outstretched hand like it's a snake slithering out of her sleeve. But in the midst of my brain scream, my manners click in. I tuck Kim's notebook under my arm, and my hand darts out to meet hers. Did she notice the delay? Do I look as freaked out as I feel? I must. She's drawing her hand back.

"I'm gonna go ahead and get going," she says, pulling her skullcap down lower, like she's disguising herself. "And look, you don't gotta worry about me squatting too long at your sister's place. I'm just passing through. I'll be on my way soon."

I suddenly feel horrible. "I'm sorry. I didn't mean to do that."

She lets out a snorty laugh, still looking down at the concrete floor of the porch. "No, it's fine. I'm— Look, trust me, you're not the first, and you sure as shit won't be the last. That's how it is."

"I'm sorry," I say again, putting my hand out more forcefully, for a shake. "Please," I say.

She looks at the hand, lets out a weary breath, and shakes with a loose, noncommittal grip.

"It's nice to meet you," I say (they found her not guilty). I step aside so she can come in. As she does, I look out past her, nervously, to the driveway and the plowed street just to be sure that, I don't know, she doesn't have a gang or something with her. As I look, I realize: There's only my car in the driveway.

Mercedes follows my gaze. "Yep," she says, "hoofed it."

"That's, like, seven or eight miles from Althea's house! And it's freezing!"

She gives me a sad grin. "Hell, taking a long walk in winter is about the easiest, most normal thing I've done in a long time."

Even with that grin on that raw, chapped face, her eyes are so shadowed. They look bruised, and I wonder, *When was the last time this woman slept?*

"I think a cup of tea will do you good," I say, leading her through the foyer.

"You got yourself a nice place here," she says, sliding her cap off her head and looking around in awe, like she's just entered a sacred place. Her hair is sweaty and grease-matted to her head. She's walking slowly and carefully, like she's testing the floor with every step, afraid it won't hold her weight.

"Are you hungry?" I ask, as we get closer to the kitchen. "Can I get you a sandwich or something? With your tea?"

She's still looking around, holding her hat to her chest with both hands. But my question, apparently, finally catches up with her, and she looks at me. I can see. She's starving.

WATER OF LIFE

I've known rivers:

Ancient, dusky rivers.

My soul has grown deep like the rivers.

—LANGSTON HUGHES,
"The Negro Speaks of Rivers"

Proctor Cochran
Federal Correctional Complex, Virginia

Tuesday, March 11, 2014

Althea,

I got something mysterious from home today. It's a postcard, and it's just sunshine yellow, that's it. Nothing else. Lillian wrote that they picked yellow for a reason, and I'm supposed to research and find out why. It's some kind of ancient Chinese secret. She said something about it being "a nice complement" to a red one they sent you to keep us connected. Do you know what that means? I guess we got plenty of time to research and write each other about it, don't we?

I got moved to my "permanent" cube today. My new bunkie seems all right. If he's telling the truth, the brother's in for some penny-ante drug stuff for a good long while. Anyway, the first thing I did when I got to the cube was get your picture out of my box and hang it over my bunk. It made me wonder about your friend Mercedes. How is she? I still don't know how much I trust her, but, God knows, I'm grateful to her. Let her know I wish the best for her in getting on with her new life. Speaking of, I got a ramp-up with my antidepressants. The Darth Vader days have been hitting your boy hard, but I'm hanging in and I hope you are, too. And I'll tell you, I do get some light in here from what you say about the girls. I hear good things from them, too.

I've got my first session with the band in a few minutes. I still can't believe I get to play sometimes with other people. Some of these boys can go. There's some real talent up in here, which is good for me but a loss for the world out there.

Anyway, I'm going to go ahead and finish getting my space set up before I go, which won't take long since I don't have much. Isn't it something that, if it comes to it, you can fit your most important possessions all in one box? It's something how when you bust your life down like that you see you don't need all that much to get by.

All right, this is me signing off from Virginia, but I'll leave you with this hint: Summer days, the park, wonder.

Short but sweet. Give me your best guess. And remember, this summer's something to look forward to even if it's not what we would have imagined in a million summers. We'll see each other when we do.

Love always,
Proctor

Althea

I read the hint again: "Summer days, the park, wonder."

"Wonder? Stevie. Definitely," I say out loud. I think for a second about the other words. "'Knocks Me Off My Feet,' I think. That's one of Proctor's favorites, at least. That much I know."

I fold the letter carefully along its crease lines and put it back in its envelope. I do this just about every day with Proctor's letters, standing here in this same spot. A letter a day, that's what we're trying for, so it's like where one ends another one begins, making for an endless conversation. The letters have sometimes been long heart-to-hearts about the girls coming out this summer, about our hopes for a future we can't see, and regrets over things that are still too hard to look at. Other times, we'll send each other a line or two. One time, it was just: *Is this for real?*

I put the letter on the shelf in my locker where I keep all the other letters Proctor's sent, along with some family pictures. They're stacked in a box with the soap sculpture, Saint Joseph, whose haloed head I touch for luck right now, like I do every day. Saint Joseph, *Soap Joseph*, is wedged up against the envelope that holds the last page from the last book of my mother's Bible, with its scripture: "The angel shewed me a pure river of water of life, clear as crystal . . . and on either side of the river, was there the tree of life." I tore that page out at the last minute before sending the book on to Lillian as an apology. I touch that envelope for courage. This is my routine. You got to have routines in here.

I glance over at my bunkie, out cold in her bed. She's just like Crazy-quiet back in jail: sleep, eat, repeat. That's her routine. With what she's done, who could blame her for wanting to close her eyes to it? But then, I'm trying not to compare.

I get ready to lock up, but I notice the red postcard Lillian sent to me. I think of Proctor's question. Yellow? I remember when Lillian was painting Nai Nai's room yellow. I took the girls over to help her. What did Lillian say in the little bit of time I gave her? Yellow means noble, I think. Yes, that's what she said. And the poppies on that bedspread she showed me. Red. That's right. Yellow or gold is usually put with red. Red, the color for luck, is what she said about an afghan Nai Nai was working on for me. It'll be waiting for me when I get home.

Lillian. She told me in her last letter that she had to learn how to knit to take over the job from Nai Nai, and of course she did. I feel this mix of awe and envy, love and loathing, for the way Lillian is. For so much of everything, if I'm honest. A sickness in the soul, Adira might say. But I mean to get better.

I lock up and walk to the entry/exit of my cubicle. I stop like I always do in this spot. I'm picturing the words from that last page from the last book of the Bible. The words my mother wrote in bold letters in the margins beside that scripture about the "river of the water of life." *Show me the way.* I quietly repeat them, like I always do here at the entry/exit of my cubicle: *Show me the way.* It's the closest thing to a prayer somebody like me'll ever say.

And I think about not just what Mama wrote but what she said to me when she was a young woman and at the end of her life: *Sometimes life can pull a lot out of you, Althea. Just squeeze you dry. And if you don't have a way to get back whatever's good and precious to you, it's like losing your soul.*

That's the way. I'm not very far along that path, but that's the way.

I look back at the sleeping mound in the bunk across the room from me. Every day, I'm tempted to be that woman. To disappear into my cell, like Proctor said. To lie down and sleep until my time here is up. Maybe even longer.

"But you're not her," I say out loud, thinking of women and water. Strong stuff. The wellspring of a fragile faith that the way is going to get easier.

I take a deep breath and step out into the hall, headed for the phones.

Viola

Althea sounds good, but she's still struggling. I can hear that false cheer in her voice.

"Everyone's good," I say into the phone, answering her question.

"And how's Mercedes coming along?" she asks.

"It's a serious one-day-at-a-time endeavor, but I think she's trying. Did she write to you about the job?"

"No. Not yet. Did she finally get something?"

"Yes. At an art store, which came down to a personal favor from a friend of Eva's. Oh, and she just got her housing this week in a sobriety group home."

Althea laughs.

"What? What's funny about that?"

"Nothing." Althea pauses. "Sober house or sober home. Just makes me think about some people I met in jail, that's all."

"Do you keep in touch?"

"No, not really anymore. Couldn't tell you where they are now. But

I guess I do keep up with one girl." She pauses. "A young girl. She doesn't have anybody else. Just a little daughter out there in the system somewhere."

There's care in Althea's voice. This is that thoughtful, reflective Althea who shows up on the other end of the line sometimes. "She must have made an impression on you," I say.

"Yeah, I guess something about her spoke to me." She clears her throat. "Anyway, they sent her up for a mercy killing. I try and write to her. Keep her company. And Mercedes knows her, so I make her write to her, too. Thank you again, by the way, for helping Mercedes."

"It hasn't been bad, really, having her here in Chicago. It's actually helpful, sometimes. Like when Eva's Good Cop and my Bad Cop and the real cop, Officer Hopkins, don't work, we call in Mercedes, the Cautionary Tale Cop."

There's a deep laugh, one from the gut. One I haven't heard from Althea in a long time.

"That's a good one, isn't it?" I say.

"Yes!"

"But seriously. Mercedes helps, and I think it helps her, too. I think it gives her a sense of belonging." I look around our family room. Here in the last days of winter, there's warmth blowing from the gas logs Lillian hates. Just beside the fake fireplace is Proctor's reconstructed stereo and the crates full of his records, adding an air of authenticity. And I'm reminded how glad I am to be back home, back where I belong. "Belonging and a sense of purpose," I say. "That's so important."

"Well, thank you again," Althea says. "You didn't need to step up like this."

"Yes, I did."

There's a silence, but it's not brittle or stretched or anything. It's okay.

"Look, Kim is here," I say finally. "But Baby Vi, I mean V., isn't back yet."

"Is she serious about that? I don't know if I like it. An initial?"

"She's serious." I think of V. telling me: "I have a grandmother's name. *Your* name. It makes me feel like not myself, or who I might be." But I don't tell Althea all of that. I say simply, "She wants her own name, and she doesn't want to be called Baby anymore. Can you blame her? We grow up, Althea."

"Yes," she says. "And no." She draws in a breath. "But I'll try and use the initial anyway."

"Good. Eva hit some traffic picking up V., but they should be here any minute. Just a second." I yell for Kim to come to the phone. "Kim will be here in a second."

"Is Baby Vi doing okay?" Althea asks.

I don't correct her about the name. "She had group today. I think we caught her eating issues on the front end."

"Good," Althea says.

"And we found this rap-session/support-group kind of thing that they'll both start next week. It's for children who have a parent in prison."

"Or both parents." She's quiet for a moment, before asking: "You're still doing okay? With yourself?"

"I am," I say, and I'm not lying this time. "Still fine-tuning and housewifing it until I figure out what comes next."

"Uh-huh. And how's the writing coming?"

"It's coming."

"I like the story you sent me. It was good."

I've been writing off and on since Althea forced me to perfect my penmanship sitting at the kitchen table when I was little. But I never had anything I felt good enough about to show anyone. I sent that short story out to her last month, offering it up like the lopsided ashtray I'd slaved over in second grade or my construction paper cutout of a

Thanksgiving turkey, a glue-gobbed best effort. Would she love it? Would she think it was good?

"I hope you keep writing," Althea says. I can almost hear her smiling. And I smile. "It's what you always wanted to do. Even when you were little. You remember?"

Tears come to my eyes. We grow up, yes. And no.

"I do," I say. "I remember." I clear my throat to steady my voice. "If I keep up with the writing, guess that will mean selling the Lexus for sure now, right?"

"Let it go, Viola. It's not you, anyway."

I laugh as I dab at my eyes. "I guess not. I'm hoping I can be more of a good, reliable economy car." Suddenly I'm reminded of an even-bigger-ticket item. "Did Lillian tell you about the house?"

"No, but Joe did," Althea says. "He said he happened to drive by the other day and he saw the new owners out on the property. I never thought she'd sell it, not after everything she put into it."

"I'm not surprised," I say, noticing the mention of Joe. Althea had stopped seeing him, but it looks like she's back in contact with him. I don't know if I'll ever see Joe again. As for Lillian, she said only that she was trying to "let loose the burden of Joe and every other thing that has nothing to do with me." "I think it was important for Lillian to let the house go," I say, back to the issue at hand. "She's in the right place now, even if it's not where she planned to be."

I stop at the sight of Kim coming in and ask Althea, "Okay, you ready?"

"Yes," she says, sounding stiff and not quite ready. She's nervous again.

"We'll talk next week. Love you."

"Love you, too," she says.

I hold my phone out to Kim. "Your mom."

“Thanks.” She accepts it and goes over to sit on the floor in front of her father’s stereo. The stereo, the records, and clothes. Those are the only things she brought with her. And that notebook, with its news clippings and website printouts from the trial: *Accused Charity Cheats in Court*; *Family Fallout on Stand as Daughter Testifies*; *Wife Goes Down in Sentencing-Day Drama.* The notebook also had pages and pages of sketches. Dark-eyed girls, some in defiant poses, but most drawn with their mouths stretched open in silent screams, up against scribbled black backgrounds.

“It’s just stuff that happened that I wanted to keep,” Kim said defensively, holding the notebook to her chest, after Lillian delivered it to her hospital bed.

Kim gave me that notebook just last week and said simply, “Get rid of it.” But I’ve kept it for her. Sometimes it’s good to view the past from the distance of another time. When we’re better able to see.

Kim is holding the phone to her ear with one hand and flipping through records in one of the crates with the other. A nervous thing, because she’s not even looking at them. Her eyes are turned up toward the window, where a bare branch is *tap-tap-tapp*ing at the glass. I hear her say, “Hi,” as I go to the kitchen to give her some privacy.

But the family room flows directly into the kitchen, so I can still see her, if I look. And hear her, too, if I listen. I don’t look or listen, but I do hear the caution in Kim’s soft murmurs. Althea has been gone for about two months, and this is only the fourth time they’ve talked. The first time, of course, was right before Althea’s transfer, when we went to visit. It was not a tearful reunion. In point of fact, it was an awkward, almost clinical visit, with Althea’s questions to Kim centering on her health: *How’re you feeling? And the doctor has cleared you?* But with every short, though affirmative answer Kim gave—*I’m fine; doctor says I’m good*—Althea simply nodded, eyes closed in relief. Any expected reprimands, Althea kept to herself.

What they do say to each other now feels so tentative. Their phone conversations always start out slowly. They wobble. They seem to lunge awkwardly sometimes, from one topic to the next. They falter and fall silent a lot before finding their footing again. They're taking baby steps.

I hear V. and Eva come in. Kim points to the phone and mouths to her sister, "Ma," then goes back to listening to whatever Althea is saying on the other end of the line. V. plops down on the floor, nearer to the fireplace but beside Kim, as Eva kisses me and grabs my hand, pulling me deeper into the kitchen to tag-team dinner. But I pause, taking one more look at the girls: Kim sits, still listening; V. takes out her own phone and starts tapping. Texting, no doubt, as she waits her turn to talk to her mother. Tucked in close to her sister.

Lillian

Hi. How are u? Waiting to talk to Mom. Still weird but better ☺ Same with Chicago. Just back from group. The girls are really nice. Told them I'm doing better on my plan and they were happy for me 👍 Can me and Kim come see u in summer after seeing Dad/Mom? Say hi to Nai and Mr. T. Miss and luv you guys lots. 😘😘😘

I text back:

Hi, V! Would LOVE for you to come! Should be settled by then. Miss you and Kim so much and so happy you're doing better and have such great support!!! Will talk to aunts V and E about summer. Tell your mom I said hi when you talk. Take care of yourself and each other. Love. XOXOXO

I put my phone away and tell Nai Nai, "Baby Vi says hi and she misses you." I don't even try using V.

Nai Nai nods a little.

"They want to come out to see us this summer. Isn't that nice?"

"Umm," she says, nodding again, but she doesn't say anything else.

We sit, watching other old people limp and shuffle and walk in slow motion to the center of the room where the furniture has been pushed back to make space for them. A couple of others roll by in wheelchairs.

"Sure you're not too tired?" I ask.

"Yes, ready," she says, her face glowing, lit by the late-afternoon sun shining through the windows of the Florida room. I glance around the pastel-colored old person's paradise (or prison). We're not supposed to be in the Florida room. We're supposed to be in the actual state of Florida. Miami. That's where she wanted to go. She asked to go a long time ago, but other things (renovations, arrests, taking care of my nieces) made that hard. And now, this.

The closest she'll ever get to Miami, now, is as close as she was before: looking at the Atlantic Ocean, as seen from Miami Beach, in that picture that hung in her bedroom in Michigan, even though it didn't go with the décor. That picture's now hanging above her bed here in the rehab facility/nursing home.

At least we made it back to New York, I say to myself. Back to New York where there's design work for me and she can get really good care. I look out the window to skeletal, bare-knuckled trees and the lonely patio furniture, waiting for cushions to be replaced in the spring.

I notice that Nai Nai's afghan is slipping down her lap. I pull it up and tuck it around her knees. "When it gets warm out there," I say, nodding toward the windows, "you'll get to go out to the park again just like before. Remember? Remember when Sam would take you to do your tai chi in the park? I mean, it's nice doing it in here"—I motion around the Florida room—"but you'll love being out in the park once the weather warms up. Like you were with Sam."

She reaches over and pats my hand with her good hand. That is to say, her *relatively* good hand. It's a gnarled, trembling claw now, after the stroke. The other hand is curled up into a tight fist and twisted close to her chest, paralyzed.

"Today good," she says.

Yeah, remember: *Be in the moment.*

"You're right, Nai Nai. Today's very good."

We sit quietly. Mr. White, another stroke patient, tilted to the side in his wheelchair, rolls by with Thelonious on his lap. I wave. Glancing over at Nai Nai again, I think of how she used to remind me of a tiny comma. But these days, she looks more like a question mark with her back more hunched and her head hanging lower, like her whole body's asking, *How much life is left in me?*

I can't imagine life without her.

Sometimes, it's like I'm trying to dam off the flow of time. I mean, I know death is coming, it's part of the cycle of life, but sometimes, it's like, if I can build up enough questions and answers about her life, I can keep some parts of her from being totally swept away. So I find myself asking her things I never would've before. Questions she wouldn't have answered before, but now she does, if she can remember.

She told me she was sixteen when she came to America. She was lonely and scared and she hated it. Her first husband, who sent for her, had a whole other family when she got here, including another "wife." He was a hard man, she said, and she was glad to see him dead. The second husband was better, but it wasn't love. She had regrets, but she had her son, and her son had Sam. Somewhere in there, she had Miami for two months. Florida. She wouldn't say exactly when, only, "It was best time for me." Then she paused, smiling with that distant look she'd get sometimes when staring off at her picture of the Atlantic Ocean. "I not always Nai Nai," she said, finally. "I was just girl, one time."

I see people turning to look at the entrance to the Florida room.

"Master Cheng is here, Nai Nai," I say. "It's about time to start your tai chi, if you're sure you're not too tired."

"Sam gone, *nǚ ér*," she says in her thin voice. "No park."

I look at her. She's looking at me. Or, in my direction at least. The stroke has made her eyes all jerky, so it can be hard to tell what she's trying to see. Does she see the tears in my eyes? The mention of Sam's name, yeah, that's part of it, but it's the name she called *me*. *Nǚ ér*. That's what got me. It's Mandarin, and I know what it means. Does she mean it? Is it just the stroke talking?

"You good girl," Nai Nai says. "You all the time think you bad," she says. "I had life. Hard life. You do bad thing sometime with hard life." She pauses, like she's trying to find the words, which she probably is. They're getting lost more and more. "You did bad thing, but you good girl. Now you home."

She has good days and bad days. On the bad days, sometimes you don't know what she means. But even with her thoughts and words wandering like they do, they've never, *never* wandered anywhere near what I did to Sam. (That's what she means, right? So, she does know?)

Master Cheng takes up his position across the room and calls out the first movement. Old bodies creak and flow into position. He gives Nai Nai and the other wheelchair patients modified moves they can do in their chairs. The tai chi master walks around, gently adjusting an arm here, a leg there, as he calls out more positions. When he instructs them to "part the horse's mane," everybody looks like they're holding a big ball or a really fat baby out in front of them, but not Nai Nai. She has the one relatively good arm raised. It's stiff and crooked and nowhere near high enough. When he says, "White crane spreads its wings," her stiff, arthritis-bent arm just kind of hovers there. But with her face glowing in the late-afternoon sun and her head haloed in hair as fine as dandelion fronds, she seems not of this world.

When the class finishes, I collect Thelonious from the lap of another old guy. Mr. Brownstone, a nice heart patient who doesn't get any visitors. Nai Nai and I say goodbye to him, to her other friends, and to Master Cheng. I wheel her back to her room and, with the help of an attendant, we get her into bed for a nap.

"I'll be back tomorrow," I tell Nai Nai. "I have to get to the new place to meet the broker." I pause and look at her. I always wait for a reaction when I talk about the move, but she's just there with her eyes closed. When I told her I wanted to sell the apartment where we used to live with Sam, she'd only nodded. I couldn't tell if she was having a good or bad day.

But it was time to let it go. I let the house in New River Junction go, too. Sold it for way less than it's worth (I'd overimproved). But the new family's nice. A mom and a dad and two little kids. Maybe they'll bring some happiness to that house. Maybe the ghosts will be able to rest. For me, the move feels good. It feels right. My new place is small, but there's plenty of space for what I need. It has good bones and lots of light, too. There's not much I'd change there. No doors I don't want to open.

As I pull the curtains closed over the windows, Nai Nai says, "Breakfast?"

I look over my shoulder at her and smile. "I'll see you bright and early. And yeah, I'll bring the goods." It was the doctor this time who'd shrugged and said, "Let her live a little," when I asked about McDonald's. "She's a tough old bird," he said, which had made me imagine her with bird bones, light and hollow, ready to float away. And I started crying, sitting right there in the doctor's office.

She's looking in my direction, like she's trying to find me with those jerky eyes.

"I'm here," I say. "What is it?"

She nods. "You home now. You have life, *nǚ ér*," she says.

I tear up again. Maybe it's *not* the stroke talking. Maybe she means to call me that.

"Okay," I say, through a closing throat.

"Go," she says, impatient now, shooing me out of the room with her relatively good arm. "Nap time."

"Okay, okay. I'm going." I go over and kiss her on the top of her head. "Sleep well." I scoop up my cat and move toward the door, but pause, lifting my eyes to the ripples and waves of the Atlantic in the picture hanging above her bed. When I packed that picture up with the rest of her stuff, I found a small, square black-and-white snapshot tucked into the frame on the back side. It was Nai Nai as a young woman—around my age—not especially beautiful, but she looked happy. She was at a bus station, standing next to a guy who wasn't either of the two guys I knew to be her late husbands. On the back of the picture was written: *Miami, 1957. Love.* I put the snapshot back in the frame and never mentioned it.

But I think of how, on the day I hung the picture of the Atlantic over her bed, she watched from her wheelchair and told me, "You keep picture when I die. Special. All I have."

"Girl have to have something," I remembered her saying about Kim and her dad's stereo. Then I told Nai Nai I expected her to be around for a long time, but I did promise that her picture would be safe with me.

I head toward the door thinking of *nǚ ér* again and translating in my head. I only know a few words in Mandarin. *Mèi mei*, definitely. That's little sister. And I know what she called me: *nǚ ér*. It means daughter. She's never called me that before. And it was weird, but that second time she said it, it was like I could hear the whisper of a voice I shouldn't be able to remember, from the mother I'm only now getting to know a little, thanks to Althea.

I pause.

Yeah, I'm pretty sure I heard that whisper.

I pull Nai Nai's door closed, but not all the way. Never all the way. And Mr. T. and I go home to the new place.

Acknowledgments

A heartfelt thank-you to my agent, Michelle Brower, who saw something special in those early pages. She was a true partner in bringing this novel to life. I count myself lucky to have found her.

My editor at Berkley, Amanda Bergeron, helped make this book markedly better with her many thoughtful suggestions and her keen editorial eye. Assistant editor Jen Monroe was also there every step of the way, keeping me updated and encouraged with each e-mail. Indeed, I am grateful to everyone on the Berkley team for their enthusiasm and care in getting this book out into the world.

An enormous thank-you to Steven Jiang and Kevin Wang for their enduring kindness and patient answers to my various questions on Chinese culture and language. A special thank-you as well to Martin Vogelbaum, law enforcement officials, and others who were so generous with their time on all matters legal, investigative, and incarceration related.

Much of *The Care and Feeding of Ravenously Hungry Girls* was written after an inspiring stay at the Sewanee Writers' Conference. I deeply appreciate the workshop leaders and fellow writers who offered comments, encouragement, and a real sense of community. But I would not have gotten far without the help of my readers: Beverly J. Armento, Gayle O'Shaughnessy, Jean K. Tomlinson, and Beci Falkenberg. Their thoughtful input through the rough patches and their friendship were invaluable.

I am forever indebted to the Atlanta Center for Eating Disorders for the work they do every day, helping girls and women understand and overcome bulimia, anorexia, and other potentially deadly eating disorders. I owe them my life.

Crucially, I thank my parents, Nathaniel and Mary Ann Wells, who helped shape me in ways large and small. The same can be said of my sisters, Chanita Vance, Patricia Frazier, and Tiffany Alexander, women with whom I share the complexity and strength of a most unique bond.

And I am incredibly grateful to my wife, Katherine Gray, who has been at my side for almost half my life, offering support, love, and laughter. For her, there simply aren't enough words.

The Care and Feeding of Ravenously Hungry Girls

ANISSA GRAY

* * *

Behind the Book

An Essay from the Author

The Care and Feeding of Ravenously Hungry Girls is not the book I intended to write. The book I first imagined is similarly named but entirely different, and it sits, unfinished, in a file titled "PossRevisit" on my computer desktop. There is, however, a common thread that runs between that unfinished manuscript and the published novel, and it exists in the character of Viola, who appears in both stories.

But I've gotten a little bit ahead of things. There is first the matter of what I was thinking before I created PossRevisit. I was a couple of years out of treatment for an eating disorder that had been with me for much of my adult life. I had, as one might expect, been giving a lot of thought to food as both sustenance and unwholesome succor. I felt I might be able to fashion a meaningful story built around my time in therapists' offices and group sharing circles. The research and planning for that novel went well. But the writing? It never came together. About eighty pages in, I put the manuscript aside in that folder and went on to another project. But the central character in that novel, Viola, never left me. That is, of course, in part because she carries some elements of my experience in treatment. But she differs from me greatly in some crucial ways, including voice—and it was her voice that kept demanding to be heard. Whether it was while I was at work or at the gym or at my writing desk doing research on that new project, she kept appearing on the periphery of my thoughts, bringing with her perspectives I had not yet considered.

Joyce Carol Oates once said, "Characters begin as voices . . . Characters define one another in dramatic contexts. It is often very exciting, when characters meet—out of their encounters, unanticipated stories can spring."

And in that way, the unanticipated did happen. Lillian and Althea stepped out from Viola's backstory with their own tales of yearning and loss, speaking in their own voices. But I was not able to truly get their stories down on paper until this reflection from one of the characters: "I'm thinking of how limits become limber. Pliable, when pressed with the *thing in you* that cries out, endlessly, *More, please*." That sentence can be found in the latter half of the book, but it is among the first lines I wrote. By exploring what it was that kept crying out and why, I was able to discover more about who these characters were, how they lived, and their shared history. And slowly, one sentence at a time, *The Care and Feeding of Ravenously Hungry Girls* became a story about a family in the midst of individual and shared catastrophes. It became a book about the myriad hungers that can gnaw at us, and the many ways—whether destructive or effective—that we try to fill the hollow places.

While some details in the novel are drawn from what I've known of life—an approximation of the Michigan towns where I grew up, being the daughter of a preacher, the eating disorder—it is its own story, made up mostly of what I could only imagine. A stark difference from the unfinished manuscript that I have tucked away in that folder on my desktop. I'd imposed too much of myself upon that story. It is less a project I'll possibly revisit than a reminder to listen. To get out of the way and allow characters to speak. To work in service to the story, even when it is slow to reveal itself. In some of the most resonant words left to us by E. L. Doctorow, "Writing is like driving at night in the fog. You can only see as far as your headlights, but you can make the whole trip that way."

And all along the winding, sometimes uncertain journey to the final pages of *The Care and Feeding of Ravenously Hungry Girls*, the characters surprised me, moved me, and challenged me, turn after turn. It was quite a trip.

Questions for Discussion

1. Early in the novel, Althea says, "I used to think I was like a river. A mighty force of nature." What does she mean by this, and how does her view of herself change by the end of the novel?

2. Why do you think Baby Viola is Althea's favored child? How does this affect Baby Vi, and what does it mean for Kim, who is so at odds with her mother?

3. Even in death, the presence of the Butler parents can be felt throughout the story. How do parental relationships affect each of the sisters and Joe?

4. How do you think Baby Vi and Kim will be affected by the long-term incarceration of their parents?

5. The relationships between Althea, Viola, Lillian, and Joe range from being warm to being incredibly fraught. How do the siblings understand or misunderstand one another in crucial ways?

6. Discuss Althea's relationship with her mother and the significance of the Bible Althea later sends to Lillian.

7. The sisters all undergo transformations over the course of the novel. Discuss the critical changes each sister experiences and what led up to those moments.

8. When Lillian, who has been the caregiver for her nieces, urges Viola to take the girls, Viola is resistant. Compare the ways in which the sisters view and approach their family commitments and how that changes over time.

9. While family relationships are at the heart of the novel, friendships are crucially important as well. Which friendship pairings—Lillian and Nai Nai; Viola and David; Althea and Mercedes—were most resonant?

10. Late in the novel, Viola says, "I'm thinking of how limits become limber. Pliable, when pressed with the *thing in you* that cries out, endlessly, *More, please.*" Discuss how this applies to each of the characters and the title of the book.

Further Reading

On Anissa Gray's Bookshelf

FICTION:

Manhattan Beach, by Jennifer Egan

Homegoing, by Yaa Gyasi

The Almost Sisters, by Joshilyn Jackson

NONFICTION:

How Democracies Die, by Steven Levitsky and Daniel Ziblatt

The Soul of America: The Battle for Our Better Angels, by Jon Meacham

Photo by Bonnie J. Heath

Anissa Gray is a senior editor at CNN Worldwide and a contributor to Emmy and duPont-Columbia award–winning coverage of some of the most consequential stories of our time. She began her career at Reuters as a reporter, based in New York, covering business news and international finance. Born in St. Joseph, Michigan, Gray studied English and American literature at New York University. She lives in Atlanta, Georgia, with her wife.

CONNECT ONLINE

anissagray.com
AnissaGrayAuthor
AnissaGrayAuthor